CLUES OF THE HEART

BAYTOWN BOYS SERIES

MARYANN JORDAN

Clues of the Heart (Baytown Boys)
  Copyright 2017 Maryann Jordan

  Cover Design by: Designs by Stacy
  Cover and model photography: Eric McKinney
  ISBN ebook: 978-0-9984832-9-0
  ISBN print: 978-1-947214-00-2

My husband worked for many years as a Certified Fraud Examiner, Certified Public Accountant, Forensic Accountant, and Investigator. While his job was very different from Gareth and Katelyn's, he was dedicated to finding the truth, catching criminals, and serving justice.
He is my biggest fan, my staunchest supporter, and the one I go to when I have research questions. And last, but not least...the love of my life.

Author's Note

I have lived in numerous states as well as overseas, but for the last twenty years have called Virginia my home. All my stories take place in this wonderful commonwealth, but I choose to use fictional city names with some geographical accuracies.

These fictionally named cities allow me to use my creativity and not feel constricted by attempting to accurately portray the areas.

It is my hope that my readers will allow me this creative license and understand my fictional world.

I also do quite a bit of research on my books and try to write on subjects with accuracy. There will always be points where creative license will be used to create scenes or plots.

Four years ago, my husband and I discovered the Eastern Shore of Virginia and fell in love with the area. The mostly rural strip of land forming the peninsula originating from Maryland, has managed to stay non-commercialized. The quiet, private area full of quaint towns captured our hearts and we rushed to buy a little place there.

It has become our retreat when we need to leave the hustle and bustle of our lives. I gather ideas, create characters, and spend time writing when not walking on the beach collecting sea glass.

1

_____

A brisk breeze blew off the Chesapeake Bay, causing her to shiver as it tossed a few strands of black hair about her face that had escaped the knit cap pulled down over her ears. The dark night provided plenty of shadows for her to hide in secret. But Katelyn MacFarlane only had one thought at the moment..._my ass hurts!_

The gnarled limbs of the tree were sturdy and she had spent plenty time during her childhood climbing up them with her gang of playmates. The boys had created a clubhouse and declared it a no-girl zone, but she quickly learned that by climbing nearby trees, she could spy on what they were doing and then report back to her girlfriends.

But, at twenty-eight years old, it had been a long time since she had attempted to climb a tree, much less sit in one. For a moment, she wondered about the folly of what she was trying to accomplish. Sighing, she pinched her lips tightly together. *I told her I would help and that's what I'm going to do!*

Hoping to find a more comfortable position, she shifted slightly but stopped as the limb underneath creaked. Uncertain if it was due to the wind, her weight, or it was about to break, she halted her movements. Inwardly cursing, she grimaced, determined to complete her task. Reaching up, she tucked a few more strands of hair into her cap, her fingers stiff with cold.

The homes along the street resembled the rest of the little town. Cottages, most over a hundred years old and refinished to maintain their original glory. Some stately brick houses, standing guard over the neighborhood as they had for years. And all with large front porches to catch the sea breeze blowing from the bay.

Sliding the binoculars to her eyes, she watched the front of the house. From her perch, she had a view of the street, driveway, the side of the dwelling, and the front porch. Most houses just had street parking, but a few homes had a driveway. Biting her lip, she thought about the back door, aware it was hidden from her view. Spying her car parked down the street, she wondered if she could possibly find out the information she was seeking while sitting in the warm interior. Glancing around, she decided there was no better position than where she was so she hoped whoever went inside would use the front door. Refusing to look at her warm car again, she turned her attention back to the house.

After thirty minutes, she began to wonder if perhaps her tree-perch lookout was a mistake. The neighborhood was quiet and there was no sight of anyone at home. After another thirty minutes, she began to doubt her sanity at agreeing to play spy.

Just as she was about to climb down, headlights turned the corner of the town street and, holding her breath, she watched as the vehicle pulled into the driveway. A lone female alighted from the car and made her way to the front door, wobbling on high heels, giggling as she dropped her keys. Finally, she managed to get the door open and staggered inside. A downstairs light came on and then a few minutes later it went off again. Almost instantly an upstairs light came on for about ten minutes before the house was plunged into darkness once more.

Katelyn sighed heavily at the lack of anything to report other than her ass was numb, her arms and legs were aching, and her nose was cold.

"You want to tell me what the hell you're doing up there?" a deep voice came from below.

Startled, she wobbled on her precarious perch and grabbed another limb for balance. Jerking her head around and down, she grimaced as she saw the man below, casually leaning against the trunk of the tree, one long, muscular legged crossed over the other as he stared up. By the dim light of the street lamp, she could see his face clearly, but it was more difficult to discern his exact expression. It appeared to be part amused, part incredulous, and part pissed. *Just what I need! The town's only private investigator catching me in a tree in the middle of the night, staring up at my ass!*

Embarrassed at her position, she lifted her chin slightly as she tucked a windblown strand of hair behind her ear and attempted to stifle a shiver—from the cold or from him, she was uncertain. Unable to come up with a plausible defense, she went on the offensive. "And just what are you doing here, Gareth? Are you following me? Spying on me?"

A long, slow smirk formed on Gareth Harrison's face. He had been in Finn's Pub with all their friends when he noticed Katelyn had slipped out. Curious, he had followed her to one of the town's residential streets and watched from a distance as she climbed a tree, staying in the shadows as she used binoculars to watch the house close by.

"Spying?" he quipped, inclining his head toward the house she had been observing. "I'd say that's a bit of the pot calling the kettle black, wouldn't you?"

Huffing, Katelyn moved her leg to the branch below and began to shimmy down the tree. Suddenly, her progress was halted as the back of her belt became entangled in one of the many branches poking her. Shifting upward did not help and as she reached back to try to pull away the offensive limb, she lost her footing. Yelping as she grabbed the rough-barked trunk, her legs jerked to find purchase.

Gareth jumped forward hearing the limb creak, his hand reaching up to guide her foot to a more secure resting place. "You comin' down or what?"

"I'm stuck!"

"Where?" he called out.

"My belt. I can't move up or down."

Hearing the frustration in her voice, he grinned as he said, "Well, since you don't like me here spying on you, I'll just head on home. Have a nice evening," he called out jauntily.

"Fine...just go. I can get myself untangled," she bit out, trying to shimmy up and down to loosen her belt. Reaching behind her again, she began pulling at the branches. A chuckle sounded out below her, only serving to make her angrier.

"Hang on, I'm coming," he called. Deftly climbing up behind her, he stood on the branch below hers, sliding his hand slowly down her back until it landed on her belt.

Her breath shallow, she stiffened as his large hand moved down her back toward her ass. Even through the layers of clothing she felt each touch. With his warm breath caressing her neck, she closed her eyes for an instant, unsettled by the closeness of him. Then his hand tugged hard on her belt and she was jolted from her sensuous musings.

Squirming, she twisted her head around, finding his blue eyes right at the level of hers, his face only a few inches away. Her ready quip died on her lips as she dropped her gaze to his mouth.

"Now, stop wiggling if you want me to get you untangled."

His voice slid over her and the chill from the evening left as warmth replaced her shivers. Irritated at her body's response to his closeness she looked away, her fingers grasping the tree trunk even tighter as he tugged the back of her pants harder.

"Okay, you're loose," Gareth spoke, his breath next to her ear, but he made no attempt to move. Being so close to her luscious body, he decided to take advantage of the moment, leaning in slightly. Her sweet scent wafted by and he leaned in, filling his nostrils.

Katelyn closed her eyes for a second, the feel of the muscular wall behind her that was his chest sent tingles throughout her body. Just then another snapping sound from a weak branch jolted her from her desire for him to press his body into hers. "Well, if you'd get out of my tree, then I could be on my way," she tried to bite out, but her words came out in a breathy rush.

"Absolutely," he chuckled. "I didn't realize this was *your* tree." Dropping to the sidewalk, he looked up, wondering what the hell she was doing in the tree in the first place. "Come on," he lifted his hands to assist as her foot slipped once more.

With another yelp, she felt her body floundering as Gareth's hands landed on her ass before sliding firmly up to grasp her waist, easily settling her feet on the sidewalk. Attempting to re-establish some dignity, she tugged on the bottom of her sweater before straightening her cap. Clearing her throat before lifting her gaze to his, she nodded curtly. "Thank you," she stated primly, as though he had simply opened a door for her.

She started to walk away, when he reached out and grabbed her arm. "Oh, no, missy. Not so fast." Seeing her attempt at wide-eyed innocence, he shook his head. "I want to know what you were doing," and before she could come up with an excuse, he added, "and I want the truth."

"Or what?" she asked, her irritation growing into full-blown anger, placing her hands on her hips. "I don't owe you an explanation!"

He said nothing, enjoying the view of her squirming at the silence. Her knit cap now sat crooked on her head, more dark hair falling around her face. His eyes raked down her body, noting the dark turtleneck sweater and jeans, both showcasing her assets. His attention, riveted to her body, almost missed the way her eyes cut back to the unlit house she had been watching before moving back to his. Clearing his throat, he continued his glare, hoping intimidation would mask his roving gaze.

"There's no sense in pretending," she admitted, with a little shrug. "I was watching that house."

"Why?"

"I wanted to know if the owner was alone or had someone with her."

"Why?"

Huffing, Katelyn said, "I was looking for a particular someone."

"Why?"

Throwing her hands up, she said, "Are you just going to keep asking why?"

"Until you give me a straight and, I might add, a complete answer, then yes," Gareth replied. He watched the blush stab her already rosy cheeks, the color matching her lips. It was hard to see her blue eyes clearly in the dim light from the street lamps, but he had them memorized. Blue. As blue as the bay on a day full of sunshine. Her hair was tucked up underneath the cap but he knew it normally hung long down her back, the thick, dark tresses waving. His fingers itched to reach out and feel the silky strands. She was not short, but compared to his height of over six feet tall, she would still tuck underneath his chin if his arms wrapped around her. And he wished they were wrapped around her instead of at his side, waiting for an answer. "Katelyn..." he prodded.

"I wanted to know if Celia was entertaining a particular male visitor. And, since it appears she's not, I'm going home."

Glancing at her small car parked a few spaces away, he nodded as he spoke through tight lips. "Fine. Go home. But then I want you in my office first thing tomorrow morning." Seeing her about to protest, he added, "Or I'll go straight to Aiden and Brogan with tales of your late-night shenanigans."

The thought of her bossy brothers halted her retort. If they found out what she had been doing, they could easily make her life miserable. Lovable, but overbearing, she wanted them out of her business and if Gareth gave up her secret, her plans would be a lot more difficult. Licking her lips, she countered, "I have to work at the diner tomorrow morning."

"Then come to me afterward. I'm sure you can spare some time between the diner breakfast crowd and the pub in the afternoon." Leaning forward, he tapped her nose, "Or I will talk to them!"

With that threat, he turned and climbed into his SUV, waiting until she hustled into her car and drove away. Leaning back in his seat, he shook his head. *What the hell was she doing?* Driving the few blocks to his home, he wondered *what the hell am I doing?*

Slamming her hairbrush down on the antique dresser that belonged to her grandmother, Katelyn dropped her head into her hands, counting to ten as she tried to calm her embarrassment. *Of all the people to show up when I'm perched in a tree, it would have to be Gareth! Sweet...nice...gorgeous Gareth.*

She had noticed him as soon as he moved into town over a year ago. Baytown was small enough that any new residents were immediately noticed. And if they happened to be male, young, handsome, and single, they caught the attention of most young, single women...older women with marriageable-age daughters or nieces or granddaughters...even cougars, single or married who wanted to check out the newest member of the Chamber of Commerce. *Oh, I noticed him for sure.*

Then, as he spent more time with her brothers, she discovered other things as well. He always held the door for anyone coming behind him when he entered a room. He tipped the servers well even though his business was new and just gaining ground. He had joined the American Legion and she watched him interact with the kids on the ball fields, patient and encouraging. Her eyes had begun to seek him out in a crowd, always noticing his presence. *I haven't done that in a long time.*

Having grown up in this tiny town on the eastern shore of Virginia, on the coast of the Chesapeake Bay, she was used to everyone knowing everyone else's business. This made the request she had received that sent her climbing neighborhood trees at night even more important.

Staring back into the mirror, she remembered Gareth's body pressed up behind hers—so close she could feel his chest against her back, his breath warm against her ear. She shivered, uncertain if it was from the cool air blowing in her window or from the memory. It had been a long time since she had shivered from a man's presence...*so it must be the air*. Standing, she walked over to the window in her bedroom, placing her hands on the window frame. The air blew in, cooling her overheated body and she knew—it was his memory that had her warm.

Irritated that Gareth had demanded she come to his office tomorrow, the idea flitted through her mind that she could just stand him up. But then, the thought that he might actually talk to her brothers had her re-think that possibility. Aiden and Brogan ran Finn's, the town's pub that had been founded by their grandfather. The idea of them hounding her to find out what she had been doing gave her pause. *The last thing I need is them riding my ass!* Thinking of her ass, she wiggled slightly, her bruised backside aching. *Damn, tree sitting is hard at my age!*

Moving back to the dresser, Katelyn stared at her reflection for a long moment, wondering at the woman staring back. Confident...yet holding back. Desiring change...yet holding back. Wanting more...*yeah, holding back*. Certain that no answers were coming tonight, she flipped off the light and crawled into bed. The slight illumination from the moon slid through the lacy curtains on her bedroom window, creating patterns on the far wall.

Closing her eyes, she tried to put the image of the handsome private investigator out of her mind, but as she flopped from one side to another, thoughts of him continued as sleep evaded her.

Outside her house, Gareth sat in his SUV until the light went off in the upstairs bedroom window. Rubbing his stubble-covered jaw, he pulled away from the curb and drove around several blocks until he came to Main Street, driving past Baytown's merchants. Turning the corner onto Peach Street he parked outside his building. His office was on the first floor and his small apartment was on the second level of the old structure. Entering through the outside door and up the stairs, he unlocked his front door and entered, flipping on the light.

The worn, wooden floors needed refinishing and the walls could do with a fresh coat of paint. The elderly landlord had given him permission to do any updates he wanted, but Gareth hoped the apartment would only be temporary. It was taking a long time to get his business up and going, so new paint was not front and center of the things he was concerned about. *Hell, it's better than what I grew up with.* Closing his eyes for a moment, he shut out thoughts of the past.

The walls were bare except for a large, flat screen TV. A non-working fireplace graced the space, the mantle providing a place for a couple of framed photographs.

Walking through the open living room to the kitchen, he grabbed a water bottle from the refrigerator and downed it while standing by the counter. Tossing the empty bottle into the recycle bin he moved into his bedroom. No more personal than the living room, the room simply served as a place to crash.

Lying in bed on his back, his arm tucked under his head, he thought of the enigmatic Katelyn. The first day he had been in town, a visit to Finn's Pub exposed him to great food, great beer, good friends, and a chance to meet the woman that had since filled his thoughts for the past year. She had cuffed her brother on the back of the head when he cursed behind the bar and then comforted a child who had spilled his drink. Funny, smart, tough...she could hold her own with her brothers. And he had been infatuated with her for a year. But he'd never made a move. *How could I, knowing her heart was somewhere else?*

Sighing, he rolled over and punched his pillow once more, attempting to find a comfortable spot on the old mattress.

But what the hell was she doing spying on Celia Ring, the mayor's oversexed secretary? He had an idea and, if it proved right, she was going to hear his displeasure tomorrow.

2

"Order up!" shouted Rupert from the kitchen.

He had been slinging breakfast and lunches at Stuart's Pharmacy and Diner for as long as Katelyn could remember. The restaurant resembled an old-fashioned drugstore and soda shop. The tourist items were in the front, while the drugstore sundry items for sale were on the right with the pharmacy in the back. To the left was a long counter with rotating stools and a small seating area filled with plastic covered booths. The kitchen was behind the counter and the smells of a greasy breakfast greeted all who entered.

Grabbing the filled plates from the serving counter, she delivered them to the table of early morning fisher-men, back from their first run. "Here you go, guys. Two diner specials and," she glanced over her shoulder at the teenage waitress, Joleen, who was bringing another plate, "one egg-white omelet, turkey sausage, and whole wheat toast?" Looking down at the sheepish expression one of the men sported, she cocked her hip and said, "George? Your wife got you watching your cholesterol again?"

Gazing at the plates piled high with eggs, pancakes, bacon, hash browns, and grits delivered to his table-mates, he looked back at her with desolate, hound-dog eyes. "Yeah," he replied.

She patted his shoulder in a show of sympathy, winked at the group, and then turned back to get the next order.

Seeing Mitch Evans, the town's sheriff, at the counter, she hesitated for a second, wondering if he were here to talk to her. *If Gareth told him about last night, I'll—*

"'Morning, Katelyn," he said after nodding toward Joleen who poured his coffee.

She moved cautiously to his side, watching his face carefully. She and Mitch grew up together in Baytown. He and her brothers had been best friends and, along with a group of others, had become known as the Baytown Boys. The nickname solidified even more when they were teenagers and named the town's base-ball team after them. Most had joined the military right out of high school and many of them made their way back to the simple, little, sleepy town as adults.

Mitch had become reacquainted with his childhood sweetheart, Tori, and they were now engaged. Katelyn's best friend, Jillian, had finally gotten with her high school crush, Deputy Grant Wilder, another original Baytown Boy.

As she leaned against the counter, she asked, "So... how's Tori?"

The smile now on his face answered her spoken

question...and her unspoken one. If Gareth had talked to him, she doubted his smile would have been so large.

"She's great and says you all have another wedding-planning meeting soon."

Matching his enthusiasm, she nodded. "Yes, and you know what that means!"

Rolling his eyes, he replied, "Uh huh. Y'all drink wine, pick out wedding shit and then me and the boys have to drive you home!"

Laughing, she agreed, "You got that right!" As his order came up, she walked behind the counter to grab it and placed it in front of him. "See you later," she said, as she moved to another group of breakfast customers, pleased that Mitch appeared none the wiser about her late-night activities.

Sitting in his office, Gareth eyed the pile of folders on his desk and sighed. Hating the sight of the messy office, he stood and moved to one of the back rooms where he kept his coffee maker.

Hearing a call from the front, he recognized the voice as he carried his cup toward the reception area. Seeing Mitch and Grant, he grinned while greeting them with a head lift.

Mitch nodded toward the empty front area, asking, "Still no receptionist?"

Rubbing the back of his neck, Gareth replied, "Not yet, but I'm working on it."

"Business picking up?" Grant asked.

"Actually, yeah," Gareth answered, inwardly

breathing a sigh of relief. "It seems that finally people are recognizing that I'm here and they aren't opposed to having a PI in their county." Grimacing, he added, "Well, maybe except the town manager."

"Silas Mills is an asshole," Grant groused. "He complains about needing new businesses in town and then gripes when they come. He gave Jillian shit when she was trying to get her galleria up and running."

Mitch's face also contorted as he grumbled. "He gave Tori hell with her bed & breakfast business."

Glad to hear he was not the only person the town manager had his sights on, Gareth asked, "This an official visit?"

Mitch nodded and Gareth led them back to his office. Plopping down in his old, wooden chair he watched as the two officers made themselves at home.

"We're still watching drug traffic come through the area," Mitch began, "and after our last big bust, we're determined to take an even tighter stance."

"I spend time in the trailer park with some of our kids and I want to keep a close eye on them as well," Grant added.

Both Grant and Mitch, as part of the original Baytown Boys, had appreciated having a welcoming hometown to return to after their military service. Recognizing that not everyone had that acceptance upon returning home, they had started a local charter of an American Legion in Baytown and made sure any veterans they knew who wanted a comfortable place to live knew about Baytown. Now the American Legion had started a community project working with local kids through sports teams.

"Got anything specific for me to look for?" Gareth asked.

Mitch glowered as he responded. "Unfortunately, no. But we know after the arrests of a few people living in the trailer park that we don't want the drugs coming back in. I know you do observations with some of your cases and we'd like to make sure to keep you in the loop and have you do the same for us."

"You got it," Gareth replied. "We've worked well together in the past and I can't see any reason why that won't continue. You know if I see or hear of anything, I'll let you know."

Mitch's gaze landed on one of the few decorations in the room—a photograph of Gareth in his Air Force uniform. Turning back to him, he commented, "I've never even asked you how you ended up on the Eastern Shore. Most people have no idea we're here."

Leaning back in his chair, he said, "After my tour in Afghanistan, I spent my remaining time in the Air Force at Dover Air Force Base in Delaware."

His words hung between the three men, all knowing what Dover AFB was most notable for—it was the place where service men and women's remains were sent and processed before being escorted to their families.

He nodded slowly in answer to their unasked question. "Yeah...I worked in the identification section of the mortuary services."

"Damn, man," Grant said, his eyes full of sympathy.

Clearing his throat, Gareth continued, "So, as you can imagine, on my days off, I had to get the hell outta Dodge, to keep my sanity. I started taking some short weekend road trips. On one such sojourn, I was driving through the Eastern Shore and saw a sign for a coffee shop." Seeing their smiles, he laughed. "Yep...Jillian's coffee shop is what brought me into town for the first time." Shrugging a little, he said, "Drove around and couldn't believe this thriving little bayside town was here. Something about it stayed with me. After that, whenever I got a weekend free, I'd come down. I had already decided that I wanted to use my investigative skills, so I got my PI license after I got out of the Air Force and, not too long after that, I moved here."

"Nowhere else to call home?" Mitch asked.

Shaking his head, Gareth admitted, "Grew up in a run-down trailer park in a small town in West Virginia. I got out of that shit-hole the second I graduated high school. Bounced around for a bit, but I couldn't get the pieces to fit so, I joined the military. Believe me, there's nothing to go back to." That was more than he usually told people, but he figured Mitch and Grant deserved to know the truth about him. Eyeing them carefully, he noted they took his background in stride, neither appearing to be bothered by his confession.

Grant, seeing the piles of folders on Gareth's desk, asked, "So who are you thinking of getting to work as a receptionist?"

Before an answer was forthcoming, Mitch jumped in. "I told him that Katelyn would be perfect."

"I know, I know," Gareth laughed, throwing up his hands in defense. "Right before you all came in this morning I was just thinking that it's time for me to get some help."

As the three men walked out into the front room to

say their goodbyes, the front door opened and Katelyn walked in. Her eyes grew large as she saw Mitch and Grant.

Gareth watched her expression change from surprise to suspicion. Hastening to speak, he explained, "Mitch and Grant just popped by for some business." Her gaze jumped to his as she nodded hesitantly.

"I see," she said, managing a smile. Floundering for a reason as to why she would be in the private investigator's office, she added, "Um...I brought your lunch order from the diner. It's...uh...in my car. I wasn't sure if you were in...so, I—"

"Thanks," Gareth said. He slid his gaze to the two officers, glad to see they did not appear to suspect Katelyn's presence in his office to be anything other than a diner delivery. Saying goodbye to them, he turned toward the irritated, dark-haired beauty standing in his reception area. Dressed in a green Finn's Pub t-shirt and jeans that fit her curvy figure perfectly, it took all his discipline to keep his eyes on her face and not allow them to drag down her body. But then, as he maintained his focus, it was clear her eyes were spewing anger.

Before she had a chance to argue, he said, "Well, it's nice to see you in the light of day and with your feet firmly planted on the ground."

"Very funny, Gareth," Katelyn replied, her hands on her hips. "So, why did you blackmail me to come see you today?"

"Blackmail?" he quipped. "I only used a little friendly coercion."

"Bringing my brothers into any discussion is hardly little or friendly!"

"Come on back. Let's talk," he invited with a warm smile before turning and heading to his office without waiting to see if she was going to agree.

"I see your office is still rather bare," she called out, the desire to see the rest of his space winning out over the desire to stay planted. Walking to the back room, she stood in the doorway, watching him pour a cup of coffee before he turned and handed it to her.

"I'm sure the coffee in the diner is better," he admitted, "but if you've been on your feet for hours, I figure you could use a break."

Sucking in a breath through her nose, she accepted the warm cup, her fingers meeting his and, once more, tingles ran up her arm. Manners overrode her irritation and she murmured, "Thank you." Glancing around the room, she observed a simple workroom with a table, counter with a sink and cabinets, and a refrigerator in the corner. The room was small but efficient.

Gareth walked passed her on his way toward his office, their shoulders brushing as he went. Looking down at her, he grinned. "Let's talk in my office."

She followed him, appreciating the view. Tall and muscular, she felt petite next to him and she rarely felt that with most men. His jeans were slightly worn, but still professional, paired with a light blue shirt and black jacket. Blinking away her appraisal, she took the chair he offered and watched as he moved to the other side of his messy desk and settled in. Lifting her chin slightly, she opted for a disinterested expression.

He noticed her attempt at casual, but observed as

her eyes darted around the room, landing on his desk. "Come on, Katelyn," he cajoled. "What were you really doing last night?"

Katelyn sighed, staring at her coffee before lifting her chin. Huffing, she said, "I'm not going to lie, Gareth. I was helping a friend."

"From the top of a tree?"

"I was hardly at the top!" she argued, then saw the twinkle in his eyes. Realizing the ridiculousness of her comment, a grin slipped out. "Okay, okay." Setting her coffee cup on the corner of his desk, the only bare space she could find, she nodded.

"You ready to let me know what's going on?"

"Helen Dorton talked to me last week after the last American Legion Auxiliary meeting and it came out that she thinks her Harry is having an affair with the mayor's new secretary. She didn't want to hire you because she was too embarrassed to have anyone else know her suspicions. So," shrugging, Katelyn continued, "I told her I would do a little snooping."

"Snooping?" he asked, sitting up straighter in his chair, his brows drawn down and his hands clenching on the desktop. "Snooping?"

"Perhaps snooping isn't exactly the right word," she said, her voice less confident.

"No, no. I think snooping is exactly what you meant and what you were doing," he clipped. "But what I can't figure out, is why you thought that was a good idea!"

"She just wanted to know what her husband might be up to," she countered, her eyes flashing in ire.

"Okay, and if you saw something, then what?" He noticed her scrunched brow and he continued. "Katelyn, you're too smart to think that what you were doing was going to help. You have no certification or license. The most you could do is tell Helen, and then what?"

"I didn't really think beyond just seeing if I could catch him with her," she admitted.

"So...you were playing at being a private investigator without actually being one," he said.

Leaning back in her chair, she huffed. "I was just trying to help a friend. You know, I've got two brothers that don't mind trying to tell me what to do...I hardly need another person in my life bossing me around."

Dropping his chin to his chest, Gareth sighed before piercing her with his gaze. "Look, Katelyn, people who get trapped can really fight back and following someone with the idea of catching them can backfire." Letting those words sink in, he confessed, "And I'd hate like hell for anything to happen to you."

3

Katelyn sat quietly for a moment, biting her lip, Gareth's warning ringing in her ears. And his confession. Deflated, she said, "Okay, I hear you loud and clear." Glancing at her watch, she said, "I need to get to the pub."

"No, wait," he hurried, anxious for her not to leave. Seeing her eyebrows shoot skyward, he glanced down at her cup and added, "You haven't finished your coffee."

A chuckle erupted from her chest as she cocked her head to the side. "Is that the best excuse that you can come up with to keep me here?"

Clearing his throat, he ducked his head. "Okay, I get it. You work in a diner and a pub, so you probably don't really care about the coffee." Capturing her gaze again, he said, "But, I'd like it if you'd stay and talk for a while. We never really get to talk." Inwardly wincing at the ridiculous excuse, he was pleased when it appeared she was taking him up on his offer.

Curious, she leaned back in her chair and picked up the coffee. Taking a sip, she said, "The coffee is surprisingly good."

"Hey, don't knock my Keurig."

They sat in silence for a moment before she set her cup back on the corner of the desk. "You know, your office is kind of...um...not neat."

"You trying to say it's a mess?"

Smirking, she replied, "That's exactly what I'm saying." Looking at his smiling face was dangerous, she realized, as she stared at his narrowed eyes, pinning her. Glancing back down at the piles of folders, she said, "Why don't you have a secretary?"

Shrugging, Gareth answered, "To be honest, when I first came to town, I had so many other expenses that paying a helper of any kind was out of the question."

"And now?"

"Now? Business has picked up. The local police use me occasionally, both here and in the surrounding counties. And I think people are more used to having a PI in town now, so I've got enough business to stay busy."

Biting her lip as she smoothed her hair back over her shoulder, she added, "Are you looking for someone?"

He wanted to shout, *Yes, you,* but managed to maintain a casual expression. "Yeah, I'd like to find someone."

"You could hang a Help Wanted sign out front," she offered.

"Well...I don't want just anyone in here."

Cocking her head to the side, she asked, "What qualifications do they need?"

Gareth stared at the beautiful woman in front of him, wanting her to be interested and, yet, afraid at the same time. "Well, for starters, I need someone who understands the word confidentiality. I need someone who can answer the phones, help with the paperwork, handle invoices, and..."

"And?" she prompted, leaning forward, her gaze never leaving his.

"And someone who wouldn't mind getting to know the private investigation business." Silence arched between them. Finally caving, he asked, "Do you know anyone who might be interested?"

Katelyn's heart skipped a beat, the idea of doing something besides being a waitress calling to her. *This is just what I've been wanting, but with Gareth?* Secretly wondering what it would be like to work day in and day out with him, now that she was right in front of him, she hesitated. "I might...but let me...uh...talk to the... person first and then I'll get back with you."

Gareth leaned back, his eyes still piercing hers. Nodding slowly, he agreed. "Okay, but let me know...or rather, have the person get in touch with me soon."

"They'll talk to you tomorrow," she proclaimed and promptly stood, sticking her hand out. "I've got to get to the bar, but thanks for the coffee." Just as she was about to leave, she turned and said, "And thanks for keeping my secret about last night."

With that, she was gone and Gareth stared after her. Sucking in a deep breath, he could still smell her fresh scent. Closing his eyes for a moment, he wondered if she were talking about herself for the job or if someone else would walk through his door tomorrow. Giving a mental shake, he turned his attention back to the files.

"Katelyn!"

Katelyn lifted her eyes to the heavens for the hundredth time that afternoon, the sound of her brother's deep voice booming across the bar. Walking behind the polished, wooden bar, she tossed her tray down. "Aiden, for crying out loud—I'm right here. You don't have to yell."

The pub had been established by their grandfather and retained the original look and appeal of bygone days. Never changing, the entrance held a dartboard to the right and an old fireplace and sofa on the left. The original building had been one of the early structures in the town. While renovated, it retained much of the original brick walls and floor from years gone by. The bar ran the length of the right side with tall, mismatched, padded bar chairs up against the counter. The left contained tables already full of patrons and the kitchens were in the back.

Aiden's long, dark hair was pulled into a ponytail and, paired with the tats on his arms, he kept the female population of Baytown coming in just to talk to him. "Aw, sis," he grinned. "Now why would I want to spend ten minutes trying to get your attention when a good yell gets it right away?"

Brogan walked over to the two of them and cuffed

Aiden on the back of the head. "Shut the hell up, asshole. You ain't gotta be yelling across the place."

With her hands on her hips, Katelyn looked at her two brothers. So alike in looks, people always thought they were twins when, in fact, Brogan was a full year older than Aiden. At one time, they both had the same Irish charm but the war had changed them. *Aiden hides behind jokes and Brogan...*sighing heavily, Katelyn knew Brogan's surly attitude hid something. He poured the drinks at the bar, but rarely touched the alcohol himself. The snapping of fingers in front of her face jerked Katelyn back to the present.

"See? That's why I gotta yell," Aiden grinned.

Eyes narrowed, leaning forward, Katelyn said, "Snap your fingers at me one more time and you'll lose them!"

"Come on, you two. Get back to work," Brogan growled, as he pulled the next beer for the men at the bar.

Rounding the corner toward the kitchen, Katelyn detoured into the ladies' room. Standing at the beaten copper sink, she looked into the mirror. It was easy to see the three as siblings, their Irish heritage shining through in the dark hair and light eyes. As children, they had bickered as siblings would, but Aiden and Brogan always considered themselves to be her protectors, even when she did not need that or want it. A close family in a small town could be as much a curse as a blessing and right now, she was feeling the curse. Dropping her chin to her chest, she sighed. She loved her brothers, but...*I need something for me. Just for me.*

All girls meeting. Tonight.

The text went out to Tori, Jillian, Belle, and Jade. That evening, Katelyn opened her door to her four closest friends and welcomed them inside. "Come on in, girls. The wine is already on the coffee table."

"Wow, this must be serious," Tori laughed, settling down on the sofa and pouring a drink, followed by Belle and Jade.

Jillian hesitated in the foyer, peering closely at Katelyn. "Should I be worried?" she asked softly.

Squeezing the hand of her best friend since birth, Katelyn shook her head slightly. "No...come on in and we'll talk."

Thirty minutes later, the four women had decimated the chips and dip, the cheese and crackers, and were on their second glasses of wine. Tori, Belle, and Jade sat on the sofa while Jillian slouched in the comfortable chair sideways, her legs dangling over one arm. Katelyn lounged on the carpet, her back resting against Jillian's chair, and gazed lovingly at her friends.

Belle grew up in Baytown but was a couple of years younger. Looking at the others expectantly, the dark-haired, petite, shy woman had slowly allowed herself to become part of the group. Jade was a new teacher at the elementary school and new to Baytown. Katelyn always thought she looked like her name with dark hair and green eyes. Tori had grown up in Virginia Beach but spent every summer with her grandmother, helping to run the Sea Glass Inn. When her grandmother passed away, Tori moved to Baytown and ran the inn herself. The natural beauty and Mitch had been childhood sweethearts who met again and now were engaged.

And then there was Jillian—best friend extraordinaire. Inseparable since birth, the two women shared confidences, heartaches, and joys. As different in appearance as they could be, with Jillian's blonde hair and slender, athletic frame, they could not be closer. She owned Jillian's Coffee Shop and Galleria and had recently gotten back together with her high school boyfriend, Grant. If anyone gave her the right advice, it would be Jillian.

Tori looked over at Katelyn and said, "Okay, girl, spill."

Katelyn replied, "I'm not sure where to start."

Belle smiled shyly, "Why not start at the beginning? Especially since Jade and I are kinda new to you all."

Chuckling, Katelyn nodded. "That's probably a good idea." Shooting a glance toward Jillian, she started, "I always wanted to go to college but had no clue what I wanted to do with my life. Graduating two years after Aiden, I watched my parents' fear when he left for the Marines just one year after Brogan joined. By the time I graduated high school, they were both in Afghanistan." Sighing heavily, she shook her head as she twisted up to look at Jillian. "Remember our plans? We were going to go to Old Dominion University."

Jillian's lips curved slightly at the memory. "Yeah, I do."

Heaving a sigh, Katelyn continued, "But that didn't happen. No way could I leave mom and dad at that time. I took a few business classes at the community college, but mostly I filled in at the pub and kept my morning job at the diner."

Sitting up straighter, she pierced them with her blue eyes. "Ladies, I'm now twenty-eight and I'm still at the diner and pub. Sure, I'm part owner of the pub, but that's just 'cause granddad left it to me and my brothers." Huffing, she repeated, "Twenty-eight. Still waitressing."

"Oh, honey—" Tori started but was interrupted by Katelyn.

"No, no, don't feel sorry for me," she said. "I made my own choices and, honestly, I would have wasted my parents' college money if I had gone ten years ago because I had no idea what I wanted to do. It's just that these past ten years have passed and I realize I'm still here...stuck in the same place, doing the same thing."

The silence was broken by Jillian's soft words. "You thought your life was going to be different."

Swallowing deeply, Katelyn nodded as a sad smile crossed her face. "Yeah...I thought I was going to be Philip's wife." Looking at Belle and Jade, she said, "You guys have heard of Philip Bayles and know about him. But, you see, before Philip left for the Army with Mitch, he asked me to marry him. I was only seventeen, but we'd been together all during high school. Looking back, I know I was too young to have made those kinds of decisions but, at the time, all I could think of was how much I loved him. I would have been twenty-one when he finished his tour and had never considered that I might not be his wife."

With a rueful chuckle, Katelyn said, "I never gave much thought to my future because I was sure that I'd be a wife, mom, and working at the pub and diner would be enough for me."

Belle's eyes teared as she breathed, "Oh, Katelyn."

"He was close to finishing his tour and when he visited on his last leave, we talked about our wedding. But then...he was killed...and with him, all my hopes, plans, and dreams."

4

Silence settled in the room that had recently filled with laughter. The five women sat, each to their own thoughts of the sadness of what all is lost when someone dies.

Jillian reached down, placing her hand on Katelyn's shoulder in a show of sympathy. After a moment, she said, "So what's got you thinking of a change now?"

Clearing her throat, Katelyn said, "I've been thinking of doing something else with my life. Something that helps other people, but will also pay the bills. Well, part time, at least, so I can still work in the pub."

"Has something presented itself to you?" Tori asked, her eyes wide with interest.

"In a round-about way, yes." Seeing the curious expressions around her, she smiled and said, "Well, the first part will sound weird but hang with me, okay?" Gaining their nods of agreement, she began, "Recently someone in town was telling me that they thought their husband was straying and—" Seeing their wide eyes, she threw up her hands and said, "Confidentiality, ladies. I won't say who."

"Spoilsport," Jillian joked. "Okay, go on."

"Anyway, I said I'd do a little checking and just did some simple things, like following him." Shrugging, she said, "So far, I've come up with nothing, but I found that I really liked the idea of helping someone and doing some investigating. And, it just so happens that Gareth Harrison has a position open. It's for a receptionist, but it sounds like a receptionist, secretary, bookkeeper, and who knows what else. He also wants someone who is interested in the investigation business."

"And you would know this, how?" Jillian asked, cocking one eyebrow, her lips barely curving.

"Uh...well, I talked to him."

"Talked to him?" Jillian prodded, her eyes now twinkling.

Katelyn could tell her best friend was sniffing out a story and she looked toward the ceiling in embarrassment. "Okay, okay. He kind of caught me snooping."

Jillian plopped her feet onto the floor, leaning toward Katelyn, mirroring Tori, Belle, and Jade's bodies. Jade giggled, "This I gotta hear."

Knowing Jillian would not give up, she started, "Last night, I thought I would stakeout someone's home to see if they happened to have company—"

"God, I want to know who it is!" exclaimed Jillian, clapping her hands together.

Katelyn cast her a narrowed-eyed look and continued, "So, I climbed up a tree outside their home—"

"You didn't!" Tori cried out, just as Jillian hooted loudly.

"Are y'all gonna let me tell my story or just keep interrupting?" Katelyn complained, finding it hard to keep from grinning as a deep blush settled on her cheeks.

"No, no, keep going," Belle begged, hiding her smile behind her hand.

Heaving a sigh, Katelyn repeated, "I climbed a tree that was next to the sidewalk and I was just looking. It was dark and I thought I was well hidden." Looking down at her lap, she flicked off a non-existent piece of fluff from her jeans and mumbled, "Then Gareth came along."

Hearing snorts of laughter, she jerked her head up, seeing all four friends bursting into giggles. Dropping her head in her hands, she said, "Oh, my God. This is so embarrassing. My pants got caught on a branch and he had to climb up to get me loose."

Laughter erupted and Katelyn leaned back, unable to keep from laughing with them. Finally, after wiping tears of mirth from her eyes, she said, "He was pissed when he found out what I was doing—"

"It does sound dangerous!" Belle exclaimed before immediately begging, "Please go on."

"Anyway, he said he wouldn't tell my brothers about my little excursion if I would come in today to see him. It wasn't about the job," she said hastily in answer to their curious expressions. "It was to make sure I knew that I wasn't to do any more investigating on my own. But then, as we chatted for a few minutes, I noticed how much he needed help in his office. So I asked what he was looking for and then told him I might know someone."

"And that someone is you!" Jade pronounced, her green eyes sparkling with excitement.

"I figure with all the years of waitressing, I've listened to hundreds of people tell me about their good times and their woes. I've helped by listening and sometimes offering my two-cents as to what they should do. With that, I've got the basis for helping people discover things."

"You want this change in your life, don't you?" Jillian asked, her eyes warm as they landed on Katelyn.

Shrugging, Katelyn looked up at her best friend and said, "I don't know. I mean, I'd love to do something besides be a waitress and it sounds really interesting." Her voice softened as she admitted, "And I haven't been really interested in anything in a long time."

"Oh, honey," Tori said, leaning over and grabbing Katelyn's hand, offering a little squeeze. "What's holding you back?"

"Fear," Katelyn whispered.

"Fear?" Belle asked, wide-eyed. "Katelyn, you're the most kick-ass woman I know!" Katelyn looked up at her as Belle continued. "You're not afraid of anyone in the bar—you set them straight if someone gets out of hand. And I've seen you on the ball field, you play as hard as any of the guys!" Belle's voice quieted as she added, "I've always admired you. I'm such a mouse and have wanted to be more like you for as long as I can remember...even back in high school."

Shaking her head, Katelyn said, "Oh, Belle, don't

wish to be anything other than who you are. I'm hard and sometimes hard-hearted."

"You've learned to be hard-hearted at times...it was self-preservation when Philip was killed," Jillian added. "But Belle's right, you're the strongest person I know. So what are you afraid of?"

Sitting in silence for a moment, Katelyn finally answered, "I've never had a job other than waitressing. That was never my goal. As I said, it was a high school job at the diner that just never ended. And then, when I was old enough, the bar was just family. It's been safe, paid the bills, but...it was never supposed to be my life-long goal. And working for Gareth? That, in and of itself, would be different. Especially for a private investigator. The work would be fascinating, and the chance to learn about the business is what really holds my interest."

"So are you more afraid of working in the PI business or for Gareth?" Jillian asked pointedly, drawing Katelyn's gaze.

"Gareth's nice," she replied noncommittally, her gaze dropping to her hands in her lap again.

"Nice? How about hot as hell?" Tori laughed.

Katelyn's lips curved up slightly, "I admit, he's good to look at, but," offering a little shrug, "he'd be my boss, that's all." She felt her cheeks warm with a blush again and hoped her friends were unable to detect her deception. Looking at Jillian's doubtful expression, she huffed, "I don't know how to flirt, even if I was interested! I'm so out of practice!"

"Well, coming from someone who works in an elementary school all day, where everyone is a child or mostly female teachers, a little eye-candy at work would be nice!" Jade added.

"Strangely enough, I've come to realize that wait-ressing has become a security blanket for me. No change. No uncertainty. Easy. Simple. But this? This would be using and learning a whole new skill-set."

"You know, bestie," Jillian said, placing her hand on Katelyn's shoulder, "I think you need to go for it. Your life needs shaking up a bit. You're smart, tenacious, driven. You've held back in your personal life for long enough."

"You think?" Katelyn asked, smiling.

"I know!" Jillian proclaimed, the others chiming in as well.

Sucking in a huge, cleansing breath before letting it out, she shifted to her knees and poured more glasses of wine. Holding hers up to the cheers all around, she toasted, "Then here's to new beginnings!"

The rhythm of his footsteps along the beach was comforting to Gareth as he sweated through his morning run. Running was one of the things he did growing up that got him out of the house and gave him a way to burn off his anger. When his stepdad decided to beat another *respect lesson* into him, learning to run and run fast became necessary. *A million years ago and a million miles away.* That was what he told himself to keep the memories at bay.

Leaving his home had been easy. Leaving the mili-tary had also been easy. But the feelings that were growing with this little town and the friends he was making...*can't imagine being anywhere else.*

The breeze off the bay cooled his skin as he brought up the bottom of his t-shirt to wipe his face. The sunrise behind the town was dawning clear, offering a glimpse of the blue-sky day in store for Baytown.

The never-ending surf washed up on the shore, cleansing the beach while also cleansing his mind as he ran, washing away old memories. The beach had been nothing more than a picture in a book when he was a kid and the idea of living near the water was a dream, that was now a dream come true.

Coming off the beach, he beat a path along empty Main Street. Early morning activity seemed to be coming from inside Jillian's Coffee Shop, where he knew she was busy at work preparing for the coming breakfast crowd.

He turned before getting to the diner, knowing Katelyn would be hard at work preparing as well. He had not been able to get her off his mind since yesterday...well, before that, if he was honest. Slowing down his pace as he neared his building, he stopped outside and performed his cool down stretches. When he first moved here, he rented a small house north of town, but when he opened his PI business, he decided to live in the apartment above his office until the business brought in more money.

Katelyn MacFarlane. A knock-out, her looks caught his eye the first time he saw her. Spirit and fire...smart and sassy. And yet, when introduced, he could have sworn he had seen a glimmer of sadness in her deep blue eyes.

Later, getting to know her brothers, along with the other Baytown Boys, he heard the story of Katelyn and the greatly-mourned, Philip Bayles. Knowing Katelyn's love was buried in the town cemetery had put a damper on his initial thoughts of flirtation with the Irish beauty. *Who can compete with lost love?* Especially one with someone the whole town mourned. So, he admired her from a distance, but admired her, nonetheless. And wondered...

Jogging up his steps and through his apartment, he headed into the shower. Dressing for work normally involved jeans or khakis with a polo. If he was meeting a client, he sometimes wore a shirt and tie. But as he got out of the shower and headed to his closet, he stood for a moment, thinking of what to wear. *Damn, what the hell is wrong with me? Since when do I give a fuck what I'm wearing?*

As he jerked a long-sleeved polo off the hanger, he knew the answer was going to be walking in his door today. After dressing, he headed into his kitchen, firing up the Keurig and mixing a bowl of instant oatmeal. Thoughts of breakfast at the diner tempted him, but he did not want Katelyn to think he was crowding her. *And who knows who she's thinking of for the job. I hope it's her, but...?*

An hour later, he was settled in his office reviewing the files from his open cases. Reading the same paragraph over three times, he finally slapped the folder closed and rubbed his eyes. Glancing at the clock for the millionth time, he was just about to give up when he heard a female voice from the front room.

"Gareth?"

Letting out a breath, he felt his heart kick-start. *Katelyn.* Just as he made it around his desk, she appeared in the doorway. Ebony hair pulled back with a headband, a touch of makeup playing up her natural beauty. He noticed right away that she was not wearing her diner uniform. She had changed into dark jeans and a red sweater with a scarf hanging from her neck.

"Hey, Katelyn," he greeted, extending his hand.

She smiled and noted once more the warmth from his fingers wrapped around hers. "Hi."

"Coffee?"

Laughing, she replied, "No, thank you, not today. I truly did have some this morning at the diner."

After ushering her to a chair, he walked back around to sit behind his desk. Trying to steady his heartbeat, he jumped to the point. "Well, did you talk to the person who might be interested in the job?"

"Yes, I did. Or rather, I talked to some friends about me. I mean, me taking the job. Or applying for it." Usually unflappable, Katelyn blushed as she stammered. "I'm sorry. Let me start over, please. I would like to apply for the position."

Holding back his grin, he simply nodded. "What qualifications do you bring, besides climbing trees in the middle of the night?"

Blinking rapidly as she blushed, Katelyn grimaced. "For starters, can we not mention that embarrassing incident again?"

Chuckling, he said, "Well, you have to admit that it won't be easy to forget getting you unstuck from that branch." Seeing her about to protest, he threw his hands up in conciliation and said, "Okay, forgotten...for now. Please, continue."

Smoothing her hands over her jeans, she held his gaze as she said, "I have no problem answering your phones, making appointments, greeting clients, and organizing your office. I admit, it's been a while, but I have taken some business classes at the community college and I can certainly run spreadsheets of your expenses and keep track of your invoices, both paid and unpaid." Looking at the stack of folders on his desk, she added, "And I can arrange a filing system that will make it easier for you to find what you're looking for. And, one more thing—I've discovered you don't have a website. I can set that up for you."

Leaning back in his seat, he rubbed the back of his neck. "I've gotta say, you've come up with some items that I hadn't thought about, but could certainly use the help with."

She smiled, encouraged, and continued, "You mentioned that you were interested in someone who wanted to know more about the investigation busi- ness...that's me as well. And not just tree stakeouts."

His eyes jumped to hers as he said, "Hey, you said no more tree jokes."

"Well, I can mention it but not you," she quipped, her eyes sparkling.

Nodding, they sat in silence for only a moment before he asked, "Tell me about your interests. Why this...why now?"

Her lips tightened for a moment as she gathered her thoughts. It had been easy to explain it to her friends last night...*well, with some wine to loosen my* tongue. *Where's wine when you need it?* Clearing her throat as she noticed him waiting patiently, she said, "I began working at the diner when I was only sixteen and," sighing, she continued, "it was a comfortable place to work. Somewhat mindless and easy. The pub is family run, of course, and I co-own it with my brothers." She hastened to add, "I help with the Pub's books and payroll, so doing it for your business would be easy, I'm sure."

Gareth's thoughts swirled in his head, excitement mixed with a strange sense of uncertainty. *This is what I wanted, but maybe I didn't think this through. She'd be my employee. How the hell can I be around her every day and not want more? And if I act on wanting more, can she stay my employee?*

Seeing him still waiting, she shrugged slightly as she said, "I've finally come to a point in my life where I want to make a change. I don't want just a job, but to have something to learn that I'm excited about. And even though I went about it the wrong way, I found it exciting to help someone who needed me to check into things for them."

Gareth smiled as he stood and extended his hand. "All right. You're hired. Welcome to Harrison Investigations, Katelyn."

Jumping up, she grabbed his hand with both of hers, pumping up and down with enthusiasm. "Oh, my goodness! Thank you! When do I start?"

5

On time and gorgeous...this may be a mistake. Gareth stepped from his door to the sidewalk and observed Katelyn standing outside the office, dressed in black slacks, a light blue blouse, and black, low-heeled shoes.

She greeted him with a smile, holding a cup tray with two cups of coffee and a pastry bag from Jillian's shop. He looked fresh from a shower, his hair curling slightly. His long-sleeve polo fit tight across his arms and chest and she refused to drop her eyes to his jeans. *He's my boss...that's all.*

Taking the proffered drink, steam still rising from the top, he shook his head. "Katelyn, you don't have to buy me coffee—"

"I know, but I thought it would be a nice gesture on my first day."

He chuckled as he unlocked the door. "I've got a second set of keys and will give those to you." As they entered the front room, he nodded toward the desk in the back corner. "It's not much, but that'll be your desk for the time being." He watched as she put her cup of coffee on the top of the desk and walked around to the chair.

She eyed the reception area appraisingly, noting the stark walls, freshly painted but bare. The tile floor clean but uninspiring. The front of the office sported full, plate-glass windows looking out onto the street, providing plenty of light, but little privacy. Her eyes roved over the simple setup, complete with a telephone and computer. Lifting her gaze back to his, she graced him with a wide smile. "It's perfect. Thank you for this opportunity, Gareth."

"I was surprised that you were able to get away from the diner with only a week's notice."

"Believe me, they had a stack of teenagers who had applied. Rupert had no problem filling my position and the long-time waitress, Betty, can train them." Looking around, she said, "So what do you want me to start with?"

"I've been on my own for so long, I hardly know," he admitted, his eyes darting around, taking in the stark room.

"How about I spend some time looking over your files and organizing them? And I'll do some basic computer work, see what needs to be done."

"I've got to meet with a client at their house this morning, so that'd be great," he agreed, grateful that she was a self-starter. "Make yourself at home and just look for whatever you need."

She watched as he made his way down the hall that led to his office, the work-room, another office, and the supply closet and bathroom. Unable to keep the grin off her face, she looked around the rather bland space. A plan already in mind, she sat down and placed a call.

An hour later, Jillian came through the door, carrying several paintings. "I was surprised when you called, but this is a such a cool idea!"

Katelyn rushed to help her, saying, "This office is so boring and I remembered you always have some extra local artwork in your galleria."

They easily hung several artists' renderings of seascapes on the walls before stepping back to admire their handiwork. Looking first at the paintings and then at each other, they simultaneously grabbed each other in a hug.

"I think you might just be really happy here," Jillian said.

Grinning, Katelyn agreed but, before she could reply, the door opened again and this time it was Tori with an oversized potted plant. Setting it down in the front corner by the large, plate glass window, she said, "Jillian called to see if I had anything to contribute. This plant is so easy to maintain. Honestly, no green thumb required."

"Thank goodness, because I have no green thumbs!" With the simple additions, the office now looked professional and inviting. Biting her lip, she hoped she had not overstepped her bounds. Saying goodbye to her friends, she sat back down at the computer, continuing to get acclimated with Gareth's invoices, payments, and business accounts.

Just before lunch, he came back in, smiling as soon as he laid eyes on her. Then his gaze jumped to the pictures on the walls and, as he swung around, the large plant came into view. "Wow, you have been busy!"

"Is it too much? I just thought it would be more inviting for clients to have a nice waiting area."

Touched by her concern, he looked back and observed her nervousness. Walking over, he placed his hands on her shoulders and said, "Katelyn, relax. It's great. Really great."

Releasing a breath in a whoosh, she smiled in return. "How did the meeting go?"

"Not bad. I finished up the case for that client and I have this to show for it," he exclaimed, holding up a check between his fingers.

"Congratulations! I know the case is over, but will you tell me about it sometime? I'd like to know some of your basic operations."

"How about now? I can go over my notes and you can type them up and file them. After that, I'll send you to the bank to deposit the check."

Grinning, Katelyn grabbed the laptop from her desk and followed him back to his office. Once settled, he began, "This was a rather simple assignment. I was contacted by a business in the county by the owner. An employee fell last year on the job, claiming he slipped on a wet spot on the concrete floor. He received compensation, but a year later, he is still off work and still receiving compensation. They had been given information that he was no longer hindered by his injury but since he lives in Maryland, no one local had been around him other than the one employee who saw him."

Katelyn, listening carefully, took notes on the

laptop. Looking up, she said, "If someone did see him, isn't that enough to stop his paid leave?"

"No, not without proof. And this is where I told you the PI license is needed. I can be a witness in court and my documentation is acceptable...not considered hearsay."

Nodding, Katelyn continued to type as he spoke. "So I did some background investigating here at the office and discovered that he actually got a speeding ticket two months ago in Baltimore, so he was driving, even though he claims he can't drive. I also checked his taxes from last year and he's working part time. Now, it's at his brother's restaurant and he gets to sit behind a counter, but it's still work. Since he doesn't know me, I ate several times in the restaurant. I was unable to catch him doing any real physical work until last week. I noticed some activity as he and another employee were going in and out."

He watched Katelyn's fingers fly over the keyboard and realized how much longer it would have taken him to type his notes. Smiling encouragingly, he continued. "So, I circled around to the back alley where I was able to take photos of him lifting heavy boxes from a delivery truck and carrying them inside. He made at least six or seven trips with the heavy boxes."

As he came to a stop, Katelyn looked up, her eyebrows lifted. "And..." she prompted.

Chuckling, he said, "I delivered the evidence to the company and got paid."

"What will happen to him?" she asked, leaning forward.

"Why? Are you out for blood?"

"No," she shook her head, smiling. "Just curious."

"Well, I don't know. It's not up to me. It's in the hands of the company. They can terminate him. Take away his compensation. My part is done unless it goes to court and I get a subpoena."

Finishing with the notes, Katelyn grinned. "What did you use to take the pictures?"

"I've got a couple of cameras and some long-range lenses." Seeing the excitement in her eyes, he warned, "You have to realize that a lot of what I do is right here, at this desk with my special computer programs. And even when I'm out, hours are spent just sitting in my SUV watching. This career is not like TV."

"I know, but I really want to help...and learn," she vowed. Sucking in her lips, she eyed him nervously, before blurting, "I've looked at the Department of Criminal Justice website and researched what I would need to become licensed. I know it will take time, but I'd like to learn."

Gareth grinned at the glitter of interest in her eyes and realized he liked that so much better than the specter of sadness he had observed in the past. "I'll help you all I can."

"Good," she said, standing. "Now, I've called in some sandwiches from the pub to pick up for us and then I'll get to the filing." As she reached the door, she looked back over her shoulder and called out, "Who knows? Maybe one day, we'll be partners!"

Gareth's gaze dropped to her ass and he leaned back and groaned. *I'd like to be partners...just maybe not the only way she's thinking.*

Katelyn looked up at the woman stepping through the door, immediately noting her unease. Standing quickly, she walked around the desk and extended her hand. "Hello. Welcome to Harrison Investigations. My name is Katelyn. May I help you?"

The woman glanced down to Katelyn's hand for a second before taking it in her own. Her other hand clutched her purse strap, worrying the leather as her eyes dropped from Katelyn's to take in the room. Swallowing deeply, she said, "Uh...hello. I'm...well...uh..."

Smiling warmly, Katelyn asked, "Would you like to speak to Mr. Harrison?"

A jerky nod was her only response as her gaze drifted to the front door, as though ready to flee. Recognizing her nervousness, Katelyn asked, "May I get you a cup of coffee, Miss...?"

"Oh, uh...yes. And it's Mrs. Milstone."

"Have a seat and I'll be glad to get you some coffee."

Looking around nervously, Mrs. Milstone said, "Is there somewhere else I can...um...well, it's just that..." her gaze drifted back to the large, plate glass window facing the street.

Understanding dawned, and Katelyn said, "Of course. Please follow me." She walked to the empty office and left Mrs. Milstone there, comfortably seated. Rushing to pop the coffee pod into the Keurig, she then hurried into Gareth's office.

"You've got a walk-in client," she said, capturing his undivided attention. "She's nervous and didn't want to wait out front, which I realized has too much glass and waiting clients have no privacy from anyone walking by, but we can talk about that later."

Gareth stood and motioned with his hands for her to slow down. "Okay, okay. You put her in the other office?"

"Yes, let me get her coffee and I'll take you in." With that she turned on her heels and rushed back out.

Gareth smiled at her enthusiasm, realizing how much different the office felt since Katelyn came on board. Grabbing a pen and pad of paper, he met her in the hall and allowed her to enter the room first.

Katelyn made the introductions and placed the cup of coffee on the table in front of the client, smiling at her warmly. Turning to leave, she heard a nervous gasp.

"You...you're not staying?" Mrs. Milstone asked, her eyes full of concern.

"Well, uh..." Katelyn stammered.

"She's just getting her notebook," Gareth replied quickly, observing the nervous woman. His gaze jumped to Katelyn's and he offered a nod.

"Yes, yes," she said. "I'll be right back." Hurrying out to her desk, she grabbed a notebook and pen before rushing back. Standing outside the door for a moment, she sucked in a deep breath, collecting herself. Once inside, she slid into the seat nearest Mrs. Milstone.

As Gareth listened to the woman, he noted her gaze drifted often to Katelyn, seeming to take comfort in another woman being present. *I've never thought of that before, but perhaps some women prefer talking with another woman.* Swinging his attention back to the matter at hand, he began gently questioning the client.

"I think my husband is hiding money and I just

want to know what's going on," she explained. "He owns his own business and makes real good money. I work part-time as well. But when I look at our bank statements, it just doesn't seem to add up. He's a good man, but something's not right and he won't tell me where the money is going. He says it just goes back into the business, but it seems to do so more than it used to."

Gareth immediately picked up on the dichotomy of her terms—*good man but something's not right*—and he instinctively knew Mrs. Milstone would most likely not like the results. Secretive spouses were rarely a good thing. Keeping his face neutral, he continued to ask more questions, creating a larger picture.

Katelyn stayed quiet during the interview, taking notes as her mind worked furiously. Having no idea how to proceed in investigating such a case, she was anxious to watch Gareth at work. He leaned toward the client, his focus entirely on her. He nodded, his face a mask of professional concern, encouraging Mrs. Milstone to continue to talk and Katelyn observed the tension in the client's shoulders seem to slip away as Gareth gently probed for more information. She realized his body language worked to his advantage as much as his questions. *But it's sincere. He really seems to care.*

Gareth finished gathering the information needed, including the bank information. Mrs. Milstone pulled out her purse and handed Gareth cash for his initial fee for taking on a case. Katelyn jumped up to retrieve the receipt book and, once she handed Mrs. Milstone her receipt, the three left the office. Shaking hands in the front room, Katelyn and Gareth watched her hasten out the door.

Turning to him, Katelyn said, "What do you think?"

He observed her wide-eyed inquisitiveness and shook his head sadly. "Chances are she's not going to like the answers we find."

Caught between his depressing answer and the fact that he included her in the investigation, she sighed. "I noticed...well, it seemed like you really cared about her...you know, as you were talking to her." Seeing his brows raise as he cocked his head to the side, she rushed, "I mean, you were totally professional. But, it's just that, you put her at ease. She seemed to relax as she talked to you and I noticed you really focused on her."

Nodding slowly, he explained, "It's not always easy for people to come ask for help, Katelyn." Lifting his hands to the side, he added, "Oh, sure, sometimes we get the client who comes blowing in and they're pissed as hell at a spouse or employee and they're out for blood. But mostly, people come when they are desperate, confused, wanting answers, hating the fact that they need to have someone probe into their lives...hell, even dreading what I might dig up."

Katelyn stood, her eyes never leaving his as he continued to explain.

"So, it's important for me to connect with the client. I'm essentially taking on their burden, so they can sit back and let someone else carry the load for a while. They know they may not like what I find, but they know someone's in their corner."

Katelyn's heart squeezed as she listened to Gareth

speak. "You're a really good person," she admired, her voice soft.

A blush crept across his face as he smirked. "Don't know about that...I just know that I really like helping people."

Sucking in a deep breath before letting it out slowly, she nodded. "Okay, so what do we do?"

Grinning, he asked, "Anxious to get started?"

"Absolutely! This is so much more exciting than working in the diner!"

"You know a lot of days are boring, right?"

Shrugging, she replied, "In the diner, I did get to hear the latest gossip, but since I'm at the pub in the evenings, I'll still catch up on it all."

Standing still for a moment, he said softly, "You're good with people, Katelyn. You put her at ease, also."

"I guess I learned to listen from all those years of waiting on people," she offered with a slight shrug. "I got adept at reading people's behavior as well as their words."

Smiling, he nodded, recognizing her value. "Come on into my office and I'll go over my plan for Mrs. Milstone."

A few minutes later, Katelyn sat and watched as Gareth began to outline his thoughts. "To be honest, her giving us the bank information makes things easier. She happens to be on the home and the business accounts so I don't have to do any special digging on that."

"What if she wasn't?"

Grinning, he replied, "Then I get creative, as long as

I don't have to testify in court. If she just wants my info, then I do what I need to get it for her."

Observing Katelyn as she bent over her notebook, scribbling furiously, her thick, dark hair falling over her shoulders, he fought the urge to reach out and touch the silky tresses. Something about her called to him... not just lust...something deeper. Jolted from his musing as she lifted her gaze back to his, he stuffed down his wandering thoughts, forcing his mind to remember, *She's now an employee.*

6

Rapping the gavel upon the podium, Jillian called the Baytown American Legion Auxiliary's meeting to order. The women in town had been excited to gain a charter for their organization after the veterans had chartered their American Legion.

"Rise for the Advancement of the Colors," she announced.

The large group of women in the building rose to their feet as Ginny Spencer marched forward carrying the American flag. As a member of the American Legion and former Army Sergeant, and current Baytown police officer, she had been voted to the position of Sergeant at Arms.

A Methodist minister from the town said the prayer before Jillian led the group in the Allegiance to the Flag. After Ginny had taken her seat again, Jillian read the preamble to the Constitution of the American Legion and then called Nancy Evans, Mitch's mom, to the podium for the reading of the last meeting's minutes. After she completed her task, Jillian called Corinne MacFarlane, Katelyn's mom, to read the treasurer's report.

Katelyn, as Vice President, called upon the committee chairs to report as well. Tori, taking the stand, said, "Our first bake sale at the American Legion's children's ball game last month brought in over three hundred dollars—"

Applause interrupted, as the group was excited about their first fund-raising activity. Tori finished with information for the next sale.

"Next, we need to discuss the Cavalcade of Memories," Jillian said. "If you look in your packets, you will find the type of things we want to collect and display. I'm sure we can gather a great number of items that reflect the history of our family members who served, but we will need to have volunteers to catalog and, then, if we have enough items, we can display them on a rotating basis."

Several other committees reported as well, including Katelyn's plan for getting more girls in the community involved in the sporting activities. Discussions ensued and after almost thirty minutes, the meeting came to a close.

With a final prayer and the retirement of colors, Jillian read the Auxiliary Charge. "Till we meet again let us remember that our obligation to our Country can be fulfilled only by the faithful performance of all duties of citizenship. Let service to the community, state and nation be ever a main objective of the American Legion Auxiliary and its members. Let us ever be watchful of our organization and ourselves, that nothing shall swerve us from the path of Justice, Freedom, Loyalty and Democracy." After that, she pronounced, "If there is no further business to come before this meeting, the meeting is adjourned."

As the women filed out of the room, the officers stayed behind to chat for a few minutes. Katelyn walked over to hug Tonya Bayles, Philip's mom and the woman she had assumed would be her mother-in-law.

"Oh, sweet girl, how are you?" Tonya asked, her smile genuine as she looked at the younger woman.

"I'm good," Katelyn said honestly.

"I've heard you no longer work at the diner," Tonya said. "I have to admit, it will be strange to go in there and not see your pretty face."

"Lord knows I've worked there for almost thirteen years," Katelyn admitted. "I miss the people, but I don't miss the smell of bacon on all my clothes!"

The two chuckled before Tonya said, "Well, gossip has it that you're now working with Gareth Harrison."

Hating to be the subject of speculation, Katelyn nonetheless knew how small towns operated. It was better to make sure you had no secrets because they would be ferreted out soon enough. "That's right. He needed a receptionist and I wanted to do something besides just waitressing."

Tonya smiled indulgently. "I understand, sweetheart. I was always afraid you had become stuck after Philip died and he would have never wanted that for you."

For once, the mention of Philip did not bring the familiar sting of tears. Instead, Katelyn was surprised to feel strangely comforted at the thought of her former fiancé being happy for her. Grasping Tonya's hands in hers, she smiled at the older woman. "Thank you for that."

With a pat to Katelyn's cheek, Tonya said her good-byes and walked out of the room with the other women.

Turning around, Katelyn noticed the group behind her, standing in both curiosity and concern. Cocking her head to the side, she peered back at them.

Her mom spoke first as she walked over to Katelyn. "You okay, honey?"

"Yeah, Mom, I'm good." Smiling, she embraced her mom, whispering in her ear, "I'm really good."

Corrine MacFarlane smiled in return and then said, "Well, let's head to the pub!"

Some of the American Legion members always had a beer at Finn's after their meetings and the women decided that they wanted to continue the tradition. Of course, on Auxiliary nights, the men were already there waiting on them.

Aiden and Brogan worked the bar, keeping an eye on the waitstaff's movements through the crowd, serving drinks and food.

"Gotta love American Legion and Auxiliary nights," Aiden said. "Brings in business during the week to match the weekend's."

Brogan grunted his agreement, his eyes continually darting toward the door.

"You got someone coming in you want to see?"

Aiden asked, noting his brother's behavior. "If I didn't know better, I'd think some honey was on their way."

"Shut the fuck up," Brogan said, scowling. "Just checking the crowd, that's all."

Aiden's attention was quickly pulled away as he moved down the bar toward some of their friends. "What's goin' on in the police world?" he asked Mitch, sitting with Grant. They were joined by Mitch's father, Ed, the former police chief.

"Not much right now," Mitch said. "Still got some drugs running up and down the county, but for now, things are quiet."

"As soon as the tourists start coming in, the department will be too busy," Grant added. "Hell, just the teen shoplifters and adults drinking alcohol on the public beach will take up time."

"Always liked the warmer weather," Ed said, "but gotta admit the tourists, which are needed for the town's businesses, can add a layer of need to the department."

Gareth, sitting on the other side of Ed, nodded toward Brogan as he served him another beer. Like the others, he found himself looking up every time the door opened, hoping to see Katelyn. *Hell, I just saw her at work today.* But he could not deny the desire to see her again. Shaking his head, he tried to empty his mind.

"Thinking of work?" Brogan asked, his deep voice cutting through Gareth's thoughts.

Startling, Gareth's gaze jumped to his friend. "Uh... yeah. Just got some cases on my mind."

"Katelyn doin' okay for you?"

Gareth knew Brogan's abbreviated verbiage held a lot of brotherly concern, but refused to wither under the intense stare. Used to doing what he wanted, when he wanted, he chaffed at feeling the need to explain himself. "She's doing great. She fits in easily and, to be honest, I now wonder how I managed without her."

Brogan stared wordlessly, non-blinking, and Gareth wondered if he caught the double meaning of his words. Before he could reply further, Brogan just nodded and walked away.

As they walked out into the night, Katelyn realized that almost all the women walking with her down the street had someone to meet at the pub. Jillian had Grant and Tori had Mitch. Their moms were all going to be meeting their husbands. Smiling at Belle, she looped her arm through hers, deciding to keep her company as the only other single woman in their group.

Entering the pub, the familiar warmth and smells hit her, bringing a sense of peace. Nodding toward her brothers, she fought the urge to move behind the bar with them on her night off.

Ed slid off his stool to greet Nancy with a kiss, mirroring the behavior of his brother, Steve, with Jillian's mom, Claire. Katelyn watched as her mom and dad embraced as well. Smiling, she realized how lucky she was to have such long-term, committed relationships amongst family and friends. She noted Mitch and Tori, as well as Jillian and Grant embracing. Feeling a pin-prick to her heart, she turned toward the bar and ran into a wall. A human wall. Throwing her hands out to catch herself, she found strong arms holding her as she steadied her feet. Jerking her eyes upward, she viewed Gareth's smiling face staring back.

"Gareth!" she exclaimed. "I'm sorry...I wasn't watching where I was going."

"My fault," he replied, his nostrils filling with her soft scent.

"I didn't know you would be here tonight."

"Any reason I shouldn't be?" he asked, reluctantly letting go of her arms.

Smiling up at his face, she shook her head. "No, I can't think of one at all."

He jerked his head toward the bar. "Do you have to work?"

Her gaze cut over to the bar and she noticed Brogan's eyes were pinned on her before she looked back up into Gareth's face. "Nope, not tonight."

"Then can I buy you a drink?"

Laughing, she said, "I might not be working, but in my bar, my drinks are free. But how about I buy you one?"

Grinning, he offered his arm and she slid her hand into the crook of his elbow as they walked toward their friends.

An hour later, as the group dispersed, Gareth and Katelyn walked toward the door. Hearing her name, she twisted around and looked over toward the bar, cocking her head in frustration toward Brogan.

"You gonna help close up tonight?" he asked.

"It's my night off—"

"We got a lot to do," he barked.

Pinching her lips together, she glanced apologetically toward Gareth. "Guess I'll help my brothers. See you tomorrow."

Not wanting to make things uncomfortable for her, he nodded, but shot Brogan a narrow-eyed glare. With a smile toward Katelyn, he walked out of the pub, leaving her fuming.

Whirling around, she stalked over to the bar. "You want to tell me why I have to help close tonight when it's my day off? I've rarely had one of those, you know. It's not like I don't pull my weight around here."

Aiden walked over, his gaze jumping between his siblings. "What's going on?"

"Just thought we could use some help closing tonight, that's all," Brogan answered, his eyes watching Katelyn closely.

"You know I've done nothing but waitress my whole life...since I was sixteen years old. I've finally got another job that I really like, where I can develop other skills besides *do you want a side of bacon with that* or *are you ready for another beer*? So, having a night off, for once, doesn't seem to be too much to ask!"

Aiden stood back, unusually quiet, letting her talk as his eyes jumped between his siblings. Brogan grunted as he mumbled, but Katelyn was not in the mood for his surliness.

"You got something to say? Then say it," she demanded, her hands planted on her hips.

"I said it just seemed like you and Gareth were kind of chummy."

The silence between the three filled the air, so thick

she thought she would choke on it. Chest heaving, she said, "You did not just say that to me."

Brogan grimaced but held his silence as Aiden stared wide-eyed at his brother.

Sucking in air through her nose, she lifted her chin in defiance. "You all need me, I'm always here. You want the books done, I do them. We need an extra pair of hands, I always fill in. I'm part owner and have never shirked my time at this pub. This very building is like family to me. But I have a chance to learn a new job with a good man and I do not expect to have to take crap from my brother. Gareth is your friend. You know him...you trust him. He's been nothing but professional to me."

Katelyn felt the sting of tears hit her eyes as her voice broke. "But if he felt more, I wouldn't mind exploring that too...and I haven't felt that in a long time." Swallowing deeply, she said, "You're not the only one with war scars, Brogan." Her finger hit her chest right over her heart and she choked out, "I carry them too."

Hanging his head, Brogan sighed heavily. Lifting his gaze, he said, "Katelyn, I'm sorry."

She felt her chin quiver as a solitary tear slide down her cheek. Both brothers looked at her aghast, having not seen her cry in years. "I...haven't had a relationship since Philip. And Gareth was not here as my date...but as my boss and someone who's becoming my friend." The air in the room hung heavily over the trio, making it hard to breathe. Sucking in a shuddering breath, her chest heaving with emotion, she added, "You know what? Close the bar yourself. I'm going home."

Turning on her heel, she stalked out of the pub, the door banging in her wake.

"Fuck," Brogan growled, tossing the rag onto the bar. He started to head toward the door, but Aiden caught him by the arm.

"Don't go, Bro," Aiden warned. "Let her be for now. You can talk to her tomorrow, but leave her alone tonight."

"I need to make this right," Brogan said, jerking his arm away.

"Then do it tomorrow," Aiden said. "You know her... she hates to cry in front of anyone and, right now, she needs to cry."

Brogan turned his gaze to Aiden and said, "Since when did you get to be such an expert?"

"Maybe you should just start paying attention to what's right in front of your face," Aiden snapped back, gaining a raised eyebrow from his brother. "You still see her as our little sister. Hell, man...she's twenty-eight years old. She got up at the ass-crack of dawn to work at the diner every fuckin' day and then came over here to work from mid-afternoon to closing just about every night. You think that's enough for her? Enough for anyone? Jesus, Brogan, she gave up college 'cause you and I went off to the military. And hell, don't even get me started on Philip!"

At Philip's name, Brogan growled, starting to turn from Aiden, who stopped him once more.

"He was our friend, but man, he's gone. And Katelyn mourned him, but she deserves a life...she deserves a love. Don't you want that for her?"

Brogan ran his hand over his face in frustration. "Of

course I want that for her. I just...I just...hell, I don't know." A heavy sigh escaped his lips as he dropped his chin to his chest for a moment. "I guess I just see her as our little sister that needs protection. I just don't want her to have any more heartache."

Aiden's voice softened as he nodded. "I get that, Bro. But that's no life for her. She's lived in the past for so long, we gotta let her move toward a future."

Lifting his face to his brother's, Brogan asked, "And you think Gareth's her future?"

"I got no way of knowing," Aiden said, sighing as well. "But a job change that she's excited about is a start. And Gareth's a good man...a good friend. He looks at her as though he knows she's special. Maybe something will happen and maybe she'll get her heart broken again. But it's living, man. It's living."

Brogan nodded slowly as he picked up the rag from the bar and began wiping down the polished wood once again. "Yeah...you're right. She deserves to live again."

7

Katelyn stormed out of the pub into the night, dashing tears away from her cheeks with the back of her hand. Fury, mixed with frustration, poured through her veins as she stalked down the street. She only lived five blocks from Main Street and while the night air was cool, it felt good against her overheated skin.

As she turned the corner of her street, she noticed headlights behind her. Going slowly. Her fury forgotten momentarily as uneasiness slithered through her, she hastened her steps.

The vehicle increased its speed and pulled to a stop next to her. She jumped back defensively just as the driver called out, "Katelyn, it's me!"

"Gareth? Oh, Jesus, you scared me. What are you doing?" she asked, her heart pounding an erratic rhythm in her chest.

He jumped from his SUV and jogged over to her, placing his hands on her shoulders. "I'm so sorry. I was worried about you walking home by yourself so I was waiting outside the pub. I was going to offer you a ride home, but you came out so fast and seemed...uh..."

Her eyes cut to the side in embarrassment at being caught crying. "Upset? Pissed? Mad as hell? Are those the words you're looking for?"

"Yeah...and then I wasn't sure I should interrupt your thoughts. I just thought I'd follow you to make sure you got home safely."

The pair stood silently on the sidewalk for a moment, each filled with uncertainty. Suddenly, Katelyn burst out in laughter, her hand covering her mouth as she giggled.

"What?" he asked.

"I'm sorry," she gasped, "but for a private eye, you weren't very invisible following me."

"Oh, thanks, smart-ass," he chuckled. "I wasn't on a case. I assure you that if I was on a mission, you would have never noticed me."

Their mirth slowly ebbed as they stood in the moonlight, staring at each other. He reached up and cupped her cheek with his hand, his thumb wiping at the tear trail. "You okay?" he asked, his voice whisper soft. He felt responsible, knowing her brothers were pissed at him.

She nodded wordlessly, leaning slightly into his warm touch. After a moment, she straightened and said, "It's late and I should be getting home. I don't want to be late for work tomorrow. My boss might not like it."

Grinning, he said, "I'll walk you the rest of the way, if that's okay. And I think your boss would be fine whenever you came in. You've already done a lot for him so he'd be real forgiving."

Nodding, she smiled her agreement. Half a block later they walked up to the front door of her little bungalow. Hesitating on the porch, she turned to him, her eyes piercing his. "Do you want to come in?"

"Yes," he replied, "but I'm not going to." Seeing her brow wrinkle in confusion, he hastily explained, "I really want to, Katelyn, but I don't want to make things complicated for you at work...or in your life."

Cocking her head to the side, she said, "I'm a firm believer in plain speaking, Gareth. So, I really need you to accommodate me and do that, please."

"I've always respected that about you—your honesty." His lips quirked up as he added, "But, I gotta admit, it was your drop-dead, gorgeous beauty that first caught my eyes."

At that, her eyes widened slightly as she waited for him to continue.

"Katelyn, I noticed you when I first moved to town over a year ago. I thought you were beautiful. Then, I as was around you more, I thought you were incredibly smart, funny, well...special. But, it's no secret that here in town, you're known as the one who still mourns your...uh...well, Philip. So, I backed off and admired you from afar, which I know sounds hokey, but it's true."

She opened her mouth to speak, but he shushed her with his fingers over her lips. "Hang on, there's more." Seeing her tilt her head, waiting for him, he said, "I always thought you'd be perfect for my office and when you walked in the door, I knew I'd hit the jackpot. But then it dawned on me that, with you working for me, it changed everything."

"Workplace harassment?" she queried.

Nodding sadly, he said, "Yeah. I would never want to do anything to jeopardize our friendship or have you feel awkward around me."

"So, let me get this straight...you'd like to go out with me, but never asked because of my reputation as the long-suffering mourner and now feel like you can't because we work together."

"You really do believe in plain speak, don't you?" he smiled ruefully.

Unable to hold back a grin, she nodded. "Hey, I'm Irish—I don't have much of a filter. To me, it's the only way to keep from having misunderstandings. Too many people get upset over too many things because they just don't say exactly what's on their mind."

Silence curved around the couple under the porch light, a calm warmth seeped throughout her. "I need to be just as honest, Gareth. I've noticed you as well. I've watched you in town and admired how you fought to get your business started. God knows, the town manager didn't make it easy on you. You're strong, determined—"

"Is that all you noticed?"

Blushing, she sucked in her lips, attempting to keep a grin from spreading across her face. "No," she admitted, shaking her head slowly. "I've watched you on the ball field with the kids...you're really good with them. And you never seem to lose your cool." Laughing, she added, "Growing up with Aiden and Brogan as my older brothers, believe me...I'm used to men saying whatever pops into their heads, and usually at a loud volume." Tucking a flyaway strand of hair behind her ear, she said, "You're the first man I've wanted to get close to in a long time...really get to know. I'm not any good at flirting or playing coy or even letting a guy know I'm interested. I don't know if those genes passed me by or if years of being with Philip, and then mourning him, knocked those abilities right out of me." Shrugging, she heaved a sigh. "But I do like you, too."

Smiling, he pulled her in for a hug, tucking her head underneath his chin. "So...what do we do now?"

"I don't want to quit my job with you, Gareth. But I don't want that to stand in our way either."

"Well, can we agree to spend some time together outside of work and go slow, to see how things work out?" he asked, hope spearing through his words.

Grinning into his shirt, she tilted her head back and pierced his gaze with her own. "Yeah, I'd like that."

"And since you're such a fan of plain speak, then I can trust that you'll let me know if things are going well or if it's affecting work."

"Absolutely!" she agreed, a full-fledged smile on her face.

Bending to kiss her forehead, he said, "Then I'll say goodbye for tonight."

Feeling the touch of his lips on her skin, she closed her eyes momentarily, allowing the warmth to rush over her. Swallowing deeply, she whispered, "Goodnight." With that, she slipped through her front door.

Throwing his hands into the air in a celebratory motion, he jumped down her front steps and jogged back to his vehicle.

Thirty minutes later, lying in bed, Katelyn smiled as her eyes closed, still feeling the heat of Gareth's lips on her forehead. A strange sense flowed through her, unfamiliar in recent years but not unwelcome. A feeling of joy. New territory to explore. Life.

Rolling over, she saw the silver frame by her bed, Philip's picture the last thing she always looked at before going to sleep. Afraid guilt would assault her, she breathed easier when all she felt was peace.

The early morning sun rose over the horizon, painting the sky brilliant colors as the wind blew off the Chesapeake Bay. Katelyn walked along the shore, her gaze downward, searching for sea glass. Bending occasionally to snatch the colored slivers from the sand, she sought the calming effect of the surf.

Standing, she stared at her handful of worn-smooth glass, the colors catching the reflection of the rising sun. Her mind, filled with tangled thoughts, interrupted the peaceful morning. Closing her eyes for a moment, she lifted her face to the sun, basking in the warmth. Memories of she and Philip running on this beach, as well as the whole Baytown gang from childhood, played across her consciousness. The peace from the night before, along with the memory of the light kiss, seemed to slide away in the bright light of day as thoughts of her argument with her brothers came back to mind.

Hearing a shout, she turned and looked behind her, seeing Jillian and Tori jogging toward her.

Catching her breath as she came to a stop, Jillian said, "We thought we'd find you here." Still panting, she said, "So, what's up with you and Gareth? You seemed chummy last night."

Her lips thinning, Katelyn said sharply, "He's my boss. He's my friend. Have you got something against that?"

Blinking in surprise, Jillian threw her hands up. "Whoa, girl. This is me."

Hanging her head, Katelyn apologized, throwing her arms around her oldest friend. "Oh, God, I'm sorry. I had a fight with Brogan last night after you all left the pub. He was being an ass and I'm still defensive, I guess."

Tori joined the group hug as the three friends held on tightly for a moment. "Honey, we want you to be happy. And you know to just ignore Brogan—he's a grumpy ass all the time, but he loves you."

Chuckling, Katelyn nodded as she let go of her friends. "I know. I'll make up with him later. It's just that...that..." sighing heavily, her words died out.

Jillian peered deeply into Katelyn's eyes and said, "You know, sweetie, for the first time I see conflict in your face instead of just grief. You've grieved Philip for so long that I figured you would never be able to move on—"

"Would that be such a bad thing?" Katelyn said, wincing at the sharp tone of her voice. *What is wrong with me? I can't even be civil to my friends.* Closing her eyes, she battled the desire to cry. "I just mean that I assumed Philip was my one love...my one chance at marriage and babies and forever." She opened her eyes and saw the understanding faces looking at her. "I know I was young, but I figured that, for some people, love only comes once in a lifetime."

Katelyn noted Jillian and Tori clasp hands as they listened and she felt their love for her. "What I said about Gareth is true. He's my boss and my friend."

"And if more grows from that?" Jillian prompted, her eyes pinned on Katelyn.

Shrugging her shoulders, Katelyn added, "Then I'd be agreeable to that." A blush rose over her cheeks as she amended, "Oh, hell, who am I kidding. I'd love that." Her gaze searched Jillian's, as she laughed, "God, it's like a burden is lifting to be able to finally say, *I want Gareth Harrison!*"

Lifting her face to the heavens, Jillian shouted, "Thank you, Jesus!" Tori and Katelyn both laughed at Jillian's expression of glee. Jillian's gaze dropped to Katelyn's tightly clenched fist. "You findin' anything good?"

Smiling at the deft change of subject, Katelyn opened her hand, showing the colorful sea glass resting in her palm.

Tori touched one of the slivers and said, "It's the rough seas of life that allow us to shine."

With smiles, the trio turned in unison and continued their search along the surf-washed sand.

Thirty minutes later, Katelyn walked along the sidewalk approaching her house. Lost in thought, she did not notice Brogan sitting on her top porch step until she was almost upon him. One look and she could tell he had spent a restless night. Tired eyes, mussed hair, stubbled jaw. She had seen him this way many times since returning from Afghanistan but this was the first time he had visited her this early.

Cocking her head to the side, she said nothing, waiting to see what he had come for. *I love him, but if he's here to rag on Gareth again, he can just leave.* Brogan said nothing, so after a minute Katelyn sat down on the step next to him, her gaze on the sleepy street she lived on.

The long silence moved around and between them, but she waited patiently. If there was one thing she knew about her brother, it was that he only spoke when he was ready.

Finally, his voice like gravel, he said, "I was an ass."

Katelyn continued to be silent for another moment, not knowing if Brogan expected her to refute his statement. Holding back a grin, she realized he knew her well enough to know she would never refute his admission of being an ass.

"You were always a happy kid."

Tears immediately stung Katelyn's eyes at his words, but she stayed statue still, allowing Brogan to talk.

"Of all of us, you were the one everyone wanted on their team 'cause you were the fastest runner. You were the one the girls all wanted to hang out with. Hell, I know once you hit puberty, all my friends did nothing but stare at you." Rubbing his hand over his face, he sighed. "Did you know I had a talk with Philip before he asked you out the first time?"

Stunned, Katelyn broke her silence as her head jerked toward him. "You did?"

Nodding, a faraway smile curved his lips as he said, "Philip came to me first. He asked if I would have a problem if he asked you for a date. Of everyone, he was probably the best of us." Sighing, he added, "I knew he really liked you. He was trustworthy...at least I knew he didn't just want to get in your pants." Hearing Katelyn's indignant snort, he continued, "I agreed, but told him that if he ever broke your heart, I'd break his face. I never got the chance to make good on that promise."

Still in shock from his admission, she shook her head and said, "He never gave you a reason."

"Oh, yes he did," Brogan said, drawing her attention. He turned and pierced her with his red-rimmed eyes and continued, "When he died, he broke your heart."

Unable to hold back the gasp, Katelyn's sob caught in her throat. Brogan wrapped his beefy arm around her shoulders and pulled her in, his big body offering comfort.

"I watched you...we all watched...you break." Swallowing audibly, he continued, "You were only twenty-two years old and I watched you change right before my eyes. And for the past six years, you've gone on working, sharing, caring, but you haven't really been living. I knew that...I saw that. But I buried myself in my own world and just figured you were okay."

Grunting again, he added, "We all miss Philip... Jesus, he truly was the best of us back then. But baby-sis, this may sound fucked up, but if I could have jerked him from the grave to shout at him for hurting you, I would have. But I couldn't. All I could do was just watch you suffer."

After another moment of silence, he said, "I watched you last night with Gareth and there was a light in your eyes that I haven't seen in a long time. And I watched him and realized he had the same light when he looked at you."

Katelyn was not sure what shocked her more— Brogan speaking so much at one time, considering he was usually a man of few words, observing Gareth's interest when she had not noticed it at first, or that his assessment of her over the years was true. Not trusting her voice, she simply nodded.

"Anyway, I wanted to say I was sorry for last night." Kissing the top of her head, he added, "You deserve to be happy again." With that, he stood and walked toward the street.

"Brogan!"

Turning, he barely had time to throw out his arms to catch her body as she slammed into him, her tears streaming as she jumped into his arms. He held her easily, the silence was now comforting. After a moment, she squeezed his neck and he placed her steadily on the sidewalk. Kissing the top of her head, he mumbled, "We good?"

Smiling through her tears, she nodded. "Yeah, big bro. We're good." She watched as he lifted his chin in acknowledgment before walking away.

8

Gareth walked into the office, his smile immediately landing on Katelyn sitting behind her desk. Before he had a chance to speak, her eyes cut over to the man sitting in the waiting area.

"Your appointment is here, Mr. Harrison," she said, her professional smile in place.

As Gareth and the man moved to the office, Katelyn went back to work. Gareth had shown her how to investigate for clues in a bank statement and she was searching Mrs. Milstone's accounts. Hearing a noise, she looked up as a large, tattooed man came through the door carrying a wooden folding screen.

"Jason!" she called out, clapping her hands at the delivery. "Oh, I'm so glad you don't need that!"

Jason Boswell was one of the new residents of Baytown, deciding to relocate after he left the Navy. Having no family to return home to, he had made a ride up the east coast on his motorcycle, stopping at the little town and deciding to plant roots. He bought the old auto mechanic shop in town and reopened it. He also leased the store next to it to open his tattoo parlor.

Even though the tattoo shop was not open yet, Jason was kind enough to let them look around while he worked on getting things up and running. Jillian and Katelyn had been inside, trying to decide on tattoo patterns, when Katelyn noticed an old, carved, wooden screen in the corner. Jason did not want the heavy, ornate screen and was willing to sell it to Katelyn for Gareth's office.

"No problem," he grinned. "Where do you want it?"

Katelyn jumped up and moved from behind her desk, beginning to move the few client chairs to the side. "I want to create a wall here so that when a client has to wait, they don't feel like they are on display inside a PI's office, since anyone on the street can look in."

Nodding, Jason said, "Good thinking. It gives them some privacy."

He set the screen up where she indicated and stood back as she observed the now divided room.

"Oh, that won't work. I still need to be able to see the clients." Turning for a moment, she cast her appraising gaze around the space. "Okay, let's move it over here."

Easily lifting the heavy screen, Jason placed it in the new position, part of it in front of the plate glass window in front and angled to be a partial room divider. He grinned as Katelyn squealed in satisfaction. "Perfect!" Standing on her toes, she placed a kiss on Jason's cheek, laughing as a blush spread across his face.

The sound of a throat clearing from behind had the pair turn quickly to see Gareth scowling as the client stood behind him. "My assistant will receipt your retainer," he said, and Katelyn smiled at the man, ushering him to her desk.

Gareth walked over and eyed the screen before swinging his gaze to Jason. "I suppose Katelyn asked you to bring this over?"

Jason smiled long and lazy, staring at his friend. "Yeah, she was in the shop and saw this antique screen. I didn't want it so I sold it to her. She said this area needed a way to provide clients some privacy."

Lips tightening, Gareth felt the sting of jealousy. "Y'all must have had a nice long talk to have covered that much information."

Laughing, Jason clapped Gareth on the back. "Calm down, I've got no interest in your...um...assistant."

Realizing he looked foolish, Gareth shook his head. Sticking his hand out, he said, "Sorry, man. I guess I'm acting like a jerk."

"No worries. If I had a woman like Katelyn, I'd be pissing on my turf too."

"I'm not so sure she'd appreciate me marking my territory," Gareth joked, "and well...she's not technically mine."

"You working on it?" Jason asked, his pierced eyebrow lifting.

Nodding, Gareth watched as Katelyn said goodbye to the client, and confirmed, "Yeah, I am."

"Good enough," Jason said with a grin. Offering a head jerk in goodbye, he moved back out through the door.

Now alone, Katelyn scrunched her nose as she stared at Gareth. "Is the screen okay? I bought it from Jason and if you really don't like it, I can take it home."

Walking over to her, Gareth smiled down at the dark-haired beauty. "I like it. In fact, I like all the changes you've made to the office, but you've got to stop spending your money."

Shrugging, she replied, "The pictures on the wall are just on loan from Jillian and I knew I could use the screen if you hated it." Staring up into his face, she added, "I just thought it would make the reception area more comfortable for clients. The ones I've met so far are either nervous about needing your services or they're pissed that they need your services...either way, I thought this would be nice."

"You don't have to convince me about the changes. I like them." Looking at the clock on the wall, he said, "Do you want to go grab some lunch?"

Furrowing her brow, she said, "I don't think we'll have time. I just made an appointment for a woman who is coming in to see you in half an hour. By the way, what did the last client need?"

The two walked back toward his office and settled comfortably into their chairs. Gareth liked the feeling of having someone to talk to about his cases. "He needs some basic security at his business. He suspects one of his employees is stealing from him so I'm going to assist him."

"Wouldn't that be something for the police?"

"Not yet. He has no proof and, well, our police staff is stretched thin as it is. So sometimes I help in the investigation stage. Once we determine someone is stealing, then we'll turn it over to Mitch."

Nodding her understanding, she said, "You want me to order something from the pub for lunch?"

"Sure. Get some money out of petty cash."

Laughing, she reminded, "Hey, I'm part owner, remember? You can get my special discount!"

Katelyn watched their next client enter the office, observing her as she nervously glanced around. Dressed in a stylish, dark wool coat, she patted her dark, slightly wind-blown hair back into place after removing her gloves and stuffing them into her purse.

Katelyn stood immediately, greeting her as she approached. "Mrs. Berry? Hello, I'm Katelyn MacFarlane."

A warm smile met hers as Mrs. Berry nodded. "Yes, I'm Eleanor Berry. Nice to meet you." She glanced around again and added, "This office is very nice. I was afraid of what I might find...I've never been to a private investigator before."

Just then Gareth walked from the back and shook her hand, saying, "Well, hopefully we can exceed your expectations. Do you mind if Ms. MacFarlane sits in with us?"

"No, no, not at all," Eleanor agreed, her eyes pleading.

"This way, please," Gareth said, leading the way into the second office. Once settled with the coffee Katelyn brought in, he waited until she picked up her notepad and turned to Eleanor. "Now, Mrs. Berry, how may we help you?"

"Call me Eleanor, please," she began. Looking down at her hands twisting her purse strap, she sucked in her lips for a moment before lifting her face. "I'm sorry... this is really hard."

"Please, just take your time," he responded and watched as Katelyn reached over and patted Eleanor's hand. The motion appeared to relax their client, who swallowed deeply before speaking.

"I need help finding my husband."

Her words hung between them for a moment and Gareth remained quiet, knowing most people talked to fill the silence. His eyes cut over to Katelyn and, with a minuscule shake of his head, he warned her to stay quiet as well.

"Uh...well...he's lost." Clearing her throat, Eleanor clarified, "Well, lost to me. I don't know where he is."

Gareth watched a blush cross Eleanor's face, embarrassment infusing her words. "When was the last time you saw him?"

"He left for work last Friday and hasn't come home. He told me he had a business trip to meet with a client in D.C. and was going to take the weekend to have his meeting and then play golf with some friends. He was supposed to get in late on Sunday." Shrugging, she blushed again. "I went to bed on Sunday night, but yesterday morning he wasn't there when I woke up. And he hasn't been home and doesn't answer his phone. So, I called his office and talked to William... uh...William Maskey, one of Walter's accountants."

Swallowing a sip of coffee, Eleanor's hand shook as

she set the cup back down on the table. Licking her bottom lip, she stared at the cup for a long minute. Lifting her gaze back to Gareth, she said, "William said he was surprised because last week Walter told him that he and I were going to take a weekend trip. They weren't even expecting him until Tue...uh...this morning." Shaking her head, she said, "Lordy, I'm so turned around, I can't remember what day it is."

"Have you spoken with the local police?"

"No...not yet. I thought maybe I misunderstood when he was supposed to come back from his trip. I did call the hospitals and the state police, but he hasn't been injured or in a car accident." Lifting her hand to rub her forehead, she said, "I...oh, this seems crazy."

Gaining a slight nod from Gareth, Katelyn patted Eleanor's hand once again. "Mrs. Berry, sometimes it's easier to just start at the beginning. We'll just listen to the whole story and then we can ask specific questions."

Offering a slight smile toward her, Eleanor sucked in a deep breath and began. "My husband, Walter Berry, is an accountant and we live about twenty miles north of here. We've been married for almost twenty-two years...um...no children." Wincing, she swallowed nervously before continuing.

"His office is actually in Norfolk and he commutes about an hour every day. We've been happy...I suppose every wife says that, doesn't she? At least I thought we were. I've never been suspicious, but I began to notice that over the last six months he's had numerous late nights, supposedly meeting with clients."

"Is this new behavior?" Gareth asked.

Shaking her head, Eleanor replied, "No, not really. He was a member of the Rotary Club, several professional accounting organizations, some organizations in Virginia Beach and Norfolk, and of course The Dunes Golf Club here in town. But he generally would ask me to accompany him to his more social meetings. Then, slowly, he began to make excuses. Like, 'oh, you don't need to drive up tonight', or 'It'll be a late night so you stay home and rest'...things like that."

"Do you work outside the home, Mrs. Berry?" Katelyn asked.

Blushing, Eleanor said, "I'm embarrassed to tell you that I don't. I have a business degree but Walter felt that, unless I really wanted to work, he preferred that I didn't. I was always available for dinner parties, or to host events for our clients or the clubs. I suppose that he liked the idea that he made enough to take care of me."

Rubbing her hands on her skirt, Eleanor said, "I truly didn't think anything about a change in him at first, but it became more and more evident that he was spending time without me. I looked...uh...for any... clues of infidelity. I mean, l looked through his pockets, his wallet, his email. I should be ashamed but I thought if I could find some reason why he was pulling back then at least I would know. But nothing." Her gaze lifted to Katelyn as she said, "And he was very loving toward me. Our...uh...marital relations were fine."

Katelyn inwardly winced at Eleanor's timidity but kept a professional expression on her face. Nodding encouragingly, she held the woman's gaze.

"But now, he's been missing for three days and I fear

he's left me. I wasn't sure if I should go to the police, knowing they would just assume he left voluntarily."

"You don't live in our county, so the North Heron Sheriff's Office would have jurisdiction and I'm sure they would want to open up a file on him. I can speak to them on your behalf if you would like?"

Jerking her head in an awkward nod, Eleanor agreed.

"What else would you like me to do, Mrs. Berry?" She looked at him in confusion, so he clarified. "When people feel the need to engage a private investigator, their reasons are as varied as the people themselves. I feel it is best if you tell me exactly what you hope I can do."

"I'd like you to find my husband. I just need to know what's going on. I don't want to think he's left with someone else, but I need to know."

Nodding, Gareth said, "Okay, I'll take this case. I'll need access to your home, your email, your bank account information, and anything of his you can give me."

"Uh...Okay, I can do that."

Explaining, he said, "That will give me a good start, seeing if he's been using your accounts recently."

Eleanor agreed. "I'll make sure you have full access to everything. Including his business..."

Eyes-wide, Gareth said, "You have that access?"

"I'm listed on his business as a full partner. I don't actually do anything with the business, but he always said that if something happened to him then it would be easy for me to have money or anything I needed."

Nodding toward Katelyn, he said, "Ms. MacFarlane

will take down all the information you have and go over the payment information. I'll get started as soon as I have it all."

Thirty minutes later, Gareth and Katelyn stood in the lobby and watched Mrs. Berry walk out the door. Turning to him, she asked, "So what do you think?"

"With her, I wouldn't make any assumptions, but I can tell you from several years in this business, he's probably in some tropical paradise with a hot side-piece."

"Oh, no!" Katelyn said, her face falling. "I hate the idea that we'll find that out and then have to tell that poor woman that the man she loves is a scoundrel!"

"A scoundrel?" Gareth countered with a laugh.

"Well, I thought that sounded more professional than an asshole."

"Yeah, you're probably right. But one term or another, that's probably what we'll have to tell her." Looking down at Katelyn's scowl, he said, "Are your ready for this? Are you ready to investigate the clues only to break someone's heart?"

She nodded, but wondered if she really was ready to search for clues, regardless of where they led.

9

Gareth picked Katelyn up early the next morning in front of her house. Grinning as she came bounding down the walk, he admired her curves. Athletic, she had a great body showcased in black jeans and a pink sweater with a leather jacket. *Professional and hot...what a combination.*

Deciding to check out Walter's business first, they were taking a day trip across the Chesapeake Bay Bridge. A seventeen-mile combination of tunnels and bridges, it spanned the bay from Virginia Beach to the Eastern Shore.

"Did you know this modern-day wonder is one of the reasons the railroad went out of business on the Eastern Shore?"

Gareth glanced to the passenger side of his vehicle as Katelyn's gaze turned to him, her eyes hidden behind sunglasses. "Nope, enlighten me."

"The whole Baytown area was formerly plantations.

The land was then purchased in the late 1800s by a man intent on running the Pennsylvania Railroad down to the end of the Eastern Shore of Virginia where a harbor would allow goods and passengers to travel by water to Virginia Beach or Norfolk. By 1885, Baytown was already bustling with commercial and residential buildings."

"Have you been secretly hiding a historian behind your amazing looks?" Gareth laughed.

Giving a playful slap on his shoulder, she said, "Oh, believe me, if you were born and raised in this area, you were taught all the local history from first grade on up!"

"And the bridge?" he prompted.

"Baytown was the epicenter of North Heron County for a long time but then took a nose dive during World War II. That's when trucks and highways took over most of the carrying of goods after the Bay Bridge and Tunnels were built. The railways weren't needed as much and, now, Baytown resembles more of a sleepy village until the warm weather vacationers come through."

"You have definitely enlightened me, Ms. MacFarlane," he replied, a gleam in his eye. He looked out over the water as the sunlight glistened over the surface. "This is really gorgeous," he said, his voice softer now. "First time I drove over to the Eastern Shore, I knew I needed to land there."

Katelyn stared at him, his handsome profile catching her attention as always, but his somber words snagged her interest even more. "Where are you from? I realize I know almost nothing about you."

His quick glance to the side found her sunglasses now perched up on her head, pushing her hair back from her face, as her eyes bore intently into his. Heaving a sigh, he rubbed his chin as he replied, "It's not all that exciting."

Reaching over, she placed her hand on his thigh. "I'd really like to know."

"I'm from West Virginia originally," he began. "My dad died in a factory accident when I was ten." Sighing heavily, he added, "He was a good man...a good dad. Mama was never quite the same after that. She kind of checked out, if you know what I mean." Gareth glanced sideways again and saw the sympathy in Katelyn's eyes and explained, "Alcohol became her drug of choice when she just wanted to forget. Problem was, she sometimes forgot she had kids. She was also the type of woman who needed to have a man around and wasn't always picky about who it was. She finally remarried but he was verbally abusive to her...well, to all of us when I was little. It wasn't until I was about 16 that I got big enough that I could stand up for her...and myself."

Her mouth fell open as she thought of his words, but she found she was afraid to ask more. "Um...kids? So you have siblings."

Smiling, he said, "Yeah, I've got an older sister. She married young—right out of high school. I think she was trying to escape our mom and stepdad. But she married a decent man who works at the same factory our dad did. They've been married for about fifteen years. I've got a thirteen-year-old nephew and a ten-year-old niece."

"Oh, nice," Katelyn said, her smile genuine.

Shrugging, he continued, "Anyway, I moved in with my sister as soon as I graduated high school and her husband got me a job at the factory, but it just wasn't what I wanted to do with my life. Not that I knew what I wanted...I just knew slaving in the factory wasn't it for me. So, I joined the Air Force, did a couple of tours before ending up at Dover Air Force Base." Unsure if Katelyn knew about Dover's reputation, he shot another glance toward her.

She scrunched her nose as she tried to think why Dover AFB sounded so familiar. Gasping, she said, "I've heard about Dover in the news."

Nodding sadly, he said, "Yeah, I was assigned a job investigating the remains of some of the cases they took. They did more than just the returning of military remains."

"Oh, wow," she breathed, her thoughts drifting off for a few minutes. Giving a slight shake, she pulled her mind back to the present. "Is that why you got into investigations?"

Nodding, he replied, "I was interested in the knowledge needed for investigating, but had no desire to go into police science. I liked the idea of working for myself."

"Do you think you'll ever want to move back? To where your family is?"

He heard the tentative sound of her voice and was unable to hold back his snort. "Hell, no!" Noticing her startle at his vehemence, he apologized. "Sorry...didn't mean to snap at you, but," shaking his head, "there is no home for me in West Virginia anymore. To be honest, it never was much of a home. Just a place to be raised. Mom died while I was overseas...alcohol poisoning. Her worthless husband is long gone. And, other than seeing my sister and her family occasionally, I've got no ties there." Rubbing his hand over his jaw, he added, "Baytown is my home now."

She smiled, his answer sliding warmth throughout her being. After a moment of quiet reflection, she decided to change the subject since it appeared he had given her more than he felt comfortable with. "Did you talk to Colt about Walter?"

"That's right, I did that last evening and forgot to tell you. With the Berry's home in North Heron County, and not Baytown, I had to involve the Sheriff and not Mitch. I gave Colt all the information that Eleanor had given us and let him know what we were doing."

"Does he have any ideas?"

Shaking his head, Gareth added, "No. Said they had no records about the Berrys at all...no calls to their house, no complaints filed. Live in a nice area."

Falling into an easy silence for the rest of the trip they soon parked outside Walter's business. Sucking in a deep breath, Katelyn let it out slowly.

Looking over at her, Gareth said, "Are you all right?"

"Strangely nervous," she admitted. "Up until now, when clients came in to talk to you, the investigation was mostly what we could dig up from our offices. Now, this seems real."

He agreed with her assessment and reached over and squeezed her hand. "It'll be fine. Just relax and, if something comes to mind, it's okay to ask. But follow my lead. Consider this a learning experience." Nodding his encouragement, he released her hand and grinned. "Come on...let's go search for clues."

Entering Berry and Associates Accounting, they were greeted by an attractive receptionist sitting behind a neat, large wooden desk. As the woman stood to greet them, Katelyn immediately noticed her youth. *Is she even twenty years old?* She was wearing a black, pencil skirt paired with a lilac, silk blouse and her hair was pulled back from her perfectly made-up face and held with a large clip.

"Hello. Welcome to Berry and Associates Accounting. May I help you?"

Gareth introduced the two of them and asked to speak to one of Walter's associates. As the receptionist walked from behind her desk, Katelyn noticed the designer boots as well. *Damn!* Leaning toward Gareth, she said, "The accounting business must be doing well. Did you see the clothes on the receptionist?"

"I noticed but had no idea of the costs," he admitted.

"Certainly not cheap," she replied.

Just then, the receptionist reappeared and asked them to follow her. They were led down a plush-carpeted hall to a closed door. With a knock, the woman opened the door and motioned for them to enter.

Making their way into the large office, they were greeted by an older man. He stood and introduced himself.

"I'm William Maskey, one of the partners here at

our firm. How may I help you, Mr. Harrison...Ms. MacFarlane?"

"We have been contracted by Mr. Berry's wife to locate him and wanted to know what thoughts you may have about his disappearance."

William's ruddy face immediately reddened more as his lips pinched into a thin line. Nodding toward the chairs, he said, "Please, sit down." Once the three were settled, he shook his head and said, "I don't understand what's going on. Walter told me last week that he was taking a trip and would be out on Friday and Monday. Then Eleanor called yesterday, wondering where he was."

"Did Walter say Eleanor was taking the trip as well?" Gareth asked.

Wrinkling his forehead in thought, he said, "I honestly can't remember. I mean, I guess I just assumed he was talking about him and Eleanor, but...maybe he didn't mention her."

"Would you consider this behavior to be normal for Walter? Either going away without his wife or lying about it?"

"No, no," William said, his jowls shaking as he shook his head.

"Do you know if he talked to others about his plans?" Katelyn asked.

His grimace caused his face to appear bulldoggish as he replied, "After she called, I did ask the other employees if they had heard from Walter. No one had." Thinking for a moment, he said, "Well, I asked Sandra, the other accountant that works here, and Beth, our office manager. Ed, our accounting intern, wasn't here yesterday morning but he came in later and, well, Carrie, our receptionist was off sick yesterday."

"Have you noticed any strange behavior from Walter lately or, say, within the last six months?" Gareth queried.

Once more shaking his head, William said, "Not that I've noticed. Walter's a very honorable man. A very conscientious accountant. I've never once noticed any behavior from him that made me suspicious of anything." He sat for a moment, his head slightly down, as he appeared to be pondering his next words. Looking back up, he asked, "Do you think something has happened to him?"

"We have no way of knowing, at this time. All we know is, his behavior from last week to now has left his wife wondering where he is. Do you have any information...or even thoughts that might shed some light on the situation?"

"I don't know. I've never thought of him as a philandering man but," shrugging a little, he added, "but I sometimes wonder if we ever really know someone."

Tuning into what William said, Gareth prodded, "Is there anyone in particular you're speaking of?"

Reddening, William admitted, "Oh, no. Not in particular. Not really..."

"But you can think of some people you aren't so sure about, can't you?" Katelyn said, her warm smile focused directly on the older man.

Meeting her smile with a small one of his own, he said, rubbing his chin, "Things are different nowadays. Used to be just me and Walter, along with a secretary who also served as our office manager...and she always called us Mr. Berry and Mr. Maskey. When she retired, he hired Beth, who is very efficient, but seems to be liberal with her sick days as well as her greetings." Shaking his head, he added, "I liked the old ways. Now, we have another accountant, who's uh...much younger than myself. Sandra's very professional—no complaints there. But then Walter hired a really young receptionist. Carrie. The first time I saw her, I thought she was just a teenager. He took a real shine to her and she's been with us for a few months now. And then Walter wanted to take on an intern, so we have Ed. He's much closer to Carrie's age, but I swear...there were times I thought Walter might be jealous of him." Sighing heavily, William said, "I feel guilty saying these things."

"I understand, but if something has happened to Walter, then it's best to look at all possible issues that might have a bearing," Gareth assured. "Would it be possible for us to talk to the others that work here?"

"Well, Sandra is off today. She called in sick this morning and Ed is in class. He only works three days a week for us. But you met Carrie when you came in. You may certainly talk to her. And Beth is around as well."

With goodbyes said after handing William a business card, they made their way back to the front, finding the receptionist behind her desk again. With a charming wink, Gareth asked, "Would it be possible for us to have a few minutes of your time?"

"Of course," she replied, a mega-watt smile reaching her eyes as she stared up at Gareth.

Katelyn mentally rolled her eyes, but plastered a smile on her face in return.

"I suppose Mr. Maskey told you that Mr. Berry

appears to be missing?" Gareth began, noticing as the smile immediately left Carrie's face.

"I was out sick yesterday, but he asked me this morning if I knew anything. I have no idea why he thinks I would know but, then, Walter has been so good to me since I started here. Perhaps William thought that Walter confided in me."

"And did he?"

Shaking her head, she answered, "No. He didn't say anything to me about his weekend plans."

"And you were out yesterday?" Katelyn threw out, her eyebrow lifted as she kept her smile in place.

"Yes. I was terribly sick. There may be something going around the office because Ed was out part of yesterday also and Sandra is out today."

"And you're sure you haven't heard anything from Mr. Berry?" Gareth continued.

"No. I saw him last Thursday as he left at the end of the day. That was the last time I saw him."

"I understand he's the one who hired you?" Gareth pushed.

A wide smile returned to Carrie's face as she gushed, "Oh, yes. He hired me and has been super sweet to me as I've learned the duties of the job. Very patient...very kind. Just a super sweet boss."

"How did you come to know about this position?" he asked.

Carrie's face scrunched for a moment. "My mom saw an advertisement and suggested I apply. I was so excited when Walter hired me. I was just sure that he would think I was too young."

Gareth, seeing Katelyn about to make a comment,

jumped in and asked, "What about Sandra or Beth? Did he also hire them as well?"

Leaning forward, her voice lowered, she glanced to the hall behind her as she said, "Yes. It's my understanding that he and William had a few words over hiring Beth. She wasn't as experienced as William thought she should be."

"And you were?" Katelyn jumped in again, earning a slight frown from Gareth. Shooting an apology toward him with her eyes, she smiled back at Carrie.

"Well, I'm just a receptionist, so my position doesn't have to be so precise."

Gareth, with a slight nod toward Katelyn, asked Carrie, "May we meet with Beth now, please?"

"Certainly," Carrie responded, jumping up and hustling down the hall.

Turning to Gareth, Katelyn asked, "How am I doing?"

"Pretty good, but you need to go slowly," Gareth warned. "You're letting your suspicions show and that can shut down a possible witness or source of information."

Katelyn's shoulders slumped, knowing he was right. "I'm sorry. I got caught up in the moment."

"This is your first day in the field. It's bound to happen. Just follow my lead, okay?"

Nodding, she clamped her mouth shut as Carrie came back in. "If you'll follow me, I'll take you to Beth's office."

As Carrie stepped back from the doorway to another office, Gareth and Katelyn observed as an attractive brunette stood from behind her desk, her smile greeting them. After introductions, they questioned the office manager as to what she might know.

Shaking her head, Beth replied, "I'm afraid I was out at the end of last week so I wasn't around for Walter to tell me of his weekend plans."

"You were out right before the weekend, Carrie was out yesterday, and Sandra is out today. Is that usual for the office?" Gareth asked.

Beth's lips tightened as she retorted, "I assure you, Mr. Harrison, this is a very professional accounting firm. No, we are not usually out, but like any workplace, employees can have sick days."

"Oh, I totally understand," Katelyn said, her smile warm as she cut her eyes toward Gareth. "My boss comes to work when he's sick, but I'd so much prefer that he didn't." Beth returned Katelyn's smile. "Can you tell if Mr. Berry's behavior has been different recently? With you or with any of the other staff?"

"Well," Beth leaned in closer to Katelyn than Gareth, "I was surprised when he hired that *child* for a receptionist! I mean, really!" Seeming to recall that she should not speak ill of her boss, Beth quickly added, "I'm not saying anything inappropriate was going on from his end, but Carrie seems to *adore* him...more than she should, if you ask me."

A few more minutes of questions followed, but it appeared they had squeezed all the information they could from William, Carrie, and Beth for the time being.

As they began the return trip over the long bay bridge and tunnels, Katelyn turned to Gareth and said, "Okay, I admit...I'm totally confused. Every time we talked to someone, I thought I might have a handle on what was going on. But now, I have no idea who might know where Walter is."

"So, how do you feel about investigating now?" he asked, glancing to the side, observing the faint glower on her face.

"It was hard to control my nerves...I didn't expect that. Hard to keep my face impassive like yours."

"Hey, don't worry about it. You're learning. We both want answers, we just have to be careful with how far and how fast to push people."

Taking in his ready and welcoming smile, she let out a relieved breath. "Thanks, for saying that. I don't want to let you down in this."

"You won't. You did great."

Looking out over the water, she was quiet for a few minutes, her mind working the new information. "Investigating's like a puzzle, but I have no idea if I have all the pieces to even work on it."

Nodding, he said, "That's about right. Katelyn, I don't solve every case. Sometimes I have to go back to the client and tell them I can't find out what they want. Other times, I have to turn it over to the police, because what I find out is in their jurisdiction."

"Oh, that would suck. You do all the preliminary work and they take it over?" she gasped in indignation.

Chuckling, he nodded, "Yeah, but you do it because as much as you like solving puzzles, if a crime is involved, you want the guilty to pay."

"So who's guilty here?"

"Too early to tell. Walter might be in trouble with

the law. He might be injured. Or maybe he just left with another woman—"

"That would break Eleanor's heart," she said.

Nodding again, Gareth agreed, but stayed quiet. His instincts told him they were not going to like what they found.

10

Gareth sat on a barstool at Finn's and watched Katelyn wink at him before she headed toward the kitchen. Unable to keep the grin off his face, he turned back to his beer, startled to find Brogan leaning his tattooed arms on the bar right in front of him. Holding Brogan's stare, he said tersely, "Got something on your mind?"

Brogan stayed silent for a long moment before he nodded and jerked his head toward the door. Gareth slid off his stool and, with his beer in his hand, followed Brogan out the front door where a couple of tables and chairs sat on the sidewalk. So alike in appearance to Aiden with his dark hair and tats, and yet so different in temperament, Brogan's quiet introspection rolled over Gareth. Family concern was a foreign concept to him, considering his mother seemed to drop her maternal instincts as soon as his dad died, but he knew he had to suffer through the MacFarlane clan's up-in-your-business attitude. The two men settled facing each other, Gareth waiting to let Brogan pull his thoughts together.

After a moment, the large man dropped his chin to his chest before speaking. "Katelyn was fearless growin' up. So fuckin' fearless. She'd play with the girls, but was just as determined to keep up with us boys as well. I can still see her dark pigtails flying out behind her as she raced each of us to see who was faster."

Gareth sat quietly, surprised at Brogan's words. He both loved hearing about Katelyn as a child and hated that he knew Brogan was going to warn him off Katelyn —something that would not go over well.

Brogan continued, "As a teenager, she kept that fearlessness. She had a spark about her...she took life by the horns and never let go. By the time the guys grew up and were thinking with their dicks instead of how fast she could run, I knew I'd have to warn them all off. But she cast her eye toward Philip Bayles and somehow, of all my friends, he was the only one I thought was good enough for her. But I still threatened him to make sure he treated her right."

Sighing, he continued, "I went off to war...hell, all of us did. What the fuck else were we going to do to get out of Baytown and see the world? Most of us found out the world we saw was a shithole compared to where we were raised. When I got the news that Philip had been killed...shocked the shit outta me."

Gareth watched the emotions play across Brogan's rough face as pain slashed through his eyes.

"But when I came back, Katelyn was gone. Her body was here, but my sister was gone. No spark. No life. Nothing. When Philip came home in a box to be buried, it was as though Katelyn was buried right along with him." His gaze drifted to the occasional car driving down Main Street, breaking up the quiet of the evening. "I wanted her happy but learned to accept that maybe it had passed her by. Like I said, Philip was the only one I thought good enough for her."

Gareth's heart plunged knowing Brogan was going to warn him off Katelyn. Bracing himself for the ensuing argument, the next words caught him by surprise.

"But I was wrong." Brogan lifted his chin as his eyes bore right into Gareth. "My sister's been happier this last week or so than I've seen her in years. I never realized how just working at the diner and here was like putting her in a box as well. Not buried...but in a box."

The two men sat quietly as the breeze from the bay blew down Main Street, Gareth sipping his beer as Brogan fought with the devils that nipped at his heels. Finally leaning back in his chair, which creaked under his weight, Brogan gave a swift nod and said, "She deserves to be happy and you do that for her. She also deserves to be loved...don't know if that's what you've got in mind, but treat her right."

From another man, those words would have pissed Gareth off, but from Brogan? His lips curved slightly as he promised, "Wouldn't have it any other way."

With a quick nod, Brogan stood to go back inside just as the front door slammed open and Katelyn burst forth, her blue eyes flashing, hands on her hips preparing for battle. Before she had a chance to berate her brother, he leaned over and kissed her forehead.

"Be happy, Sis," he whispered, then walked back into to bar.

Katelyn stood statue-still, her eyes pinned on the closed door. Jumping slightly as Gareth placed his hands on her shoulders from behind, she twisted her head to peer up into his face. "What was that about? What did he say to you—"

"Shhh," he murmured against her ear. "He and I just had a little chat, that's all."

"But—"

Turning her around to face him, he bent low, his lips a whisper away from hers as he paused...waiting. Her heart pounded, both in longing and in fear. She wanted him to kiss her, more than she had wanted anything in a long time. Lifting her eyes to his, she saw the fire of desire staring back at her. Realizing he was waiting on her, she dropped her gaze to his lips and wondered if they were as strong and soft as they appeared. Licking hers, she lifted on her toes while circling her arms around his neck.

The kiss started soft...sweet...the bare touching of lips. Warmth, combined with the unique colliding of their tastes, quickly sent her lifting further on her toes as his arms banded around her tighter. What started as a tingle in her belly flared into a full butterfly assault as his tongue swept into her mouth, caressing hers. Gasping, her fingers dug into his shoulders as her legs threatened to give out from underneath her.

Intoxicated from her essence, Gareth held the back of her head, angling for better access as the kiss went from mild to wild. His tongue tangled with hers as he pressed her body into his, the feel of her lush breasts against his chest causing his eager cock to swell against his zipper. Wanting to argue against the knowledge that they were standing on the street in full view of anyone, he nonetheless slowly pulled back, smiling as he peered into her blue eyes, hazy with emotion.

Dragging in a deep breath, he said, "I don't want to stop, Katelyn."

"Then don't," she whispered, her breath sweet against his face.

"Slow," he murmured. "We need to go slow...and perhaps find a more private place next time."

Her kiss-swollen lips curved into a smile as her eyes darted around quickly, finding no spying gazes on them. His arms relaxed slightly, allowing her to slide back onto her heels as his gaze stayed on her.

"I liked that," she admitted, her heart still beating erratically in her chest.

Nodding slowly, he loved her no-bullshit attitude. "Yeah...me too."

"Maybe we can do that again sometime...even if you are my boss."

Catching her grin, he said, "I don't want to make any problems for you, Katelyn. But I want to do this again. I want to see where we can go. But I sure as hell don't want to do anything that would take you out of my life."

"I know it might be difficult, but if we promise to be honest with each other and take things slow...I really want to see where we can go also."

"Can I escort you home, Miss MacFarlane?"

Smiling widely, she replied, "Why, Mr. Harrison... I'd love for you to."

A few minutes later, the two stood on her front porch, arms wrapped around each other and lips locked once more. With more privacy, the kiss flamed hotter until she finally gasped, "Do you want to come in?"

Leaning his head down to touch her forehead, he sucked in a ragged breath. "God, I'd love to, Katelyn. But...no, not tonight." Seeing her about to protest, he touched his finger to her moist lips. "I want to take you to dinner. Not the usual *Let's grab a sandwich*, but an actual date." Standing taller, he looked down at her and smiled. "Would you do me the honor of going to dinner with me tomorrow night?"

Beaming, she nodded. "Yes, I'd love to."

"Alright, then I'll pick you up at seven." With a light kiss goodbye, he watched her go in, listening for the deadbolt to click before he jogged down the front path to his SUV.

Peeking out the window, Katelyn watched his progress, smiling as her fingers lay on her lips, the feel of his still tingling.

Sitting at her desk early the next morning before Gareth came in, Katelyn stared at the computer screen. She had begun developing a simple website for Harrison Investigations, but with thoughts of the kiss still filling her mind, she found it hard to concentrate.

The old-fashioned bell over the door jingled and her smile wobbled, anxious to see him walk through the door while nervous about how their workplace demeanor would change after the kiss.

Surprised, she watched as Eleanor Berry walked into the office, her eyes darting around nervously as she clutched her coat about her middle. Her hair appeared to only have had a quick brushing and she was wearing sweatpants instead of neat slacks.

"Eleanor," she greeted, jumping up from her desk. Before she questioned as to why she was back so soon, Eleanor gushed, "I found something!"

"Okay...uh...follow me, please." Taking her back to the conference room, she rushed back to reception as she heard Gareth come in.

His warm smile landed on her but before he spoke, she grabbed his arm. "Gareth!" she whispered excitedly. "Eleanor Berry is here, just walked in the door a minute ago, and she said she found something and I—"

"Got it," he nodded, giving her shoulder a squeeze. "Come on."

They entered the conference room, Gareth noting the difference in Eleanor's appearance from the other day when they met. He held out his hand but, instead of shaking it, she leaped from the chair as she pulled a few sheets of crinkled papers from her purse.

"I found these—" her voice cracked, as she swallowed deeply.

"Please," Gareth started, assisting her into a chair. "Do you need some coffee or maybe some water?"

Katelyn was almost to the door to get whatever the distraught client needed, but halted as Eleanor denied the offer.

"No, no. I just needed to get this to you."

Gareth and Katelyn settled quickly into chairs and he said, "What do you have, Mrs. Berry?"

Sighing, she said, "Yesterday, I opened up the mail and in his company credit card statement were several charges at a hotel in Norfolk. Each was only for one day, all within the last month. I don't know why he would need these because until three days ago, he's been with me at home each night."

Gareth and Katelyn shared a quick look before turning back to Eleanor.

"I'm not stupid, Mr. Harrison. My assumption is that he checked into the hotel during the day for an assignation. Who with? I don't know." Eleanor blinked back tears.

"I don't want to make any assumptions, at this time, Mrs. Berry," Gareth said, "but is there anyone you suspect?"

"He meets so many women professionally, both at the office and with his various organizations all over the place...The Dune's Golf Club here in town...I have no idea," she replied, her hands twisting on the table-top. Her gaze lifted to Katelyn's before shifting to Gareth. "I've always trusted him, but if I'm honest, he could have met a beautiful, poised woman in many places. I've..." she swallowed audibly, "seen the way some women look at Walter. He might not be the most handsome man in a room but he has such charm."

"Let's start at his workplace," Gareth suggested.

Shaking her head sadly, she replied, "There's a new accountant in the office. I've met her and she is very young...very pretty...and very into climbing upward.

Since my husband is the boss, it would not be a huge leap to think that perhaps she thinks husband stealing is a way to climb. But then, they recently hired a new receptionist also," she sighed, "also very young and very pretty."

Katelyn detected a touch of resignation in the last words and began to see that the more a client talked, the more they began to let go of their reservations and really said what was on their minds.

"I...I never thought my life would come to this," she said softly, her chin quivering. "I don't know what's happening...it's like I'm trapped in some kind of nightmare."

"Again, at this time, I'm not going to assume anything," Gareth said, "but we'll start with the hotel and see what we can find."

The sun peeked through the clouds creating a perfect view of the bay as Gareth and Katelyn drove back over the bridge toward Norfolk once more. Neither mentioned the kiss from the evening before as they focused on the case. Heading to the hotel listed on the credit card statement, she wondered what they would find.

Thirty minutes later, looking out her window, she commented, "This doesn't look much like where a man who golfs at the country club would stay."

The older hotel had been refurbished but had still seen better days. Entering the lobby, they saw a thin, young man behind the registration counter. The man looked between them and grinned. "You want a room for a couple of hours?"

Bristling at his assumption, Katelyn opened her mouth to protest, but a quick squeeze from Gareth caused her to hold her tongue.

"Naw, Tim," Gareth said, looking at the name badge on the man's shirt. "But I do need some information and I'll make it worth your while. I'll give you the money that you woulda charged for a couple hours on a room."

The man's eyes lit and he grinned bigger. "Well, all right. Now you're talkin'!"

Gareth threw several twenties on the counter along with a picture of Walter. "This man's been in here a couple of times this month. Paid with a credit card. You remember him?"

The man looked at the picture carefully. "Yeah, he looks familiar, although he looks like a lotta men who come in here. But if he's who I'm recollectin', he came in with some broad."

"Can you describe the woman? Was it the same woman each time?"

"It's kind of hard to say. She wore a scarf over her head and sunglasses. Hell, I knew she was trying to be all discreet and shit."

"Could you tell what color of hair she had?"

Scrunching up his face, Tim said, "Blonde...not a real yellowish blonde, but more of a sandy kind of color. I could see a bit peeking from her scarf." He snorted as he added, "And the guy? He'd wear sunglasses too, along with a hat...like they were trying to be all secret-like."

"Did you see them leave? How long did they stay?"

"I never saw them after check-in, but they paid for a night, so if they only stayed a couple 'a hours, I didn't care."

"When was the last time you saw them?" Gareth pressed.

The man's face scrunched even more in thought as he shook his head. "It's been a week or two," he finally replied. "But, then, I only work days so they coulda come in one night."

With a glance to the corner, Gareth said, "Any chance I can get a look at your security camera feed?"

Hooting, Tim leaned forward and whispered loudly, "They ain't real. The owner put 'em in here to make it look like we got security, but they ain't real cameras."

Lips thinning, Gareth nodded as he took Katelyn's arm and gently started to lead her out of the lobby. Just as they reached the door, Katelyn turned back and asked, "What color lipstick was the woman wearing?"

At that, the man scratched his head as Gareth stared at her in open curiosity.

"Pink, coral, peachy, dark red..." Katelyn prompted.

"Kinda pinky, now that I think of it," he said. "Yeah...'cause I always thought it looked like the bubblegum I used to get as a kid."

With a nod, Gareth continued to lead her back to his vehicle. His eyes scanned the area and locked onto a security camera on a nearby building.

Once inside the SUV, Katelyn turned and said, "Okay, this goes a lot slower than I thought it would."

"Patience, Katelyn. In this business, it's not like on

TV where suddenly things are wrapped up in an hour. We confirmed that Walter was here several times and in the company of a woman who was not his wife. By the way, lipstick?"

Shrugging, she replied, "Some women change their lipstick to match their clothes, but if this woman wore bright pink lipstick every time, then she falls into the category of a woman who has a favorite color and that's what they wear every day."

Brows drawn down, Gareth shook his head. "I can see you'll bring some skills to the table that I obviously don't have."

"Hey," she protested. "I'll be worth a lot more than just women's knowledge of lipstick."

Feeling contrite, he immediately apologized. "I'm sorry, I didn't mean that the way it sounded. Honestly, I just meant that I would have never thought of that."

Smiling at his face, his eyes full of concern, she reached over and grabbed his hand. "I'm just teasing! Right now, you're teaching me and, if I can throw out nuggets of ideas, then that's great...lipstick and all,"

With a relieved sigh, he grinned back. Starting the engine, he said, "Let's go back and talk to the others at Berry and Associates and then I want to check on the security cameras from the business next to the hotel."

11

The woman walking from the back of her desk to greet them was wearing a designer suit of soft, cream wool paired with an ice-blue silk blouse. A strand of pearls wrapped around her throat and as she stuck out her hand, a diamond tennis bracelet glistened around her wrist. Her makeup was impeccable, with a soft blush, pale silver eye shadow, and pink lips. Her blonde hair was pulled back from her face in a loose bun at the base of her neck.

Sandra Posten smiled as she waved them to two plush chairs in her office. "Please make yourselves comfortable." As she settled behind her desk once more, she said, "William has filled me in and I'm so concerned about Walter. Do you have any new information?"

"No, not now," Gareth said smoothly. "We're assisting the North Heron Sheriff's Office, but since there's no evidence of a crime at this point, we're working for Mrs. Berry. What we'd like from you is your opinion of Walter Berry...his habits here at work, any social settings you may have seen him in, any conversations you might have had that would give us an idea of where he might be?"

Wide-eyed, Sandra said, "Oh, I assure you that I have absolutely no idea where he might be. He's always so prompt...very professional. In fact, I'm not sure he's ever even been late to a meeting."

"You were hired last year I believe?" he prompted.

Sandra's face relaxed as she replied, "Yes...actually almost a year and a half now."

"And you're happy here?" Katelyn asked.

"Absolutely," Sandra nodded. "My father is an accountant and, since I didn't want to go work for Dad, this has been a wonderful place to work right out of college. Both Walter and William are easy-going and the business is extremely successful." Leaning forward, she said, "That's important, you know. I wouldn't want to work for just any old run-of-the-mill firm."

With a glance around the office space, Katelyn easily recognized the expensive furniture and artwork on the walls. "This is your first accounting position?"

A light blush stained Sandra's cheeks as she licked her lips. "Yes...I actually traveled a bit in Europe right after college. I was married briefly but, that relationship ended badly, I'm afraid. So, I had not used my accounting degree but Walter was wonderful to take me on."

"Do you consider yourself close to the other members of this firm?"

Chuckling delicately, she smoothed her hand over her hair and replied, "William is a father figure...a bit curmudgeon at times. And Walter? He's been..." she paused as she gazed at her wall for a moment with a faraway smile playing about her lips, "he's been very good to me."

Katelyn and Gareth shared a look before he asked, "And what about Beth and Carrie?"

Immediately Sandra's gaze shot back to his as her expression hardened momentarily before softening again. "Well, Carrie's just a child, but Walter asked me to make sure she was welcome here and to take her under my wing. She's...sweet."

"And Beth?" Katelyn prodded.

Rolling her eyes as she lifted her shoulders slightly, Sandra quipped, "Adequate...for an office manager."

"Did Walter mention a trip to you last week?"

"He said he would be gone on Friday and Monday... I just assumed it would be a long weekend trip. Mr. Maskey told us on Tuesday that Mrs. Berry called, concerned about Walter, but I didn't have any way of contacting him. It was just one day, so I didn't really know what to think. It's so unusual for him not to contact anyone. Then yesterday, I was really sick so had to call in. I didn't know he was still missing until today."

"And you have no idea where he might have gone or who he might be with?"

Tapping her fingernail on the desk again, she gave a jerky shake of her head. "Walter was a very charming man and if you are asking me if he had a...lady friend other than his wife that he could be with, I can assure you that I don't know."

"But it's possible?" Katelyn asked, her voice soft.

With a wince, Sandra replied, "Anything's possible, Ms. MacFarlane."

Driving back over the bridge, Katelyn sat in silence as she turned the information about Walter Berry over and over in her mind. Finally, with a huff, she said, "You're awfully quiet over there. What do you think?"

Chuckling, Gareth said, "I could hear the wheels turning and was waiting for you to finish running through everything that we know so far." Glancing to the side, he said, "I'm curious about what you've come up with."

Puffing her cheeks out with an exhale, she said, "Okay. One...we have a professional man who's very socially active. So he meets a lot of people, used to involve his wife, but in the last several months has become more secretive and now we know was seeing a blonde woman with pink lipstick at a hotel. Two...his older partner is a bit baffled by the younger generation but has no reason to suspect Walter of any cavorting. Three...Walter's been filling the office with younger women, all of whom seem to like Walter, but not each other very well."

"And his wife?"

"Eleanor? Oh, geez...I guess four would be that he's married to a nice woman who has been clueless about her husband's extra-curricular activities."

"And next step?" he pushed.

Pressing her lips together, Katelyn plotted. "Uh...I think we need to check out his finances and check into some of his other social outlets, such as the country club in Virginia Beach and our own local Dunes Resort, since he played golf there as well." Turning back to him, she asked, "So how am I doing?"

Laughing, Gareth nodded. "Good, you're doing good. But you must remain objective and see Eleanor as our client and not our friend. Assumptions can give you a direction to investigate but don't jump to conclusions. Now, since there are just the two of us, we will need to split up some of the tasks and, while you're probably going to protest, I'll check out the organizations in Virginia Beach and you work on compiling some of his finances. Since you're used to the bookkeeping from the pub, you'll have a good understanding of what to look for."

"Hmph. So I get some of the grunge work," she joked. "It's all good. I know a lot of what we do is office work anyway."

"Then we can both check out The Dunes Golf Club. You'll know more people there and can set them at ease talking to us." He thought for a moment and then added, "I think I'll have you also go back and visit with Eleanor at her home. Sometimes when people are in their personal environment, they think of things that fly out of their minds when they are in a strange place, such as our office."

Silence filled the SUV again for a few minutes before Katelyn turned back to him and said, "Thank you, Gareth."

Looking at her, he smiled. With her dark hair, the rich waves pulled back from her face showcasing her classic, Irish, porcelain complexion and startling, blue eyes, the words caught in his throat. His brain screamed, *You're beautiful. You're so smart. And I want to be with you*—

"Are you all right?" she asked, her forehead scrunched as she stared at him.

"Yeah, yeah," he said in haste. "I was just thinking that...uh...you don't need to thank me. You're helping me out and...uh...you're really good at this."

The praise washed over Katelyn, causing her to grin. Nodding, she replied, "Good."

Blinking rapidly, he realized that while his cock was always at half-mast when in her presence, this time, it was his chest that twinged. As he watched the delicate blush creep over her cheeks he felt a jolt straight to his heart.

"We still on for dinner tonight?" she asked, her voice uncharacteristically uncertain.

"Wouldn't miss it for the world," he replied, his smile widening as he observed her lips curving up as well.

Gareth sat at the conference room table in the Baytown Police Station, looking at his friends, Mitch and Colt. "I wanted to keep you up on what I'm finding since we are now on day four of Walter Berry missing...well, day seven if you go all the way back to last Friday."

The two lawmen nodded, both looking over the notes Gareth had provided.

"I don't have much, other than the evidence points to him having an affair with at least one woman, whom he saw more than once, according to the hotel receipts and the statement by the hotel receptionist. The only thing his accounting firm has given us is that the three women who work there, another accountant, the office manager, and the receptionist, are all young, pretty, and appear to be somewhat jealous of the attention that Walter gives to the others."

Mitch's eyebrow rose at that statement and he glanced back down at the picture of Walter and Eleanor Berry.

Chuckling, Gareth said, "I know. It's not that he's young or particularly handsome, but he apparently has a certain charm that turns the ladies' heads."

"I've got my deputies talking to the wife and checking the county, but nothing so far," Colt said. "I also talked to the State Police and had Mrs. Berry file a report with them. Since he works and lives in two different jurisdictions, I knew they would need to be involved."

"What do you need from me?" Mitch asked.

"Nothing, right now. I know you're stretched in personnel, but since he golfed at The Dunes Golf Club, I'm also heading over there to see what I can find out. Since that's in town, I wanted you to be aware that I'm asking questions."

Nodding, Mitch said, "No problem. Just keep me up on whatever you find or whatever you need."

"What about a money trail?" Colt asked.

"Katelyn's working on it," Gareth replied. He noted Mitch and Colt shared a look before turning back to him. "It makes sense right now," he hastily replied.

"She's got the bookkeeping background to do a preliminary check for me."

Throwing up his hands in defense, Mitch said, "Hey, you've got no problem from me. I've thought Katelyn would be a good fit for you...and your business."

Colt laughed at Mitch's double meaning as Gareth blushed. "She's good, I have to admit. Not just a good receptionist, but she's got good instincts for the business."

"And..." Colt threw out.

"Jesus, we're not a bunch of women," Gareth grumbled. Seeing the two stalwart men staring at him, uncharacteristically grinning, he added, "Okay, okay. She and I are friends who are willing to see what else might happen. There. Are you happy?"

Scraping their chairs back across the tile floor, they grinned as they stood. "I don't need to be happy," Mitch quipped. "But it's nice to see that you are."

Gareth placed his hand on Katelyn's lower back as he escorted her into the Sunset View Restaurant that evening. Her hair hung in dark, silken waves, the ends tickling his fingers and he fought the urge to wrap the ebony strands around his hand. Her lush curves were displayed to perfection in an emerald-green, jersey wrap dress. As they followed the hostess to the corner window booth, he noticed the other patrons eyeing them with a few nods and smiles. Suddenly nervous, he realized he was out with one of the town's iconic darlings.

Approaching the booth, Katelyn turned, her smile slipping as she noticed his expression, and cocked her head in silent question. He assisted her into her seat before sliding in on the opposite side. His gaze shifted to their perfect view of the setting sun.

"You had a funny look on your face when we walked over here," she prompted after the waitress took their drink order.

"I was just thinking about how you know everyone here. Growing up in this town...working here for all these years." Pulling on his shirt collar, he looked discomfited. "It suddenly seemed like a lot of eyes were on us."

Her gaze roamed around the beautifully decorated restaurant and she nodded slowly. "Yeah, I guess I do know most everyone." Looking back at him, she admitted, "It can be nice but also very restricting."

Cocking his head to the side, he said, "Restricting?"

"It's like everyone is pigeonholed in a small town. We get accustomed to how everyone acts and thinks." Fiddling with her napkin, she admitted, "I think that's why I stayed a waitress for so long...it was simple, comfortable. No one expected anything different."

Placing his hand over hers, stilling her nervous movements, he confessed, "Well, I, for one, am very glad you took a chance on working for me."

Her lips curved into a slow smile as she lifted her eyes to his, blue eyes twinkling. "Just working?"

A chuckle erupted from deep inside his chest as he

shook his head. "No, no. I should say that I'm glad you took a chance on me." With a quick finger squeeze, he reluctantly let her hand go as their drinks were delivered.

"Do you know what you'd like to order?" the waitress asked, after repeating the specials.

Katelyn, without looking at the menu, stated, "I'll have the scallops with butternut risotto and green beans."

"I thought about the prime rib—"

"Gareth!" Katelyn interrupted. "Why would you want to come here and get something besides seafood?"

Eyebrows lifted, he grinned at her exuberant interruption. "Because I love steak—" Seeing the incredulous expression on her face, he turned to the waitress and said, "I'll take the She-crab bisque and we'll have the crab-cake popsicles for an appetizer...then I'll have the steak."

Giggling, Katelyn nodded enthusiastically. "I'll have the soup as well," she agreed. After the waitress left, she turned back to see Gareth staring at her.

"Beautiful," he breathed.

She shifted her gaze to the multicolored, setting sun through their window. "It is," she agreed.

"I was talking about you," he said, his voice raspy as his eyes pierced hers.

Blushing, she looked down at the wine glass stem she was fingering. She lifted her gaze and said, "It's been a really long time since I've done this."

"This?"

Nodding, she explained, "Go on a date...a nice date. With someone I...uh...you know..."

Saying nothing, he simply waited her out. After

swallowing deeply, she said, "With someone I want to get to know."

Interrupted by the soup being placed on their table, they shared a smile before digging into their dinner, stopping only to watch the sun's final drop into the orange sea.

The full moon hung over the bay, illuminating the stark, blank walls of Gareth's apartment. Sleep eluded him as memories of the evening filtered through his mind. Katelyn's beauty...her full belly laugh that always made him chuckle as well...her attentive kindness to the wait-staff...her pleasant greeting of the other patrons who were more used to seeing her in the diner or behind the bar. The memory of the kiss on her front porch ignited his blood as he replayed the way her body felt against his. His hands finally fisting her silky hair. Her breasts crushed against his chest. Her lips, red and plump from their fiery kisses.

Tossing to his back, he flung his arm over his forehead as his legs kicked off the offending covers. Letting the cool breeze from his open window blow across his body, he thought of standing under her porch light at the end of the evening. *She looked up at me, her eyes full with an open invitation. All I had to do was walk in...to her house and probably her bed.* Jerking up, he swung his legs over the side of the mattress and stood quickly. Stalking into the kitchen, he poured a glass of filtered water from the pitcher and drank it thirstily. Setting the glass into the sink, he walked through the living room and stared out of the large window. The full moon was visible as he viewed the quiet town.

Why did I hesitate? I could see the disappointment in Katelyn's eyes when I turned her down. Sighing, he dropped his chin to his chest and knew the answer. *Uncertainty. What happens to our relationship if she decides she can't move past Philip's memory?*

12

Driving through the security gates of The Dunes Resort, Katelyn smiled at the perfectly manicured landscapes. Several neighborhoods split off the winding entrance road, leading to modest houses in some, while others contained multi-million dollar homes backing to the golf courses. Two nationally known courses drew in visitors from the area, as well as all across the east coast.

Gareth had visited several times in his investigations, as well as eating at the Dunes Clubhouse Restaurant.

"You play?"

Katelyn's question cut into his thoughts and he jerked his gaze to the side. More casual today, she was in nice jeans and a simple navy sweater, her hair pulled away from her face. Following her gaze over the course, he realized what she was asking. "Yeah," he responded before adding with a chuckle, "But not well. What about you?"

Laughing, she replied, "I've played a couple of times but, honestly, golf was never my thing." She looked at the restaurant as they pulled into a parking spot and said, "I thought of working here at one time, but then I couldn't stand the thought of one more waitressing job. I knew that while the tips might be better on the weekends when they had golf tournaments, the restaurant really is kind of seasonal. And..." she added with a shrug, "I hated the idea of all the out-of-towners." Seeing his lifted eyebrow, she explained, "The diner is just more homey."

Nodding, he said, "Yeah, at the diner you didn't have to worry too much about strangers hitting on you."

"Exactly," she agreed as they alighted from his vehicle. Looking over at him, she asked, "How do you want to work this?"

Standing for a moment with his hands on his hips, his gaze drifting over the clubhouse, he said, "How about you go into the bar and start some questioning of the staff and I'll head to the pro-shop. I'll meet you in the restaurant as soon as I'm finished."

With a nod, Katelyn set out, Gareth watching her as she moved into the building, a smile playing about his lips as he realized how seamlessly she fit into his business...and life.

A few minutes later, he stood at the counter in the pro-shop, glad to see someone he knew at the register. The fact that the shop was not busy was also in his favor.

"Gareth, my man! How's it going?"

Nodding, he smiled at the young man. "Slow day, Bob?"

"Oh, yeah. Boring as hell in here when no one's playing golf. You thinkin' of playing?"

"Sorry, no, not today. But I do have some questions, if you don't mind."

"Sure thing."

"Do you know Walter Berry and, if so, what can you tell me about him?"

Bob scrunched his face for a few seconds before his eyes widened and he said, "I heard he was missing."

Rearing back in surprise, Gareth said, "From who?"

"His wife was in here a couple of days ago asking if I'd seen him this week." He looked at Gareth and said, "Whoa...she's hired you, hasn't she? Damn, he really is missing."

Hoping to quell the young man's inquisitiveness, Gareth just shrugged and said, "So, what can you tell me?"

Leaning his arms on the counter, Bob replied, "Nice guy. Decent golfer."

"He usually in alone...with a group...his wife...some other friend?"

Laughing, Bob said, "How about all of the above? He's a real regular and I've seen him come in with a group that he'd introduce as clients of his. Sometimes he'd just play with whatever members were here to play. His wife played some, but usually she'd come and sit with a book while he played."

Nodding slowly, he asked, "So you never saw anything suspicious in his behavior? Or a change of behavior?"

Shaking his head, Bob replied, "Nope, sorry. I told his wife the same thing. He was just a real good guy."

Thanking him, Gareth walked out of the pro-shop and headed into the restaurant. Finding Katelyn at the bar chatting with one of the bartenders, he had a flash of jealousy seeing the man leaning his arms on the bar perilously close to her. Hearing him come in, Katelyn's beautiful smile filled her face as she beamed at him, causing his heart to skip a beat.

The bartender leaned back, his face showing his disappointment as he poured Gareth a beer. Katelyn greeted him before inclining her head toward the bartender, saying, "Chris remembers seeing Walter numerous times, with all sorts of people. Groups, friends, and his wife."

"Bob from the pro-shop said the same thing."

"He was a good tipper," Chris joked. "He came in almost weekly."

"Ever see him with a woman...uh, not his wife?"

Chris' eyes widened for a millisecond before he replied, "Yeah...but not alone. You know, not like he was hookin' up or anything. Just sometimes there might be a woman golfer with some of the men he was with."

With a nod, Gareth stood and picked up his and Katelyn's beers from the bar and walked to one of the tables overlooking the course. Settling in chairs, she turned and said, "So what do you think?"

Taking a sip, he said, "I figured this was a long-shot. This place is too well known...too close to home and his wife. Odds are, he'd never bring another woman here, but I thought it was worth checking out."

Finishing their beers, they nodded to Chris as they

headed back out into the sunshine. Driving back to town, Katelyn said, "If it's alright, I need to leave a bit early this afternoon. I've got an AL Auxiliary officers meeting."

"No problem. I'll spend the afternoon going over the Berry's financial statements that you started on," he replied, glancing to view her smiling face. "How's the Auxiliary going?"

"Really good. Just like with the AL, there are a lot of women who are interested in serving. We'll keep doing fundraising to help with the programs you all are working on. We're also getting a memory wall going, and we'll have the newspaper do an article when we're finished."

"Did you walk to work today?"

"Yeah, so can you just let me out at the AL building? It'll just be a short walk home when it's over."

Pulling up to the curb, he turned toward her, wanting to lean over to kiss her but unsure what she would deem acceptable. Kissing at night on her front porch was one thing, but he knew it was entirely different for her to kiss him in front of others. Before he had more time to wonder, she leaned over and met him halfway. Her lips hit his and his hand automatically reached up to cup her cheek. Rubbing her soft skin, he smiled as he pulled back regretfully. "See you later," he said, as she met his smile with one of her own.

"Yeah," she breathed against his lips, sighing before she hopped down from his SUV. Jogging over to the door, she stopped to chat as a group of women was walking up to the building.

Gareth watched as Tonya Bayles greeted Katelyn

with a hug and, for a moment, he panicked. *Will Katelyn be upset if Tonya saw us kissing?* Immediately chastising himself, he drove away, forcing the thought of Katelyn and Philip's mother out of his mind.

"Fabulous!"

The pronouncement by Jillian, as the temporary chairman, in response to how much the Auxiliary's officers had accomplished in their meeting, was agreed upon by all.

"Okay, ladies, we're ready for the next month's meeting." With that, the women stood and scooted their chairs back. Hugs and goodbyes took several minutes before the room was emptied.

As Katelyn began walking down the sidewalk, Tonya called out to her. Turning back, she smiled as Tonya jogged over to her.

"I couldn't help but notice that nice young man who brought you to the meeting," Tonya began and, with a huge smile, added, "And the kiss you gave him."

Blushing, Katelyn ducked her head, her grin slipping. Lifting her gaze back to Tonya's, she said, "Gareth's the first man in a really long time that makes me feel like there might be more out there for me."

"Oh, darling girl," Tonya gushed, throwing her arms around Katelyn. "Yes, yes, there's more for you."

Leaning back, Katelyn peered into the face of the woman she would always care for deeply.

Tonya cupped Katelyn's face and, with tears in her eyes, said, "I've prayed for so long that you'd find someone. Someone that deserved you as much as Philip did. And it looks like my prayers have been answered."

Swallowing hard, Katelyn felt the familiar stinging behind her eyes before a tear slipped over her cheek. "I would have lived and died his wife, you know?" she whispered.

"Oh, Katelyn, I know. Philip loved you so. His father was so worried that you two were too young to be so committed, but I told him not to fret. I never worried about how young the two of you were."

"I just never thought I might find that kind of love again," Katelyn whispered, her voice rough with emotion.

Tonya smiled through her tears, one hand still cupping Katelyn's cheek. "If you've found it, then don't let it go. Don't let the past...or fear, keep you from it." Leaning over, she kissed Katelyn's cheek before nodding and turning away, walking toward her car.

Katelyn stood, rooted to the sidewalk for a moment, swallowing deeply. Changing directions, she hustled down the sidewalk in the opposite direction from her house, not seeing Gareth in his SUV parked on the road, watching.

How can I compete with a memory? Heart heavy, Gareth sat in his vehicle, parked outside the Baytown Cemetery. His gaze still on the woman kneeling at a tombstone, he leaned his head back as a long sigh left his chest.

A rapping on the passenger side window had him

jerking his head around in surprise. Aiden's face stared back at him. Shaking his head, he unlocked the doors, observing as Aiden climbed up into the SUV.

Silence filled the vehicle until Aiden, unable to stand the quiet, said, "So...you doing a stakeout of the ghosts of Baytown now?"

Rolling his eyes, Gareth looked over, his quip choking in his throat as he saw Aiden's pained expression. Saying nothing, he turned his head back to watch out his window.

"She does this, you know," Aiden finally said, breaking the silence once more. "She comes here to talk to him."

Silence.

"It's just something we've all come to accept," Aiden continued. "It's harmless and seems to make her feel better."

Silence.

Shifting in his seat, Aiden confessed, "Sometimes me or Brogan will come out here, just like you are now, and watch. You know...to make sure she's all right. Years ago, she'd fall asleep out here after crying her eyes out and one of us would pick her up and carry her back home."

Twisting his head back toward Aiden, Gareth's brows lowered as he growled, "And you call that harmless?"

"That was years ago, man. When it was all...I don't know...fresh. Hell, Philip's death just about tore all of us up." Aiden let out a deep sigh and said, "We were all young, idealistic...hell, foolish. From this little town and we were going to go out, see the world, and save

America." Scrubbing his hand over his face, he said softly, "Jesus, we were stupid. Thought we fuckin' knew it all. I guess we were lucky that only one of us didn't come back."

Silence filled the vehicle once more only, this time, less strained. More introspective. Comforting.

"I really care for her," Gareth confessed, "but don't know that I'm up to competing with Philip's memory."

"Oh, hell, Gareth! That ain't what's happening here!" Aiden rushed. "She does this now when she has something on her mind. Sometimes she comes to talk to him about good stuff and, if I had to guess, that's exactly what she's talking to him about now."

Doubt in his eyes, Gareth stared back at Aiden.

"I'm telling you, I know my sister and she's been happier in the past week being with you than I've seen her in years! Katelyn's not hanging on to Philip's memory to keep her from moving forward. She's just..." sighing again, "she just finds some comfort out here. It's almost like talking to Jillian...only less loud."

A chuckle rumbled out of Gareth's chest at Aiden's description of Katelyn and Jillian together. As his mirth ebbed, he said, "I hope you're right."

"I know I'm right," Aiden confirmed. "And I gotta tell you, not to get all emotional and shit, but I'm real glad. She deserves someone like you."

Praise now from both MacFarlane brothers, Gareth dared to smile. Nodding, he said, "Appreciate it, Aiden."

"No problem. So, uh...you gonna wait on her now?"

"Yeah, I'll be here when she's finished. I just hope she doesn't mind."

"Like I said, if I had to guess, she's telling Philip about you right now."

With that, Aiden jumped down from the SUV and, with a quick salute, jogged over to his truck, leaving Gareth wondering who would be walking home from the cemetery—a woman still devastated by her memories or a woman ready to take a chance on him.

13

Kneeling on the grass, Katelyn leaned her forehead against the cold, marble headstone. "Oh, Philip..." A silent tear dropped onto the marble base as her fingers trailed over the indentations that made the words she had traced a thousand times.

SPC. Philip Michael Bayles
He loved his family. He served his country.
He is not forgotten.

"I would have waited forever for you to come home to me," she whispered. "My heart was yours from the time we were so little." She smiled sadly, remembering his blond hair curling over his ears as the wind swept in from the bay. Freckles lined his cheeks and by the time he was a teenager, she loved to run her fingers through the long curls.

"You were my first kiss...my first everything. And I thought you were going to be my last." Wiping her cheeks, she said, "But there's someone new...someone that's given me hopes that I might have all that I thought was lost. And as crazy as this sounds, I think you would approve. He's a lot like you. He doesn't feel like he needs to be the life of the party...instead, he makes me feel like I'm the only one in the room. But I'm older now, Philip...I know more about what I want out of life. When you loved me, I was such a child. Gareth likes me for who I am now."

A raw chuckle erupted as she added, "And we've only kissed. Who knows if he'll be my everything but, for the first time, I feel like living again."

Leaning back, her fingers dropped into her lap as she realized she had been sitting for a long time. The sun was dipping low in the sky, painting it with orange and red. Exhausted, she stood stiffly, wobbling slightly as she regained the feeling in her legs. Bending over, she kissed the top of the headstone before turning and walking out of the Baytown Cemetery. As she passed the iron gates, she startled, seeing Gareth leaning against his SUV, one booted leg crossed over the other, his hands shoved into his jeans' pockets.

Her heart pounded a staccato in her chest as she wondered if her eyes were deceiving her. If the fates had conjured him up from her dreams to place him directly in her path. Glad to see him, she took in his knitted brow. Walking up to him, she placed her hands on his forearms. His hands stayed in his pockets as he stared at her warily.

"Hey," she said, softly, her lips curving upwards. "What are you doing here?"

"I came to the meeting to offer you a ride home, then followed you here," he replied, his gaze never leaving hers. "Are you okay?"

Nodding slightly as she squeezed his arms, she answered, "Yeah. I come here sometimes." There was no response, so she continued, "I know it seems silly, but I talk to Philip. Or rather, I talk out loud to myself and just happen to do it here."

Heart pounding so loud he was sure she could hear it, he asked, "Anything in particular you needed to talk about today?"

"Yeah. I needed to tell him..." she swallowed audibly as tears formed again. Gaining control, she said, "About you. I needed to tell him that I've found someone special. Someone that I want to take a chance on. Someone that I have no idea what the future will hold with, but I want to work on finding out."

At her words, Gareth's eyes widened, his breath catching in his throat. Slowly pulling his hands out of his pockets, he felt hers slide down until their fingers were clasped.

"I'm not afraid of us...of trying...of becoming," she whispered, drawing closer until her body was pressed against his. "I think I'm cautious. It's scary opening my heart again." Lifting on her toes, she kissed him. Soft. Slow. Sweet.

He tasted the salt from the tear that escaped her eye and moved his lips from hers to kiss it away. He held her gaze as he said, "I was afraid...that maybe this wasn't what you wanted."

"Oh, no. My heart's sure. It absolutely knows you are what I want."

Leaning over until his forehead touched hers, he said, "You want a ride home?"

Nodding, she smiled. "But this time, will you come in?"

His voice raspy, fear mixed with longing, he asked, "You sure?"

A smile was his answer.

Entering her house, Katelyn stepped hesitantly into the small foyer, glancing over her shoulder at Gareth as he followed her. Turning, she asked, "Do you want something to drink...or eat...or—"

Her words were halted by his lips on hers as his arm slipped around her. Melting into him, she gave over to the sensation of his body. The strength of his arms as her fingers dug into the muscles of his biceps. The softness of his lips as they moved over hers. His body, angles and planes of muscle, surrounding her as he nibbled at her mouth before plunging his tongue deep inside.

Gareth stroked his tongue along the recesses of her mouth, relishing the taste of her, memorizing the feel. The physical pleasure zipping along his spine meshed with the overwhelming desire to claim her with his heart as well as his body. Pulling back, he chuckled as she moved forward, her lips attempting to stay in contact with his.

"Hang on, Katelyn," he begged, not giving back into the pleasure until her eyes opened and focused on him. "I know you said you were ready for us...but we don't have to do more...not now—"

"I want more," she breathed into his mouth,

dissolving any concerns he had. Looping his arms around her waist he lifted her up and she quickly snapped her legs around his hips, pulling him tight. He felt her core pressing hot against his crotch, his dick aching to be set free from the confines of his jeans.

Their lips latched once more, he mumbled, "Where?" as he began to walk to the stairs.

"Door on right," she managed to say, her body flaming as he carried her up.

Once in the bedroom, he allowed her body to slide slowly down the front of his until her feet were firmly planted on the floor. His hands lifted to cup her face as he peppered her lips with kisses, nibbling at the corners until she gasped and he plunged his tongue inside once more.

The moonlight filtered into the room through lace curtains, creating patterns across their bodies. Slowly pulling back, his eyes locked onto hers and he said, "Tonight is about us...taking it slow. I want to worship every inch of your body. I want you to feel every move-ment. I want you sure so when you look back, you'll remember it as the beginning of you and me."

Her mouth opened slightly, the weight of his words moving through her, the only response she had was to nod.

His hands slid to the bottom of her sweater and as he pulled it upward, she lifted her arms above her head, allowing him to continue to pull it until the soft material fell away onto the floor. His eyes held hers for a moment until dropping to her breasts, spilling out from her black bra. Lifting his hands, he clasped her waist before moving them torturously up, halting at the underside of her bra cups. He flicked over each lace-covered nipple with his thumbs, watching her eyes fill with lust as the hardened points begged for more.

Reaching to the front, he unclasped the bra and his breath caught in his throat as the material joined her sweater on the floor. "Beautiful...perfectly beautiful," he breathed as he palmed her breasts, the silky flesh filling his hands.

Bending, he lifted her once more so that her breasts were at the level of his face and his lips pulled one deeply into his warm mouth. Sucking, nipping, soothing, he moved between the budded mounds as her fingers clutched his shoulders.

Katelyn threw her head back as each pull on her nipples sent shockwaves straight through her core. It had been a long time...longer than she wanted to admit and her body was awakening from a long slumber. Before her mind had time to travel down that road, she felt her body being lowered backward and she clung to his massive arms as her back landed softly on the bed.

Pulling away from her luscious breasts reluctantly, Gareth wanted to see all of her. Standing, he reached for her pants and unzipped them before sliding them down her legs, snagging her panties along the way. With a quick toss, the rest of her clothes lay on the floor and her body was presented to him.

His breath hitched once more as he viewed her lying on the bed with the lace-filtered moonlight creating patterns across her pale skin. Her dark hair spread across the comforter underneath her and the slight light allowed him to see her dark blue eyes carefully observing him as well. Her kiss-swollen lips curved into a smile as her arms lifted to beckon him.

Meeting her smile with one of his own, he crossed his arms in front of him grabbing the bottom of his t-shirt. Pulling it over his head, he allowed it to join the pile of discarded clothing on the floor. Pulling a condom out of his wallet before tossing it to the night-stand, he toed off his boots before unzipping his jeans over his erection.

Leaning up on the bed, resting on her elbows, Katelyn watched the play of muscles in the moonlight as Gareth stripped for her. His body, honed to perfection, held her gaze.

As his jeans slid to the floor along with his boxers, his erection sprang free, capturing her complete attention. He stroked himself, smiling at her, his cock eager to seek her warmth. *But not yet...this is about her.*

Bending, he placed whisper soft kisses along her calves, over her knees, and up the sensitive skin of her thighs. His nostrils filled with the scent of her arousal as he placed his lips on her wet folds. Licking his way toward her clit, he slid his shoulders between her thighs, opening her legs up wider.

Katelyn's head fell back to the bed, the sight and feel of Gareth between her legs almost causing her to erupt immediately. She did not want to think of how long it had been since she had had sex—she did not want to think of anything other than the man with her right at this moment, giving her all he had to give.

With only a few nips on her clit, she came undone, her orgasm overtaking her, causing a gasp to slip out as the electricity shot from her core outward in all directions.

As Gareth continued to kiss his way up her body, over her tummy to each breast, she clapped her hands over her face. He paused, saying, "Katelyn? Babe? Are you all right?"

Lowering her hands slowly, she peered into his crystal blue eyes, swallowing audibly as a tear slid from the corner of her eye, landing on the comforter. Before he had a chance to ask, she threw her arms around his neck and pulled him closer. "I'm sorry," she cried.

"Shhh, don't apologize," he whispered. "What's wrong, please, tell me."

She looked at his anguished expression and gushed, "No, no, nothing's wrong. I'm just...it's just that it's been...I don't know. I was suddenly overwhelmed."

He rested his weight on his forearms, planted on the mattress, as he cupped her face. "I want you to feel nothing but good, right now, sweetheart. So we can go slow and we can stop now. I'm fine with that—"

"No," she hurried to interrupt. "I want this. I want you." Sucking in a deep breath, she added, "I was just overcome. It's been a long time since...well...since. And it all felt so right. So perfect."

"I want you, too. Not just this," he said pressing his erection against her stomach, "but all of you. Your spirit, your life, your everything."

As she smiled once more, he captured her lips with his, his tongue delving to taste her essence. Sitting up just long enough to snag the condom packet from the nightstand, he ripped the foil and covered his cock. Placing the head at her entrance, it took all his might to hold still, his gaze seeking her permission one last time.

Grabbing his shoulders, she pulled him into her as her legs wrapped around his waist. The sense of fullness had her digging her fingers into his back as he moved slowly until fully seated.

Trying to go slow, sweat popped out on his forehead, as he gave her tight channel a chance to acclimate. His voice, gravel rough, barely managed to form words. "You okay?"

"Yes, please, please," she begged, not sure what she was begging for. She just knew her body was screaming for more. More movement...more fullness...more friction. Desperate for another orgasm, this time with him buried deep inside, she thrust her hips up hoping to get him moving.

Chuckling, he said, "You got it," and began to thrust, slowly at first and then harder and faster as she urged him on.

The friction she sought began to build until her mind was no longer cognizant of anything other than his body joining with hers. The muscles in his back rippled with each movement, her feet resting on his firm ass. Soon, her inner walls grabbed at his cock as she was rocked once more with an orgasm.

The feel of her tight, slick core pulling against him had Gareth flying along with her. His lower back tightened as his balls drew up, finally thrusting inside a few more times until he emptied himself inside. Continuing to move through his orgasm, all thoughts left other than this woman underneath him and in his heart. Crashing down on her, he barely had the presence of mind to roll slightly to the side. Keeping his arms around her, he pulled her forward until she was resting, draped halfway over his body.

Neither spoke for several minutes as their bodies slowly cooled and their heavy breathing began to slow. Resting her head on his chest, her fingers splayed over his heart, she felt the comforting sensation of it beating for her.

For a second, Gareth wondered what she expected. *Should I offer to leave? Does she want me to stay?*

As though she could hear his thoughts, she raised her head to smile down at him. "Please, stay. I really want you to stay."

"Nowhere else I'd rather be," he vowed. "Give me just a minute and I'll be back." With that, he stalked to the bathroom to take care of the condom. Coming back into the bedroom, he saw her raised up on her elbow, head in hand, staring at him.

Before he could ask, she said, "You're gorgeous."

Climbing into bed, he jerked the covers over their bodies, pulling her soft curves tightly against him. "I think you must be looking into a mirror, 'cause those were the exact words I was going to say about you."

Sated, satisfied, and smiling, Katelyn closed her eyes as his warmth enveloped her.

14

"George! Where are you?"

The shout came from one of the groups playing golf at The Dunes. A golf tournament was to be held the next day and the grounds crew were busy. A local group of townies were playing regardless of the hustle and bustle of the landscapers.

Roger Thorpe, The Dunes general manager, drove around on his golf cart, overseeing the work. Hearing the shout from one of the golfers, he observed as another man used his club to whack a path through the azaleas. Lips pinched in irritation, he turned and drove quickly over the cart path to where they were.

Hoping out of his cart, he approached the three men standing nearby. "What the hell is George doing?" he barked.

One of the men shook his head, saying, "Sorry, Roger. His ball went in there and he's determined to find it."

"Idiot! He's ruining the landscape!" Marching

toward the now still golfer, he approached him from the back. "George, this is your warning. One more infraction and your club privileges will be revoked—"

Coming to the side of George who was staring down at the ground, he halted at the sight now before him. "Oh, Jesus...oh, Jesus."

One week. Katelyn knew it had been one week since Eleanor had seen Walter. She tried to keep her mind on the task of delving through Walter's finances, but her night with Gareth kept slipping into her thoughts. Grinning to herself, she forced her eyes back to the pages of numbers.

Viewing an unusual withdrawal, she went back to look at it again. It was buried amongst a lot of other mundane office withdrawals, but the abbreviation C Col caught her attention. The withdrawal was only for a thousand dollars, but as she flipped through several more months, she discovered it there again. Not trained in the computer programs Gareth had at his disposal, she grunted in frustration as she shoved the papers into the file and headed back to his office.

Rounding the corner, she came to a halt as his head lifted and his warm eyes landed on hers. Memories of their lovemaking the night before filled her mind as all other thoughts fled.

"Hey," he greeted, grinning at her rooted stance and unabashed stare. When she did not speak, his gaze dropped to the files in her hand. "You got something for me?"

Blinking out of her lust-filled musings, she blurted, "I need your Superman computer programs to figure out something."

"My Superman computer programs?" he laughed.

"You know, the ones where you can be a spy and find out all sorts of things," she huffed, hurrying over and placing the file on top of the open one on his desk. "How do we find out what C Col is? Walter made seven months of payments and this is the only notation he used for it. They are a thousand dollars each. And what's weird, they're buried in the business accounts, but only by him...not Beth. Do you think he was paying blackmail money?"

"Hold your horses," Gareth chuckled, enjoying her enthusiasm. His eyes raked over her face, cheeks flushed and eyes bright. His voice dropped as he lifted his hand to touch her warm cheek. "Are you all right this morning?"

Smiling, she pressed her lips against his while mumbling, "Oh, yeah. More than all right."

Holding each other's gaze for a moment, they slowly pulled back and he said, "Okay...work..."

Laughing, Katelyn pulled a chair up to his side of the desk so she could see his screen. Frustrated at how fast his fingers flew over the keys, she grumbled, "You'll have to teach me how to work these programs soon."

Nodding his agreement while he continued to probe, he said, "Okay, looks like I've found the actual money trace. The payments went to Virginia Beach Community College."

"Huh? For him? Is he taking some kind of class when he already has an MBA?"

"Let's see if I can find an account associated with the payments." It took Gareth a while to search and Katelyn's leg bounced continuously next to his. Clamping his hand down on her knee, he said, "Be still. You're breaking my concentration."

"Sorry, I'm just nervous." Seeing his eyebrow lift, she explained, "I want so much to find something that will lead us to Walter but hate like hell having to find anything negative that we have to tell Eleanor."

"Can't have it both ways when investigating."

"I know, but—"

"Got it!" He clicked once more as she leaned over. Both stared at the screen as the account owner popped up. Carrie Reynolds.

Turning, they looked at each other in silence for a second before Katelyn burst out, "He's paying Carrie's college tuition?"

Both leaned back heavily in their chairs, air leaving their lungs in a whoosh. Gareth silently checked a few more screens before nodding. "Yep...the money's been paying Carrie Reynolds' college tuition for months."

"Do you think there's something else going on between them? I know she's got light blonde hair, but she could have worn a wig to the motel."

"Don't know and at this point, we don't have enough information to make any kind of conjectures," he warned. "And I need to have you keep searching."

Nodding, she leaned over to snag the file off his desk when she found her cheeks captured in his hands. His kiss was soft at first and then nipped at her lips, causing her to groan into his mouth.

Losening his hold, he mumbled, "That was a bad

idea. Now all I want to do is take you upstairs to my apartment."

Laughing, she pushed back, "Not now. I've got to figure out where else he was spending his money...and maybe his time!"

Back at her desk, she was now fully focused on what other secrets Walter Berry held.

Turning into the Berry's driveway, Katelyn pulled up to the front of their house, appreciating the landscaping that surrounded the bayside home. In a neighborhood on the waterfront, the Berry's impressive home was modest compared to a few of the others, but Katelyn knew the true value was in the land.

Answering the door, Eleanor pushed her hair back from her pale face, dark circles clearly visible underneath her eyes. "Please, come in, Katelyn. I'd love the company and to hear anything you might have found."

The two women settled, Eleanor on the sofa with Katelyn in a comfortable chair facing her. Deciding to stall no longer, Katelyn waded in. "Eleanor, we have found some movements in money that Walter controlled and I want to ask you about them."

"Okay," Eleanor said slowly, sucking in her lips.

"I know you have looked through the personal accounts that you and Walter share and we have gone through the firm's recent books. We have discovered that Walter has another account set up in the firm's name and he is the only one who has access to it. It does not go through the other accountants."

Eyes wide, Eleanor shook her head. "I had no idea."

"We assumed you didn't. It appears to be a petty-cash type of account with the withdrawals only being for a few items."

Hesitating, Katelyn watched as Eleanor's face morphed from surprise to anger. Lips pinched, Eleanor said, "And what has he been spending on from that account?"

Clearing her throat, Katelyn said, "Well, because the money has come out as cash, it is hard to say where he has been spending, but we did manage to find a notation that we then could trace." Sucking in a fortifying breath, she continued, "It appears he has been paying the college tuition for Carrie Reynolds."

"Carrie? His receptionist, Carrie?"

Nodding, Katelyn bit her lip, watching the other woman carefully. Eleanor blinked, her face a mask of confusion. "But...why would he...I mean...what..." Taking a deep breath, she shook her head slightly, her eyes staring at Katelyn unfocused.

"Are they particularly close?" Katelyn prodded gently.

"No," Eleanor responded just before doubt clouded her eyes. "I...well, I don't think so. But..." Her voice tapered off as she shook her head.

"I'm sorry to be the one to tell you," Katelyn offered, reaching over to clasp Eleanor's hand. "And don't read any more into it than what we know right now."

"I...I suppose the firm could have decided to assist her...I really don't know." Looking back up into Katelyn's eyes, she added, "But will you continue to see what you can find out?"

Nodding, Katelyn agreed. "Of course, we'll keep investigating until we find him and know what has happened."

Driving back to the office, Katelyn hoped she would be able to keep that promise.

15

Katelyn paced the office, unable to settle the unease filtering through her mind. Gareth was not in, having gotten a call from Mitch. She checked her phone to see if she had missed a message, but it was as silent as the office. Sighing, she leaned back and squeezed her eyes shut, tired from looking at bank statements.

Jumping when her phone's ring sounded out in the quiet, she grabbed it, pleased to see Gareth's number. "Hey, what's up?"

"Katelyn, I've been at The Dunes golf course with the police. An early morning golfer found a body. There's been no official identification, but I've got a bad feeling."

"Oh, shit," she breathed, her mind racing to Eleanor. "What can I do?"

"I would have you come here but, honestly, it's a zoo. Zac's here with the ambulance to take the body in. The county coroner has been here. The whole area is now off limits as a crime site—"

"Who's yelling in the background?"

"Roger Thorpe is having a shit-fit because the golf tournament tomorrow will have to be cancelled."

Thinking of The Dunes' manager, Katelyn knew he would be purple with frustration. Before she could ask anymore, Gareth said, "There's really nothing to do except stay in the office and take care of things there. And keep going over Walter's books. If this body is his, I'd like to have something to go on before it all ends up with the police, although I know Mitch'll work well with us."

"Okay, Gareth. I'll take care of the office."

"Thanks. And Katelyn? I'm sorry."

"Sorry? For what?" she asked in confusion.

"I would have preferred to spend time after our first night together with you and not on a golf course with a dead man."

Unable to stop the smile that curved her lips, Katelyn agreed. "Well, for the record, I'd rather be with you also. I'll see you when you get back." With that, they disconnected and her momentary mirth fled in the face of Eleanor possibly getting worse news than her husband was on a trip with a mistress.

Gareth stood to the side as Mitch and the rest of the Bayside Police Department moved about the area. Ginny walked over and stood next to him as the medical examiner gave Zac the okay to move the body.

"You think it's Walter Berry?" she asked.

"From the pictures I've seen, I'd say yes." Sucking in

a deep breath, he shook his head. "God, I hate for his wife to have to come in to identify the body."

"What do you think of her?" Ginny asked.

"Seems strong...and fragile all at the same time."

Nodding, Ginny said, "Well, let's hope the strong side comes out now." Moving away, Gareth watched her make her way back over to the officers then he turned as more vehicles came into the area. Colt and another deputy from the North Heron Sheriff's Department alighted from their SUVs and, with a nod to Gareth, headed to Mitch. Several minutes later Mitch and Colt walked over to Gareth.

"We're fairly sure the body was Walter Berry but I'll be going out to pick up his wife to take her for the identification," Mitch said. Looking over, he added, "Do you want to be there also?"

Rubbing his chin, Gareth said, "I'm thinking yes, but Katelyn might be a better support for her."

Mitch nodded his agreement, "I'll give you a call when we're ready."

With that dismissal, Gareth walked back to his SUV to drive back to the office. Sighing as he pulled into a parking space, his gaze landed on the beautiful woman sitting at the desk in the reception area. Rubbing his chest, he closed his eyes for a moment, the previous night's memories sliding through him. With a mental shake, he stepped out of the vehicle and smiled as Katelyn met him at the door.

North Heron's Medical examiner, Dr. Warren stood

outside the room with the body, his observant gaze on Eleanor's pale face. Glad her hand was clasped in Katelyn's, he said softly, "Mrs. Berry, normally this type of thing is done at the hospital where they use a camera from another room for identification purposes. We don't have a camera here at this facility, but it's my understanding that you want to identify the remains now, before we transport him to the hospital for further examination?"

A shaky nod met his question and Katelyn felt her fingers squished by Eleanor's nervous hand.

"All right, then this is what we will do. I have taken pictures and have them here," he explained, patting his lab coat pocket. "I will place them on the table and you will look at them closely. You may certainly keep Ms. MacFarlane in the room with us and, for legal purposes, Officer Spencer will remain with us as well."

Katelyn glanced over to Ginny, sharing a tight-lipped grimace with her. She was glad for Ginny's presence, not knowing how Eleanor would react.

Eleanor nodded jerkily once more and they stepped toward the table after Dr. Warren laid five photographs down, side by side. Before Katelyn had a chance to study them, she heard a gasp from Eleanor just before she cried, "No! Oh, no!"

Feeling Eleanor's body slumping into hers, Katelyn tried to steady her, grateful as Ginny rushed forward to support Eleanor as well. Dr. Warren slid a chair behind Eleanor and they assisted her to sit.

"Oh, God. Oh, God, no," Eleanor repeated, her mouth opening in gasps, as though no air was reaching her lungs.

The nurse stepped in and the medical staff attended to Eleanor for a few minutes, keeping her from fainting. Katelyn stood back with Ginny at her side as they silently watched the scene unfold. As Eleanor's sob finally worked its way to the surface, Katelyn jerked, the woman's raw emotion hitting her in the stomach. Feeling punched, she fought tears herself as Eleanor's grief took over.

"Mrs. Berry, I just need to hear you identify the man in the pictures," Dr. Warren said softly, his hand comforting on the back of her shoulders.

"Yes," her voice croaked. "That's my husband. That's my Walter."

Katelyn and Ginny moved to assist Eleanor from her seat as the doctor explained the next steps in the procedure. Katelyn saw Eleanor nodding but knew she was not actually hearing anything the doctor said. Her heart ached for the woman whose journey of grief was just beginning.

Ringing the doorbell, she waited a moment until it swung open, Eleanor greeting her wanly. "I hope you don't mind, but I wanted to come by to see how you were doing."

Eleanor's red-rimmed eyes filled with tears as she reached out to clasp Katelyn's hand, pulling her forward. "Thank you...please come in." Trying to force a smile to her lips, she followed Eleanor though the entrance foyer into the den, passing a formal living room. The den, in contrast, appeared to have been very much lived in. A plate with leftover pizza sat on the end table and the coffee table contained several half-empty cups and glasses.

Stopping suddenly, Eleanor turned quickly and, with a blush, said, "I'm so sorry. I'm seeing this room through the eyes of a visitor and realize how horrible it looks."

"It's fine," Katelyn said. "In fact, I like to work while I'm talking, so maybe I can help."

Eleanor gave an embarrassed nod and within a few minutes the two women had rinsed the dirty dishes and placed them in the dishwasher. Giving the kitchen counter a swipe with a clean, wet cloth, Katelyn observed Eleanor standing at the window staring into the back yard. Looking at the same view, Katelyn appreciated the landscaped yard that eventually ended at the dunes and the bay beyond.

"You have a lovely home here," she said honestly.

Eleanor turned, her eyes blinking with tears, and offered a small smile. "Walter actually enjoyed yard work. We didn't hire a landscaping company...we did it all ourselves." Swallowing deeply, tears filled her eyes once more.

Pulling her into a hug, Katelyn felt Eleanor's shoulders quake with silent sobs. Not speaking, but hoping to simply offer comfort, she stood for several minutes until Eleanor took a shuddering breath before lifting her face.

"I feel so guilty," Eleanor admitted.

"Let's go sit and talk a bit," Katelyn suggested.

Once settled in the den, Eleanor said, "I thought the

worst I was going to find out was that he had run off with another woman. I never...never..."

"Have the police told you anything?" Katelyn asked.

"Not much. I know they said that it appeared he had been brought to the golf course by boat...from the bay and then up into one of the many inlets around the courses."

Katelyn immediately tried to envision where Walter's body could have come from...and when...but without more information, her imaginings were halted. Reaching, out, she grasped Eleanor's hand. "Do you have relatives who are coming? What can I do?"

Sighing, Eleanor replied, "I've got family coming in this afternoon. I can't plan the funeral until the police release his...his..."

"I understand," Katelyn rushed to say.

"Walter's mother is still living and he has a brother. They'll come when I have the arrangements made."

"What can I do to help?"

Eleanor focused on Katelyn, shaking her head. "Oh, my dear, just being here is a help. And the cleaning you just did...it's more than enough."

As she walked Katelyn to the door, she said, "Will you and Mr. Harrison continue to find out what happened to Walter?"

Katelyn hesitated before answering. "Uh, well, it's a police matter now, Eleanor. We'll turn over our information to them for their investigation."

"Oh," Eleanor replied, her voice low. "I thought... well, I really hoped..."

"I'll talk to Mr. Harrison and if the police would still

like our assistance, then we'll be more than happy to work with them."

Eleanor's face lifted for the first time that morning as she nodded enthusiastically. "Yes, please. I feel like a horrible wife, accusing my husband when he was actually...uh..." wiping her eyes hastily, "well, it would make me feel better if you kept working on finding out what happened."

Squeezing her hand, Katelyn cautioned, "Eleanor, what we find might not make you happier."

Letting out a deep sigh, Eleanor nodded. "I understand what you're saying. You might find that he was having an affair. But I still want to know, and I think if he was, it might be tied to his death."

With a final nod, Katelyn turned and slid into her car. Driving back to the office, she wondered what they would find...and if it really would give Eleanor peace.

16

"Murder?"

Mitch stood with the medical examiner, Gareth with him, both men carefully reading the report.

"Yes. The blow to the back of the head would have rendered him unconscious, and then he was in the water. Official cause of death is drowning, but being unconscious, he would not have had a chance."

"So, someone hits him near the water, he falls in and drowns, and they transport the body to the golf course."

Nodding, Dr. Warren said, "That's my assessment. There were no drugs or alcohol in his system."

"Time of death?" Mitch queried.

"My estimate is approximately eight or nine days ago."

"So, the weekend before last, when he was supposed to be gone on a trip, he was killed some-where, then transported and deposited at the golf course where it took over a week for anyone to find him," Gareth commented.

Dr. Warren added, "Just so you know, I'll be releasing the body to the funeral home this afternoon."

Mitch thanked the medical examiner as he and Gareth walked out of the building into the sunshine, both men sliding their sunglasses on in unison. "You said he told his staff he was going on a trip, and that's not just the word of his wife?"

"Yeah...they were not expecting him back until Tuesday. They assumed he was taking a trip with his wife."

"And his wife thought he was going on a business trip?"

"According to her though, she assumed he would be back on Sunday evening, checked with his staff on Monday, and came to see me on Tuesday."

Driving back to Baytown, Mitch said, "I'll take all the evidence and notes you've collected. In fact, why don't you come meet with my staff and we'll call in Colt, since the Berry's live in his jurisdiction."

"No problem," Gareth replied, rubbing his chin in thought. "I gotta tell you, Katelyn'll have a hard time letting go of this."

Chuckling, Mitch glanced at the passenger side. "So, is she liking the investigation business?"

"Taking to it like a duck to water. In fact, she's taking a private investigation class at the community college to get her license."

"No shit?" After a moment, Mitch added, "Good for her. Nothing wrong with waitressing, but I always felt like Katelyn was stuck in the past and didn't know how to move forward."

"That's what Aiden and Brogan said."

"Whoa," Mitch exclaimed. "You've got the brothers talking to you about Katelyn." Shaking his head, he added, "I gotta tell you, that's big, man."

"I kinda got that feeling," Gareth admitted, smiling in return.

Sighing, Mitch said, "Okay, back to Walter Berry. Listen, I'm not going to lie. I'll throw everything my department has into this investigation, just like always, but as long as you and Katelyn run everything—and I mean everything—by me, I've got no problem having you keep working the case. You'll need to inform Mrs. Berry that everything will go to us, and you'll probably have to stop billing her as of now, but I'll take whatever help I can get."

Pulling into the parking space directly in front of Harrison Investigations, Gareth hopped out of the BPD vehicle, turning to Mitch just before shutting the door. "Let me know when you want to meet, and Mitch? I appreciate the vote of confidence." With a wave, he headed back into the office.

Parking at the church where the funeral was to be held, Gareth looked to the passenger side where Katelyn was quiet. His hands still on the steering wheel, he hesitated before asking, "You okay with this? I could have come by myself."

She turned, a slight smile on her face as she shook

her head. Reaching over to place her hand on his thigh, she said, "I'm good. Living in a small town, you go to a lot of funerals 'cause you know everyone." Sighing, she said, "It's just...I really thought we'd find him...alive, and probably with another woman, but still...this isn't the conclusion I thought we'd find." Looking out the front windshield at the mourners, she added, "They might not have been able to have children, but they had hopes, dreams, plans. They say funerals are supposed to be a celebration of a person's life...but really? It's all about saying goodbye to dreams."

Nodding, he curled his strong hand around hers, saying, "Let's go in and pay our respects to Eleanor."

"And do a little more investigating?" she asked, her brow lifted.

"Unfortunately, yes. Murder is usually committed by someone the victim knows and this is our chance to see all the players."

The church was filled to capacity with friends, family, and co-workers all present to say goodbye to Walter Berry. Katelyn sat a few pews behind Eleanor, noticing that she sat with a woman that looked so similar to her, she must be Eleanor's sister. An older woman, probably Walter's mother, was seated next to them with a man that appeared to be Walter's brother.

The Berry office staff was seated on the other side of the church and Katelyn leaned slightly forward so she could observe them with ease. William was with a distinguished woman who occasionally brought a handkerchief up to her eyes. *Probably his wife.* Behind them, Sandra and Beth sat. *Funny...no one is between them, but they're at least four feet apart on the pew.* Behind them, she recognized Carrie and sitting with her was a couple, the woman also dabbing her eyes. *Wonder who they are?*

Katelyn, so intent on observing the crowd, startled when Gareth took her hand. Darting her eyes sideways, she blushed before turning her attention back to the service.

The minister's words sang Walter's praises before allowing a few to offer their eulogy. William, dignified as ever, spoke of Walter's unwavering ethical professionalism and his kindness toward others. Another man from one of the social organizations Walter belonged to also commented on Walter's sense of fun and his dedication to charities.

A slight hiccup sounded and Katelyn's eyes moved back to see Carrie and her mother wiping tears.

The service was finally over and Gareth walked over with Katelyn to offer condolences to Eleanor. She grasped their hands and introduced them to her and Walter's family. "These are the private investigators I hired to find out who did this to my Walter," Eleanor said, turning to her sister, an attractive blonde attending the funeral by herself.

"We're working with the police," Gareth supplied, catching Walter's brother's narrow-eyed stare.

"So, this little town's police needs assistance?" Ken Berry asked, barely concealing his irritation.

"No sir, our police are more than capable, as well as the North Heron Sheriff's Department. But as the firm that had been hired a week ago by Mrs. Berry, we will be giving our findings to the officials. And if we can continue to assist, we're more than happy to do so."

"Hmph, just make sure you're not being charged for this, Eleanor," Walter's brother said. "It'd be just like this little town, having a PI charge you when the police should do it for free."

Eleanor bristled as she glared at him. "I am perfectly able to handle our affairs, Ken." Turning to Katelyn and Gareth, she apologized, "I'm sorry." Cutting her eyes over to her in-laws, she said, "I...well, I need to be at the wake. I hope I see you soon."

"I'll come in a couple of days," Katelyn promised, squeezing Eleanor's hand before taking Gareth's arm and walking back toward the church's vestibule, where they could observe some of the others.

"What do you think of the co-workers?" Katelyn asked, leaning closely to Gareth.

"I'm curious about the couple with Carrie...the woman was discreet, but shed as many tears over Walter as Carrie did."

Katelyn hissed as she stood on her toes, whispering into his ear. "I noticed that. How can we find out?"

"Let's try the most obvious way," he replied and with Katelyn's hand still tucked onto his arm, began walking toward the co-workers.

Approaching William and his wife first, Gareth shook his hand while commenting, "Your remarks about Walter were very moving."

"Thank you, Mr. Harrison." William's arm was around the woman who had been sitting next to him and he said, "Let me introduce you to my wife, Theresa. She's the one who actually introduced Walter to me, for which I'm grateful, since our partnership came from that introduction."

"Mrs. Maskey, nice to meet you. I'm Gareth Harrison and this is my associate, Katelyn MacFarlane."

"The service was lovely," Katelyn commented. "Had you known Walter long?"

"Walter and I served on one of the charitable committees that he so loved," Theresa said, still dabbing her nose with her tissue. "I suppose I must have met him almost fifteen years ago. He and William hit it off and we stayed good friends."

Katelyn's gaze drifted to the other Berry employees standing nearby and she said, "I suppose this is a great shock to everyone."

Theresa stiffened, a grimace replacing the sad frown as she sniffed, "There are a few that I don't understand why Walter courted—"

"Now, Theresa," William interrupted.

"Courted?" Katelyn prodded, her head cocked in curiosity.

"Oh, she doesn't mean *courted* in that way," William rushed. "Just that he persuaded them to come work for us."

"You have our condolences again, Mr. and Mrs. Maskey," Gareth said with a nod of his head as he and Katelyn moved away, allowing the Maskeys to join Eleanor.

"What do you think?" Katelyn whispered.

"Let's see what else we can find out," he said under his breath as they walked toward Sandra next.

The elegant accountant shook their hands as they approached. "I assume your work is finished, Mr. Harrison. I'm just so heartbroken that it ended like this."

"Finished, Ms. Posten?"

She fiddled with her clutch, casting her eyes down. "Well, after all, Walter is no longer missing. And for him to drown accidentally...I assume your work is complete."

Katelyn opened her mouth to retort but the squeeze on her fingers halted the words in her mouth. Keeping her expression neutral, she waited for Gareth.

"Yes, he may have been found, but the police will be investigating the circumstances," he stated, his eyes never leaving Sandra.

Sandra looked up, her mouth opening and shutting several times before she said, "Investigating? But...I..."

"Even though a death might appear accidental, the police have to make sure."

Paling, Sandra nodded before rushing her goodbyes and moving away. Gareth and Katelyn shared a glance before moving toward Beth, standing to the side. "None of the office women are talking to each other," Katelyn whispered.

"Not surprising when you consider they all seemed to be in competition for Walter's attention," Gareth whispered back.

Stepping up to Beth, they had barely greeted her before she bit out, "I see Carrie brought her parents to Walter's funeral. And, of course, Ed is all over her."

Katelyn fought to keep her mouth from hanging open, but was unable to keep her eyes from darting over to the side where Carrie stood with the couple that had been sitting with her.

"We just wanted to offer our condolences," Gareth began, but Beth interrupted.

"I mean, it's bad enough that he hired her to begin with...I wonder if William will keep her around." Sniffing, she barely glanced at Gareth or Katelyn before walking away, muttering to herself.

Turning to where Carrie and her parents had been standing, both Katelyn and Gareth looked around briefly before seeing that the trio was already in the parking lot, getting into a car.

"Damn," they murmured under their breath at the same time.

17

"So, who do you think killed him?"

Katelyn rolled her eyes at Jillian sitting on the swing in the back yard, one leg tucked underneath her and the other used to push the swing along with her toes on the ground. "Your fiancé is one of the police officers...you tell me what Grant thinks."

Huffing, Jillian complained, "He doesn't tell me enough! I get more information sitting in the pub and listening to everyone guess."

Tori popped another mini blueberry muffin in her mouth and nodded. "Yep, Mitch is the same. That's why we thought you could tell us more."

Belle leaned forward a bit in her seat, quiet but ever alert. Jade sipped her mimosa, her eyes pinned on Katelyn's.

"You know, this is a weird way to spend a Saturday morning," Katelyn stated, throwing her arms up to her side. "Talking about a murder."

"I can't imagine being the golfer who found him," Jade said.

Unable to stifle a snort, Tori said quickly, "I'm sorry! I'm not laughing about Walter, but I was just thinking about Roger Thorpe. Mitch said he was literally purple in the face at the thought of having to cancel the golf tournament."

"I know that's an expensive event to have to reschedule or just cancel, but Grant said that Roger was more worried about his azaleas getting whacked by a golfer to begin with," Jillian added. "And I can't imagine what Silas, the town manager, is doing! He hates the idea of any blight on the town and with the cancellation of the tournament, he'll be in a blaming game with Roger."

Sighing, Tori said, "Well, I know Silas and the mayor always come flying in to see Mitch whenever something goes wrong in the town. They'll be demanding the case be solved immediately!"

"At least tell us what you know about the will," Jillian begged Katelyn, planting both feet on the ground as she brought the swing to a halt, almost sloshing Jade's mimosa out of the glass. Shooting her an apologetic smile, she turned back to Katelyn. "Well?"

Katelyn's face scrunched as she said, "They had no children, so I suppose everything goes to Eleanor."

"Yes, but what if it doesn't? I mean, he was murdered...maybe by a jealous lover or an enraged lover's boyfriend or husband."

Katelyn started to refute Jillian's imaginings, but had to admit, she thought the same things herself.

Someone killed Walter...someone had a reason to want him dead. Maybe Jillian's wild speculations were not so wild.

"And that's all I've got right now."

Gareth sat with Mitch and Colt, as well as the other officers of the Baytown Police Department, Burt, Sam, Grant, and Ginny, having just delivered all his investigative information. "Katelyn and I informally talked with the Berry employees at the funeral, except for Carrie. I was frustrated because she was the one I wanted to speak to since finding out Walter was paying for some of her college costs."

"You said she was there with her parents. Do you think they know?" Grant asked.

Shrugging his shoulders, Gareth replied, "I don't know. I was going to go to William first to see if he knew anything since it's not too uncommon for employers to assist with educational costs."

"Do that," Mitch said, looking up from the report. "We've got to finish processing the body recovery scene and work to determine where his body came from." Glancing at Grant and Burt, he said, "I'll have you two continue to work the golf course scene. Sam, you and Ginny check to see what the body might have been transported in and from where. I'll be talking to Eleanor again, but with the town's needs still in place, I'll have Gareth and Katelyn investigate as well and report to me."

Colt added, "I'll go with Mitch when he talks to Eleanor. I want to introduce myself to her and, since they live in the county, I'll have my deputies do a preliminary search of the property."

As the group prepared to finish, Gareth looked down at his phone and said, "Just one more thing. Katelyn just sent me a text. It appears Eleanor has asked her to accompany her to the lawyer's office and they'd like me to go as well."

Mitch nodded as he stood. "Sounds good. Keep us up on what you learn."

Gareth swung by the office and watched as Katelyn flipped over the CLOSED sign and locked the front door as he rounded the front of his SUV to open her door. She smiled as he offered his hand and stepped up into the vehicle.

He had barely made it into the driver's seat when she peppered him with questions. "What do you think the lawyer wants to talk to her about? Do you think he changed his will? Do you think Eleanor's going to have a surprise?"

"Babe, slow down," he chuckled, pulling out onto the road heading out of town. "Remember, when investigating, use your imagination but don't get ahead of yourself. Take the information that comes in and look at it from all points of view."

Leaning back, she huffed, "I know, I know. It's just so hard...I hate this for Eleanor."

Reaching over, he placed his hand on her thigh, palm up in invitation. She responded immediately, linking her fingers with his.

"You've got to be careful. I know you really like Eleanor, but you're getting personal with a client and that can be difficult when we have to deliver bad news."

"Can she possibly get worse news than her husband being killed?"

Shaking his head, he replied, "Probably not but, then, we have no idea where this investigation will take us. There could be more bad news on the way."

With that heavy statement hanging between them, they drove the rest of the way in silence.

Bushy eyebrows peered over his glasses at the assembly before him. Settling on Eleanor, the attorney, Mr. Bashor, cleared his throat.

"Mrs. Berry, I want to offer my condolences on the passing of your husband. His will hasn't changed since the two of you came to see me years ago."

Katelyn glanced sideways at Eleanor whose face was pale, but serene. The only expression of nerves was her clutching the leather straps of her purse in her lap.

"Walter's will was very simple. He set aside a small trust to be used for his mother's care and the trust is to be administered by my office. He left a nominal amount to his brother, as well as one-time monetary gifts to three of his favorite charities. The rest of his estate is left, in its entirety, to his wife, Eleanor, since there are no children."

Eleanor nodded, a sigh heaving from her chest. "Thank you, Mr. Bashor. I appreciate all that you've done. Is there anything else I need to do?"

"No, no, my dear. My office will handle everything and we'll be in touch."

With that, they shook hands and Gareth walked

Eleanor and Katelyn out to the parking lot. "Did that go better than you were afraid of?" Katelyn asked.

Eleanor blushed as she replied, "It was a lot of fuss over nothing, wasn't it? Walter and I made our wills out years ago and never changed them." Sighing heavily again, she said, "Everything just seems so hard now...so many decisions to make...I don't know where to turn."

"My unsolicited advice," Gareth began, "is to not make any major plans right away. Take time to let things settle and, when you feel stronger, then you can make decisions."

She nodded her agreement as she approached her car. "Would you two like to come to the house? I have more food than I know what to do with since so many people brought things over after the funeral. And..." she hesitated, her gaze on her shoes before lifting her head, her eyes pleading. "The police are back at the house, going over all of Walter's things to try to see if they can find what he might have been doing or who he might have been with. I'd really like the company."

A quick shared glance between Katelyn and Gareth had them agreeing to follow her there and soon the three were ensconced in Eleanor's den overlooking the back yard. Gareth excused himself to go out and talk to the detectives.

"What all were they looking at?" Katelyn asked, her eyes following Gareth as he walked outside.

"They asked if he kept any journals, diaries, appointment books, address books...that kind of thing. As far as I know, he had all his important dates and information on his phone and I haven't seen that since he left on Friday morning.

"You know Gareth and I shared about the woman at the hotel..." Katelyn's voice trailed off in embarrassment.

"I know," Eleanor nodded sadly, her chin quivering. "I know it's horrible of me, but Katelyn...I'm so mad at him! And I can't talk about it with anyone else because I don't want just anyone to know that he was having an affair and must have been with the other woman when he was killed." She sniffed before leaning over to grab a tissue from the ever-present boxes around the room. "I keep wondering if that had something to do with it...a jealous lover...or an angry lover's husband. God, my mind just keeps rolling to all sorts of notions."

Leaning her head back on the sofa, Eleanor added, "But then I lay in bed and think, if he were just here, I could yell and scream and then make him love me again."

"I think your feelings are completely understandable, Eleanor," Katelyn said, torn between wanting to comfort the grieving woman and trying to keep an eye on the yard where Gareth and a few detectives were moving around. Unable to contain her curiosity, she asked, "Did you and Walter ever go boating, or canoeing, or kayaking?"

Letting out an inelegant snort, Eleanor replied, "No, neither of us did, which seems crazy considering we live out here. At first Walter wanted to get into boating, but it was never something I cared about doing. I get motion sickness on the water and he had fair skin that burned easily." Her gaze drifted to the window but her eyes were unseeing of the activity in the yard as her face took on a wistful expression. "We drove out here one evening and had dinner at The Sunset Restaurant and watched the sun set over the bay. We were newly married and it was magical. We looked at each other and just knew we wanted to live where we could see that sunset every day." Lifting her shoulders in a slight shrug, she added, "So we bought this place and we spent many evenings sitting out on the beach with a glass of wine. I thought we were happy."

Patting her arm, Katelyn remained quiet, knowing Eleanor needed to talk out her memories. Just then, Gareth walked back inside and said, "Eleanor, the detectives will be leaving soon." Giving Katelyn a pointed look, he said, "And I need to get back to town for a meeting tonight."

Standing, Eleanor hugged them both, thanking them for coming before walking them to the door. Once outside, Katelyn waited until they were in his vehicle before asking, "Did you find out anything?"

"So far, they've found no evidence of Walter being killed in his house, yard, or their dunes—"

"Wait...what?" Katelyn jerked her head around to face him. "What do you mean? If he was killed there, Eleanor would have seen or heard something!"

Gareth met her incredulous stare with a patient one of his own. "Katelyn," he said softly before sighing.

Shaking her head, she said, "No, no. How can you even think that Eleanor had anything to do with his death?"

"I didn't say I thought she did. But the police have to check every angle. More often than not, a family member is involved when someone is killed, so the police have to check." He reached over and grabbed her hand, giving it a reassuring squeeze. "But, like I said, there's no evidence in the house or yard."

Her lips pinched together, she said, "It's bad enough she's lost her husband and has to deal with the fact that he cheated, but to be treated like a murderer—"

"Look at me," his voice carried authority and she turned back to him. "No one's treating her like a murderer, Katelyn. But the police have to do their job. And, once she's cleared, they will start focusing on other places he could have been murdered."

Sighing heavily, she nodded. "You're right." They drove in silence for several minutes, passing rural farms on their way back to Baytown. "This is harder than I thought."

"What is, babe?"

"Becoming involved in a case," she said, her voice barely above a whisper.

With another hand squeeze, he said, "Most of the time, this kind of investigation doesn't happen. I've never been involved in a murder before. The majority of PIs just follow people or do a lot of computer searches. This..." he met her sigh, "is different." Looking at her again as they pulled up in front of her pub, he added, "I'm glad you came to work for me, Katelyn."

Her lips curved into a slight smile as she leaned across the console, "Me too. Working for you has given me a purpose. An excitement about getting up each morning and going to work."

Their lips met, a soft kiss, just a taste before pulling back. Grinning, she said, "And being with you also gives me an excitement about what happens at the end of the day."

Chuckling, he met her lips again. This time, his hand cupped the back of her head as he angled her mouth, taking the kiss deeper, wetter, hotter. His tongue swept inside, plundering as she met him stroke for stroke. His cock pressed against his zipper, an uncomfortable reminder of where they were and what he had to do. Reluctantly pulling back, he let out a deep breath, his forehead touching hers. "I hate this, but I do have to go. I promised Mitch I would get some records ready about the American Legion youth teams before our meeting tonight."

Nodding, she said, "I've got to work this afternoon on the pub books." She waited as he alighted from the driver's seat and jogged around to her side. Taking his hand as he assisted her out, she raised up on her tiptoes to kiss him once more. "I'll see you tonight?"

"Absolutely," he replied with one last kiss.

18

Mitch, as commander of the local chapter of the American Legion, rapped the gavel on the podium. Brogan, the Sergeant-at-Arms, closed the doors of the meeting room, located in the basement of the Baytown Community Center. With another three raps of the gavel, the members stood as Mitch called out, "The Color Bearer will advance the Colors." Jason, standing in the back with Brogan, marched forward, the American flagpole in his hands, and set it in the floor stand.

"The Chaplain will offer prayer." The Presbyterian minister, a member of the American Legion, stood and prayed as the group bowed their heads in unison.

The POW/MIA Empty Chair Ceremony followed. A chair was designated as a symbol of the thousands of American POW/MIAs still unaccounted for from all wars and conflicts involving the United States of America. The POW/MIA flag was placed on the Empty Chair.

The eclectic assembly included men, plus a few

women, ages running from about twenty-five to almost ninety. At the moment, there was unity as all faces turned toward the Empty Chair, a haunted expression on many of them.

After the Pledge of Allegiance and the Preamble to the American Legion Constitution, the gavel was rapped once more to indicate that everyone could take a seat.

After the secretary's and treasure's reports, Mitch called on Gareth to report on the statistics of the youth baseball teams they created. Walking up to the podium, Gareth nodded to the assembly. "So far, we've had the teams up and running for several months now, and the response from the community has been overwhelming. We have almost fifty children, ranging in age from five to seventeen, who come out almost every weekend. We now have the support of the community and the parents. Many of the parents cannot afford to give financial assistance, but they offer what they can and have participated in some fundraising. Our budget was just reported on from the treasurer's report, but we're always interested in any businesses in the area who would like to assist."

He took several questions from some of the members and with the vote to continue the program, he moved back to his seat, a grin on his face. Lance, a new resident living on the outside of town, sat stoically on one side. Gareth knew very little about him, but from what he heard, that was exactly what Lance wanted—peace and privacy. Aiden, his ever-present smile firmly in place, sat on the other side. Behind him sat Callan, one of the original Baytown

Boys. He was still in the Coast Guard but luckily served at the small station in the Baytown harbor with his CG buddies, all of who had joined the American Legion. Jason, Grant, Zac, Aiden, and Brogan sat on the other side of Ginny, and Gareth noticed Brogan had managed to sit next to her. Grinning, he wondered when the big guy was going to finally ask her out...if ever.

Bringing his attention back to the meeting, another committee member was discussing the American Legion Auxiliary.

"They've done great work so far in the few meetings they've had and their fundraisers are going well. They wanted me to let you know that they are working on the Cavalcade of Memories and if you have any articles or items you would like them to display, please get them to Katelyn MacFarlane."

At Katelyn's name, Gareth's heart jumped. Reaching up, he rubbed his chest, unconsciously trying to ease the tight feeling. Glancing to the side, he saw Aiden grinning at him and he smirked, knowing he was caught.

Mitch nodded toward another member, Bill, who made his way up front. Standing for a moment, his hands gripping the podium, he appeared to gather his thoughts and his strength. Swallowing deeply, staring down, he began. "I know Ms. Ginny Spencer talked a while ago about the counseling that's offered here locally for former military. Figured I didn't need it. I was doin' good. But I recently got word that a buddy of mine—we got out about the same time and he headed home to Oklahoma—well, he killed himself last week."

His shoulders shook and Mitch stepped up to place his hand on Bill's shoulder, providing steady support.

Sucking in a cleansing breath, Bill continued, "Anyway, it hit me hard and I decided to give the Eastern Shore Mental Health Group a call." Finally lifting his head to survey the gathering, he concluded, "Should've done it sooner. So if me telling you this gets you out to do it too, then I hope it helps."

The members were quiet and Gareth remembered reading that those, like him, who served in the mortuary identification section had a high depression rate. Scrubbing his hand over his face, he sighed.

As the meeting came to a close, he jumped up, ready to head to Finn's Pub and see her again. *It's only been a couple of hours since I've been her, but it feels so much longer.* As Gareth parked his SUV down the street and began walking toward Finn's, he noticed Katelyn's father standing near the door talking to another man he had seen at the meeting. As he approached, they turned toward him, Katelyn's father calling out.

"Gareth, that was a good report about the sports teams," Eric MacFarlane started. Clearing his throat, he said, "I'd like to introduce you to one of our members...this is David Bayles."

Bayles...he must be Philip's father. Uncertainty fled in the face of the man's open expression. Shaking his hand, he said, "It's nice to meet you, sir. I've heard wonderful things about your son, Philip. I'm sorry for your loss."

Shaking his hand, David said, "Thank you, Gareth. And, please, call me David."

As Gareth nodded, he noticed the hesitation in

their eyes and cocked his head in silent invitation, girding himself for what might come.

Rubbing his chin, David said, "Uh...I know this might sound...well, odd." Then he rushed, "And you don't have to, but...well, I wondered if you could tell me..." Sighing heavily, he turned his dark grey eyes to Gareth and finally said, "Can you tell me what it was like...at Dover...for those who..."

Inwardly sighing in relief, he nodded in understanding. Gareth motioned toward the small table and chairs outside the pub and said, "Why don't we sit, sir?"

The three men settled into the seats and Gareth leaned forward, resting his forearms on the table. "The first thing I can tell you is that the servicemen and women were always treated with the utmost dignity." His mind slid back to a different time and place, as he continued. "I was struck, the first time I witnessed it, how each fallen servicemember, from the time they arrived until they left Dover to be transported to their place of burial, was so respected—as much as humanly possible."

David inhaled a shuddering breath, his voice raspy as he claimed, "No matter how many years have passed, I still feel Philip's death as though it were now."

"I cannot imagine your grief, sir...but know that his treatment was filled with honor. And not just at Dover. From the moment a servicemember falls, they are treated with dignity."

"Can you tell me what you did at Dover?" Eric asked.

"I was assigned to the Office of the Armed Forces Medical Examiner, involved in some investigating. Officially, I was a medical-legal examiner. I reviewed the circumstances of the death. I worked with the doctors who scientifically identified the decedent and performed an autopsy. Specifically, I would perform fingerprinting, dental analysis, and assist with DNA analyses."

David nodded silently, so Gareth took that as permission to continue. "There were changes made about the time I came in...it appears there was mishandling of...remains, and once made public, regulations changed and new military leaders came in. By the time I was assigned there, it was running the way it should have always been run. It was part of my job to do the forensic investigation, so that we knew how each servicemember died and the family could have closure."

The slight breeze from the bay swept over the trio sitting at the table, the stars filling the night sky, each to their own memories.

David finally looked up, holding Gareth's gaze, with a slight smile on his face. "Thank you so much for telling me this. It does help to know my son was handled so carefully. And it's my understanding that you are now dating Katelyn?"

Shifting uncomfortably under both men's stares, Gareth nodded. "Yes, sir. I...I'm completely aware of her former relationship with your son, Philip. I...well, I care for her greatly and I'm not trying to take away from their past—"

Raising his hands quickly, David interrupted, "Oh, no, no. Please don't explain. My wife and I are thrilled that she's finally found someone to be with."

Eric's eyes twinkled as he leaned back in his chair. "You already know, Katelyn's mother and I are happy as well."

Letting out a deep breath, Gareth allowed a grin to slip out. Not since his father had died had he felt such acceptance from those older than he. "Thank you, both."

"Katelyn's a good girl," David said. "She'll always be special to my wife and me."

"Sir, I'd never try to take away that relationship," Gareth assured.

David nodded in appreciation. "Thank you. I was worried she'd never begin to move forward, but now I feel like you're the perfect man for her."

"Well, then, let's go inside and share a beer!" Eric said, slapping his hand down on the table. As the three men stood, their metal chairs scraping on the sidewalk, none noticed the pub's slightly open window.

Katelyn stood in the pub's ladies room, her hands on the counter, staring into the mirror before dropping her chin to her heaving chest as she fought to blink back tears. She heard the door open and felt arms encircle her from behind, knowing whom they belonged to. *Jillian...of course, Jillian.*

"Hey, sweetie," Jillian greeted softly from behind, muffled, as her face was pressed against Katelyn's back. "You okay?"

Nodding silently, Katelyn said nothing, not sure she trusted her voice.

"I saw you at the front window before you rushed in here. And I saw Gareth come in with your dad and Philip's dad."

Nodding again, Katelyn swallowed deeply.

"Should I be scared for you?" Jillian asked, her words still barely above a whisper.

This time Katelyn shook her head before lifting it as Jillian slid around to the side, both women staring at each other's reflection.

"They were talking about Philip...and Gareth's time at Dover Air Force Base. And then David told him that he would always think of me as a daughter, but that he was glad that I was moving forward with Gareth."

Jillian's sky-blue eyes peered closely at Katelyn's darker blue ones and she asked, "Isn't that a good thing?"

"Yeah, it is," Katelyn admitted. "But it also seems very final. You know...like we're all finally moving ahead, leaving Philip behind." Sighing, she added, "I've held on to a dream for a long time. I never thought I'd love again, but the truth of the matter is that Philip might not have been my forever. I wanted him to be...I thought he would be. But we might not have been able to make our love last in the adult world."

She closed her eyes for a moment, swallowing back the lump in her throat. Opening her eyes, she pinned her best friend's gaze with hers in the mirror. "I've fallen for Gareth. Mom and Dad approve of him and seem happy. Hell, even Aiden and Brogan are on board."

This time Jillian said nothing, offering a slight smile, her eyes warm and accepting, allowing the distant noise from the pub to fill the space. Katelyn turned on the tap and splashed cold water on her face as Jillian reached over to pluck some paper towels and held them out to her. Invigorated, Katelyn turned to face her oldest friend. "Come on...let's go back out there. I'm ready to face the crowd...and my future."

Grinning, Jillian threw her arms around Katelyn, squeezing her tightly. "I love you, you know."

Laughing, Katelyn nodded, squeezing back. "I know." Pulling away slightly, she added, "And thank you."

Arm in arm, the two women walked back into the pub, heading directly for Grant and Gareth, sitting in a booth. Sliding next to their men, Katelyn met Gareth's worried expression.

"You okay?" he asked, leaning in to whisper.

As his breath washed over her ear, she shivered. "Yeah...I'm great. But how about we get out of here."

Eyes wide, he grinned as he hip-bumped her out of the booth and grabbed her hand. With a wave to their group of friends, the two left the pub, fingers as well as hearts, linked.

19

"My place or yours?"

Giggling, Katelyn replied, "Which is closer?"

"Mine, but your bed is more comfortable," Gareth stated, firing up the SUV and pulling onto the road.

"Then mine it is," she said, and within two minutes he parked on the street in front of her house. She barely let him put the brake on before she launched herself over the console, claiming his mouth. With her hands clasping his face, she dove in, her tongue immediately tangling with his.

Breaking apart only long enough for them both to leap from his vehicle, she jumped into his arms. Carrying her to her front door, he felt inside her purse for her keys. Unlocking the door with difficulty, he maneuvered them inside before kicking the door shut.

Grabbing his stubbled jaws in her hands, she held him in place as her tongue vied for dominance. Sucking on his tongue, she felt his groan rumble through her chest.

Twisting, Gareth walked forward until coming to the bottom of the stairs with her in his arms. He felt her legs move behind him then heard her shoes land on the floor. Setting her ass on the steps, he pressed her backward as he leaned over her, his body still pressed against hers.

She released him long enough to slide up two more steps so she had room to unsnap her jeans. His hands replaced hers as he slid the pants down her legs before undoing his as well. Giggling at the sight of him fumbling when he forgot to take his boots off first, she watched as he jumped around, finally disentangling himself from his clothes.

Her lips were kiss swollen as he leaned over her reclining body once more. She used her hands to scoot up two more stairs, giving her enough room to pull her shirt over her head. His face was at bra level and he leaned in, pulling her bra cups down with his teeth.

Sucking a nipple in deeply, he grinned as her primed body began to writhe underneath his. "Bed," she moaned as she twisted and attempted to scramble up the stairs.

She managed to make it up three steps before he wrapped his arm around her waist, turning and lifting her. Slamming his lips on hers again, he carried her the rest of the way up, he in his boxers and she with her bra hanging off her body.

They separated for a moment, breaths ragged and chests heaving. He stepped closer, his nimble fingers unsnapping her bra and letting it fall down her arms, her nude body now gloriously displayed.

He slid his hand from her shoulder down her arm, soothing her skin as he admired her beauty. Her pale skin appeared luminescent in the moonlight streaming through the lace curtains on the windows. Her curves were inviting and his breath caught in his throat that she wanted him.

Her nipples begged for his mouth and he obliged lifting her breasts to his lips. Her fingers held onto his shoulders, the short nails digging in as his mouth did wondrous things to her breasts. She heard moans, but was uncertain if they came from her or from him.

Gareth, lost in the feel of her luscious mounds against his face, moved from one breast to the other, deeply sucking, nipping with his teeth before soothing with his tongue.

Lifting his head, he grinned just before tossing her onto her back on the mattress, following as soon as he rid himself of his boxers. Laughing as the bed bounced, he captured her giggle as he kissed her once more.

Moving his mouth over hers, he felt her fingers dig into his shoulders as her legs pulled him in. Sliding down her body, the scent of her arousal filled the air, intoxicating him. Lapping her juices as he plunged his tongue inside her warm channel, he knew there was no other woman for him.

He moved his lips upward to latch onto her clit as he inserted one finger deep inside. Curling it, he found the exact spot that caused her hips to buck off the mattress. Smiling against her folds, he watched as she leaned up on her elbows to watch him, her eyelids half closed in passion.

"I...I...need..."

Answering her with another suck on her clit, she flung herself back on the bed, her hips unable to stay still as she pressed them upward against his face. Her core tightened and her breathing became more ragged. Lifting one hand to her breast, he rolled her nipple between his fingers while giving one last tug on her clit. Her senses on overload, she cried out as her orgasm roared through her.

Quivering, she allowed her body to go along for the ride until the last spasm slowed. Katelyn was aware of the soft mattress underneath her and her legs draped over Gareth's shoulders as the cool of the room finally penetrated. Lifting her head to peer down at him she saw his slow, easy smile as he licked her juices from his fingers.

Moving up her body, he kissed his way over her stomach and breasts on his way to her lips. She tasted herself on his tongue—the heady combination of her juices and his own scent leaving her body needing his.

Lifting an eyebrow at her as she rolled over to straddle his hips, she grinned, sliding down his legs until she was sitting on his ankles. Eyes wide, the idea of her lips around his dick knocked all other thoughts from his mind. She smiled as she leaned her body down further, sliding her full lips around the head of his cock. He groaned as her swirling tongue moved around the sensitive rim.

Pressing her hand down on his stomach when his hips bucked up, she moved her lips up and down his impressive girth, relishing in the taste of him on her tongue. It had been a long time since she had given head and she worried if she was effective.

He leaned up, the sight of her mouth sliding up and down his length nearly undoing him. She peered up, his cock sliding from her lips as she asked, "Am I doing this okay?"

"Oh, hell, babe. If you do it any better, I'm going to blow too soon!"

She grinned as her lips slid back over his dick, her tongue working its magic. The tightening in his lower back alerted him to the oncoming orgasm, but he wanted to be buried in her again. Lifting her shoulders, he pulled out of her mouth with another groan.

"I want to be buried deep inside of you when I come," he growled.

Flipping her underneath him, he stopped suddenly. Pulling away from her arms as he raised up, he twisted his body, his eyes searching before he realized the condom was in his wallet, which was in his pants, which were at the bottom of the stairs. As he started to climb off the bed, her hands on his stopped him.

"I'm clean...and I...uh...I'm on birth control."

His breath left him in a rush as he grinned at her implication. "I'm clean too. Are you sure this is what you want?" he asked, wanting to feel her with no latex between them, but wanting her to make the final decision.

Her brilliant smile was his answer as she nodded, lifting her arms up to him. Nervous energy pulsated from him as he realized this was the first time he would ever be bareback during sex. Pushing slowly into her tight warmth, he let out a sigh as his body found its home. Moving deliberately, he refused to give into the desire to rush. Thrusting, first slowly and then faster, he found his pace as his cock dragged along the inside of her sex, the friction causing his arms to quiver as he held himself over her body.

Katelyn bent her legs, opening herself as wide as she possibly could to accommodate his body as she looped her feet on his muscular ass. His pelvis rubbed against her clit, the shivers it elicited starting from somewhere deep inside and beginning to shoot outwards. The pressure built as she climbed higher and she threw her head back on the mattress, her eyes never leaving his.

"I'm ready, baby. Are you close?" he panted, using all his control to keep from blowing before she had a chance to come again.

Still thrusting, he leaned down, taking a taut nipple into his mouth, biting slightly as he tugged on the sensitive flesh. "Come on, baby," he encouraged. "Let go and come with me." His order was gentle, but the meaning was clear. He was holding on by a thread and wanted her to go with him.

Whispering his name, her voice hoarse with need, she fell apart, the sparks finally igniting the explosion ripping through her body. He watched as her face tensed with the power of her orgasm, his balls tightening and his own climax roaring through him and into her. His arms quivered as they held him up, the muscles in his neck standing out as he strained before collapsing onto her waiting body.

His legs quivered with the force of his orgasm, expending all his energy. Pulling out reluctantly, he fell face first to the mattress, arms spread out to the side, breath coming in gasps.

For a moment they lay, their breaths labored, as the euphoria washed over them. Realizing he weighed her down into the mattress, he rolled to the side, taking her with him, their bodies still crushed together, slick with sweat. Her breasts pressed against his chest, heartbeat to heartbeat.

"You okay, Katelyn?" he asked.

Not trusting her voice, she simply nodded. Rolling to the side, he stalked into the bathroom, coming back with a warm, wet cloth. Gently, he cleaned between her legs before taking the cloth back to the bathroom. Sliding back into bed, he rolled her body so that she faced him, her head on his shoulder. Tracing patterns on his chest, he reached up and clasped her fingers in his, over his heart.

"Do you feel this?" he asked.

Not sure what he was asking, uncertainty settled in her gaze as she sucked her lips in.

Brushing a few dark tendrils of hair back from her face, he cupped her cheek, his thumb rubbing over the soft skin. "I noticed you the first time I ate in the pub. I saw you behind the bar, smiling at everyone but barking at your brothers to behave. I thought you were sexy as hell, with your dark hair, blue eyes, and curves that don't quit."

She smiled but stayed quiet, wanting to hear his thoughts.

"I was going to ask you out but held back...first because I was new in town and had to focus on getting my business going."

"And then you heard about Philip, right?" she whispered, her fingers feeling the pounding of his heart.

"Yeah...I figured I had no chance. I tried to fight my feelings, but you stayed in my mind. As I set up the office, I imagined you being there with me, but gave up hope that it might happen."

Leaning over to place a soft kiss on her lips, he murmured, "I've fallen in love with you, Katelyn."

Her lips curved slowly before her smile blossomed, beaming on him, warming him completely. Nuzzling her nose alongside his, she whispered, "I'm in love with you, too." Tracing his jaw with her finger, she said, "I never thought I'd find love again after having my heart broken. But you've found all the pieces and have put them back together. Now I know...you have my heart. All of it. Not just what's left...or part of it. But all of it, Gareth. All of me."

His heart leaped at her words, understanding what she was confessing. Leaning down, he grabbed the covers, pulling them up over their still tangled bodies. Tucking her in closely, he placed a gentle kiss on her forehead as they slept with the moonlight watching over them.

The incessant knocking on the front door ceased just as Katelyn managed to pry her eyes open. The first thing she saw was the mouth-watering, defined muscles of Gareth's chest. Lifting her head, she grinned down as his blue eyes opened and peered back at her.

"Did you hear knocking?" his sleep-rough voice asked.

"Yeah, but they're gone." Leaning up, she looked over his body at her clock and said, "Oh, my God, we slept late. It's already nine o'clock."

"But it's the weekend, baby, so we can stay in bed all day if we want." He rolled so that she was underneath him. Just as his lips were about to mesh with hers, a call from downstairs halted him.

"Katelyn?"

"She's probably in the shower. Where's her coffee maker?"

"Katelyn, are you—oh my! Eric, she's got *company* and we're interrupting!"

Katelyn and Gareth's hearts pounded as they stared at each other for a few seconds before being hurled into action.

"Shit, my parents came over! I forgot what day it is... they always come over on Sundays after early mass!"

Pulling on his boxers, Gareth looked around frantically for his jeans. "Oh, fuck, my pants are downstairs."

Katelyn realized her parents had already discovered the evidence of the stair-strip and began to giggle while blushing. Pulling on a sweatshirt and a pair of yoga pants, she fled down the stairs. At the bottom, she saw her dad's flushed face and Gareth's jeans held in her mom's hands.

"Uh...hi. I'll...take those," she said, snatching them out of her mom's grip and whirling, running back up the stairs, snagging his shirt on the way. Throwing them at Gareth, she rushed over. Lifting on her toes, she kissed him soundly. "It'll be fine," she laughed. "Seriously."

He jerked his legs into the pants and pulled the shirt over his head, the whole time trying to figure out if her dad was going to deck him when he reached the bottom of the stairs. With a quick swipe of his hand over his hair, he followed her back downstairs.

The entry foyer was blessedly empty and as they moved around the bottom of the stairs, he could see the living room was also unoccupied. Katelyn headed toward the kitchen and he followed, the sound of pans rattling meeting his ears. Entering, he found Eric sitting at the table in the dining room, a cup of coffee in front of him and the newspaper opened.

Lifting his eyes over the top, Eric nodded at the couple entering the room. "Morning," he greeted as Katelyn leaned over to kiss his cheek. "Guess we'll need to start calling before we come to visit."

"Oh, Dad," Katelyn laughed as she moved to her mom, who was busy scrambling eggs and frying bacon.

"Gareth, dear," Corrine called out. "Can you pop the toast in the toaster?"

Just then the back door opened and Aiden and Brogan walked in. Stiffening, Gareth eyed the two men as they greeted their mom and Katelyn first before nodding toward Gareth. Aiden poured a cup of coffee before he sat down with their dad, taking a section of the newspaper. Brogan stared at Gareth for a long moment, his eyes dropping to Gareth's bare feet. Lifting his eyebrow as he lifted his head, he continued to stare before a slight grin slipped across his face. Turning, he also poured a cup of coffee before sitting at the table.

Feeling surreal, Gareth shook his head as he watched Katelyn's family make themselves at home for breakfast, acting as though his presence was not only expected, but wanted.

Catching Katelyn's smile, he winked as he turned to make the toast.

20

The drive back over the seventeen-mile bridge was beginning to become commonplace as Katelyn looked over the water and Gareth fiddled with the radio.

"I used to only go to Virginia Beach a couple of times a year," she confessed, "and now, it feels like we go all the time."

Nodding, he agreed, "Some cases take me over here a lot but, other times, weeks will go by without me having to leave the Eastern Shore."

"So, what's the game plan today?"

"We need to get back into Berry and Associates Accounting and do some serious digging. We need to know about Carrie's relationship with Walter, why he was paying for her education, did he spend money on anyone else, all of that."

"We've got this," she replied, smiling as her fingers trailed over the hair at the back of his head.

"Speaking of going over the bridge, when does your class start?" he asked.

"Next month. I'll be in Virginia Beach every weekday for two weeks, so I won't be able to be in the office on those days." She sighed as she added, "Or the pub!"

"I haven't even asked how you're doing with both jobs," he confessed. "I honestly thought that you'd just handle the office work...things were so much slower before you came on board!"

"Hey! Are you accusing me of bringing in the business...and not in a good way?" she joked.

"No accusation, but if the work is coming in, that's a good thing."

"Aiden and Brogan have done fine with me not there as much. The pub runs smoothly and I still have plenty of time to do the books and keep up with the bar's local gossip."

A few more miles passed in silence before he added, "When you are gone those two weeks, it'll seem strange. The office will be so lonely."

She looked over at his somber expression and laughed as her fingers continued to trail along his neck. "Well, if the days are lonely, we'll just have to make sure the nights are more exciting!"

Entering the accounting firm once more, their eyes settled on Carrie at the reception desk. She stood as they walked toward her and gushed, "Oh, it's nice to see you. Do you have any word on poor Walter's death?"

"It's a police matter now," Gareth replied smoothly, his warm smile in place, "but we are assisting. We'd like to talk to you for a few minutes before we go see the others, if that's all right."

Mentally rolling her eyes, Katelyn watched as Carrie preened under Gareth's charm.

"Of course. Anything I can do to help," the young woman insisted, motioning to two chairs in the reception area.

Once settled, Gareth cut to the chase. "Ms. Reynolds, we have found that Mr. Berry was paying you money for your college education. Is that correct?"

"Yes," she replied, her eyes jumping between the two. "Is that a problem? Will the money stop now?"

"That's not for us to say," Gareth continued, "but you did not mention this when we interviewed you before. Nor did you mention it to the police."

Eyes wide, Carrie said, "But lots of businesses help employees with college expenses. I...well, I didn't mention it because," she shrugged slightly, "it didn't seem important." Scrunching her nose, she said, "I do hope it doesn't stop now that he's gone."

"May I ask who accompanied you to the funeral?" Katelyn asked.

Her face brightening, Carrie answered, "Oh, that was my mom and dad."

"Did they know Mr. Berry?"

With a slight shoulder shrug, she replied "I think my mom might have met him once when she came to see where I worked, but Walter never met my dad. They came to the funeral because they knew how upset I'd be."

Katelyn eyed Carrie, noting the professional dress and manner belying her young age, but after having seen her mother so classily dressed at the funeral, it made sense.

Carrie took them back to Beth's office next and Katelyn felt the chill rolling off Beth. As soon as Carrie left the room to go back to the front, Beth turned her smile to Katelyn and Gareth.

"We'd like to check on a few financial facts and you are certainly the one to ask," Gareth said, and once more, Katelyn observed as Beth sat up straighter at Gareth's attentiveness. "To begin with, can you tell me about the different accounts this firm uses for its purchases and employees?" If Beth were surprised at his question, he noted that she did not hesitate in her answering.

"There is a major checking account that receives all of the paid invoices and is the account from which I make purchases, pay employees, things like that. The firm also has a few investment accounts that I make deposits to, based on what Walt..." sighing heavily, she continued, "Walter or William would tell me to do."

"And Sandra?"

"Oh, no, the two senior accountants made those decisions...not a junior accountant," she replied, with a sniff. "I, of course, handled the transactions, overseen by either Walter or William."

"And what about miscellaneous payments to employees?" Gareth pushed.

Knitting her brow, Beth said, "I...I don't understand."

"Well, like the business account that Walter used to pay for Carrie's college education—"

"I assure you that no matter what *she* may have led

you to believe, Walter did not pay for her college!" Pinching her lips, she continued, "I have no idea why she insists on trying to appear as though she and Walter were closer than what is appropriate!"

Katelyn, confused, kept quiet, allowing Gareth to continue leading the discussion.

"We have found that he was paying for her college expenses," Gareth replied, watching as purple fury crossed Beth's face. "And it was a firm account—"

"That snake!" she bit out, her lips no longer pinched but in a full-blown snarl. "I asked him a year ago about helping me take some accounting classes and he said there was no company policy that allowed that type of expenditure and yet he pays for that... that...aughhh!"

Thick silence blanketed the trio but before either Gareth or Katelyn could break it, Beth jumped up and said, "Let's go to William's office," and she moved toward the door.

Katelyn and Gareth hustled to follow the irate woman down the carpeted hall. He looked up, a smile of greeting on his face, which quickly fell as Beth immediately launched into a tirade.

"I've just been informed that Walter paid for Carrie's college classes, but when I asked him a year ago for some college tuition assistance, I was turned down! On top of that, he paid from an account of which I know nothing about! So, am I the bookkeeper or not? Am I trusted to do this job or not? And do I need to pursue legal representation about the different treatment of employees?"

Her last question, ending on a shout, had William

throwing his hands up to placate her. "Now, now, this is the first I'm hearing about any of this." As Beth sat down heavily in one of the chairs, he continued, "I have no idea what you're talking about, but I assure you, I will find out." His ruddy cheeks puffed with exertion and he leaned back in his chair, the creaky leather sounding loudly in the room. Shaking his head, he looked over at Gareth, breathing, "My Lord. I hardly know what to say."

Turning to Beth, Gareth smiled in sympathy and said, "Would you allow us to talk alone with William? We appreciate your candor and honesty and will certainly have more questions, at a later time."

Standing while smoothing her skirt with her palms, she offered Gareth a tight smile. "Of course." Looking back at William, she inclined her head politely before adding, "I will be expecting to discuss this later, when you've had a chance to figure out what has been going on in this office!" With that, she turned and walked out of the room, closing the door behind her.

William turned his beleaguered face to Gareth and Katelyn, his mouth opening and closing several times. "I don't know what to say...I had no idea Walter was acting surreptitiously." His hound dog jowls shaking as he hung his head, he added, "Secret accounts, treating one employee differently from another...oh, lordy. Now I need to sort this mess out and make sure the integrity of the firm isn't compromised."

Katelyn spoke softly, "So, from what you're saying, you knew none of this?"

"No, no. Well, I do remember, a year ago, Walter told me that Beth had asked if there were any business funds for helping her out with some college classes. We decided that wasn't something we wanted to take on, at least not for a new employee. What if she took the money for tuition and then left the firm? So, we decided together to deny her request. Now...to find out that he was doing it for Carrie?" Sighing heavily, he said again, "Oh, lordy. What a mess."

With a slight nod from Gareth, Katelyn prompted, "And the money coming from an unknown business account?"

At that reminder, William's eyes focused as his lips became a grim line. "I have no idea what that is about... but I will find out."

Like air slipping out of a balloon, William slumped back into his chair. "I thought I knew him. I thought I could trust him."

Thanking William, Gareth and Katelyn stood and moved out into the hall. "Let's find Sandra—"

Just then Ed walked by, his eyes widening as he said, "Are you the investigators Carrie told me about?"

"Yes. I'm Gareth Harrison and this is Katelyn MacFarlane. And you are?" Gareth asked. He recognized Ed from the funeral, but since they had not been formally introduced, he feigned ignorance.

Sticking his hand out, Ed said, "Oh, sorry. I'm Ed Rogers. I'm an accounting intern here...well, at least for another couple of months, until the end of the semester."

"Can we talk to you for a few minutes?" Katelyn asked, her smile focused brightly on the eager young man.

His eyes lighted as he raked his gaze over her beauty. "Sure...come to the workroom and we can talk."

As they followed him, Katelyn felt Gareth's possessive hand on her back and stifled a grin at his growl. Sparing him a quick glance, she turned her attention back to Ed as they settled into chairs.

Katelyn was beginning to feel overwhelmed, as they had bounced from person to person, but found the information they were pulling in to be fascinating. *So much better to see everyone's faces as they are questioned.* She opened her mouth to speak, but Ed jumped in first, eyes alight.

"This place is becoming quite the talk of my classes. I go back and tell my professors what's going on in this office. And I come in today and Beth is in her office fuming about something to do with Walter and now she's not speaking to Carrie." Looking eagerly at Katelyn, he said, "So what's going on now?"

"Were you aware that Mr. Berry was paying some of Carrie's college tuition?"

His forehead scrunched as Ed replied, "Is that really a big deal? Lots of businesses help their employees." He thought for a moment, then grinned. "Oh, is that what's got Beth in such a snit?"

Not answering him, Gareth asked, "What did you think of Mr. Berry? We didn't have a chance to talk when we were here the week before last, so I'd be very interested in your opinion."

Chuckling, Ed said, "He was a good accountant, but I kind of thought he had a particular eye for the ladies, if you know what I mean." Glancing at the open door, he quickly rectified, "I never saw anything inappropriate but, well, let's face it, he's got three gorgeous women working here and I got the feeling it wasn't William who hired them."

"Besides their looks, what else is your opinion of the office employees?" Katelyn quipped, inwardly wincing as Gareth shot her a look.

"Sandra's got a very high opinion of herself, being so young and already considered for a partner—which she'll undoubtedly get now that Walter's out of the picture. I used to think that she had the hots for him, but I've seen she and William holed up in his office a lot lately."

Surprised at Ed's easily presented rendition of the office, Katelyn smiled encouragingly, but it appeared Ed needed little prodding to keep talking.

"And Beth...she's strict on the money here and likes to think she runs the place. She flaunted that she and Walter were close friends. Of course, I've only been here for three months, but I could tell from day one that she hated Carrie." Leaning back, he grinned. "Hell, how could anyone hate her? She alone is worth walking through the front door of this place! It's not hard to see why Walter hired her!"

"Did Mr. Berry seem infatuated with Carrie?"

"Sure...who wouldn't be?" Ed replied, his smile still firmly in place. "Have you looked at her?"

Katelyn bristled, but Gareth's hand on her knee under the table stilled her.

"I suppose by infatuated, I mean anything inappropriate?" Katelyn probed.

Ed thought for a moment and said, "Not really.

Although, the first time he saw us going out together after work, I could have sworn he acted jealous."

"So you and Carrie are seeing each other?"

"Not seriously, if that's what you mean. But yeah, we hang out. She's certainly closer to my age than he was. And, I can tell you, she was never interested in him in that way!"

Thanking Ed, Gareth rose and escorted Katelyn into the hall. Looking at her upturned face, he said, "Sandra next?"

Leaning in to whisper, she admitted, "My head is spinning!"

Grinning, Gareth nodded as they approached Sandra's office. Knocking on the doorframe, they were invited in. Settling once more into chairs, they looked at the pale face of the younger accountant.

"I didn't realize you were coming in today," she began, glancing down at a few files on her desk. "We closed the office for a few days and now, I'm afraid, it's catch-up time."

"We won't take up too much of your time," Gareth said, his smile firmly in place once more. "We've come across some information that we are checking into. First, is that Walter was covering some of Carrie's tuition and it appears to be from an account that neither Beth, nor William, knew about,"

Sandra's expression did not change, but Katelyn could see the wheels turning.

"I see," Sandra replied smoothly. "I did not know about that, but as a junior member of the firm, it's not surprising for me to be left out of that sort of business. Beth, while office manager, is certainly not the boss around here, although she would like you to believe she is. So, if Walter was executing things the way he saw fit, then it's hardly her place to complain."

Nodding politely, Gareth noted Sandra did not seem upset and was sure in her defense of Walter. "Did you ever see anything that caused you concern about the way Mr. Berry conducted himself in the office...or out of it?"

"Not at all! He was a gentleman, through and through," she defended. Barking out an unladylike snort, she added, "Carrie? Really, the idea is too absurd. She's a child. He had no interest in her other than a very solicitous concern."

"Did you know Carrie and Ed are in a relationship, of sorts? "

"It's none of my business, but this is a small firm so, yes, I am aware that they spend time together. Everyone is aware—they don't exactly hide it."

"Do you think that bothered Walter?"

"Oh, please...Walter had more important things to deal with than a college office romance between those two!"

"And the secret account—"

"Mr. Harrison, I don't know what the others have implied, but Mr. Berry ran a respectable accounting business. But the bottom line was it was *his* business, so if he had various accounts, there is nothing illegal, nor unethical, about that. Not wanting his busy-body office manager to know about all of them is more of an indication of what he thought of her, not anything to do with him."

A few minutes later, as Gareth assisted Katelyn up

into his vehicle, she turned before he shut the door, and said, "I'm confused. Utterly and completely confused!"

Sandra entered William's office and closed the door softly. Turning, her professional face dropped and in its place, a snarl erupted.

"What the hell are we going to do about this mess?"

"Now, now, Sandra, if Eleanor hadn't hired those two, things would not have gotten this far," he replied.

She leaned over his desk, her weight resting on her fists, knuckles pressed against the hard wood. "Yes, but she did. And now things are being discovered that you said would be left unfound. So, I repeat. What. The hell. Are we going to do?"

"Mom, I just found out that with Walter gone, my college money will dry up. What am I going to do?" Carrie cried.

Beth, just around the corner, listened carefully, a grin playing about her lips.

21

"So, any idea how the body was moved?"

Gareth sat with Colt, his top detective, Mitch, and the rest of the Baytown police officers, reviewing their information.

"Right now, we've got two lines of thought. One, he was transported near the golf course in a larger boat, which would not be hard to find living on this peninsula, and then transported via a small, flat-bottom boat up the inlet at the golf course and dumped there. Or, he was transported there entirely by a smaller craft, which is an important distinction because it means he couldn't have been transferred as far," Colt replied.

"The ground disturbance and tracks near where his body was found would indicate the flat-bottom boat was the last point of transportation. The shoeprints around the area were disturbed when his body was dragged but, we've managed to gain impressions, and they don't match the boots worn by the groundskeepers. Men's size 11," Mitch added.

"So, was this a crime of passion, happening quickly, or a planned murder? While Gareth has given us a list of the women Walter worked with or was involved with professionally, one woman alone could not have taken his body out of the boat. Walter Berry was not a large man, but at the place where his body was found, there were no marks other than the one pair of boots."

Sam, the oldest member of the Baytown Police Department, said, "I keep coming back to where Walter said he was. He indicated to his co-workers that he was going away for the weekend and wouldn't be back until Tuesday. None of them can remember him mentioning his wife going, but they all made that assumption. Eleanor states that he told her that he was going to be gone just for the weekend to meet with some clients and, according to her, she thought he was going to be in the Virginia Beach area but would be back on Sunday night. So, what the hell was Walter doing?"

"And who was he with?" Burt added.

Gareth leaned back in his seat, his mind going over the possible reasons for Walter's death, but coming up empty. He caught the others staring at him and he shook his head. "I know we need to look close to Walter but his co-workers were women except for William and at his age, he'd never be able to haul Walter around, even if he had a motive. As far as his workplace goes, there's a lot of jealousy and petty feelings, but nothing that would warrant murder and certainly not against Walter. The will was straightforward—Eleanor got most everything and the will had not been changed since she and Walter had it drawn up together years ago."

"Who else was mentioned in the will?" Ginny asked.

"His mother, who he set aside a small trust for that the attorney's office will administer, and then his brother, who he set a small amount for," Gareth answered.

"What about his brother? Was he listed as administer for their mother?" Burt asked.

Shaking his head, Gareth replied, "No, but Eleanor didn't seem surprised."

"He might be worth looking into," Mitch said. "How about you and I go talk to him in about an hour?"

With a nod, Gareth said goodbye and headed back to the office. Walking in, he saw Katelyn at the reception desk working at the computer, the office phone propped between her ear and shoulder. She grinned at him, holding up a finger while mouthing *almost finished*.

He nodded and as he walked closer, his gaze moving around the room, smile widening as he took in the changes she had made. Jillian's pictures and Jason's wooden screen filled up empty space. The folding chairs he had used at first were now replaced with comfortable, padded, wooden chairs. The potted tree Tori had donated gave the room a homey feel. Katelyn's desk, while slightly messy with work, was a hundred times more organized than his office.

Just as his attention turned back to the beautiful woman at the desk, she hung up the phone. "I've got us ad space in the Baytown News, the North Heron Herald, and the Accawmacke news, as well sponsoring ad space with the Eastern Shore radio station."

"Damn, woman, you're gonna put us on the map!" he joked as he walked around to her side of the desk.

Standing, she grinned as his arms encircled her, pulling their bodies close. "I just want to be useful...I'd hate to think you'd fire me for not being productive." Pressing her pelvis against his, she felt his cock jump. Her giggle was cut short as he swooped in, his lips capturing hers.

All thoughts jumped from her mind other than strong and soft. *His lips are strong and soft.* But as he plunged his tongue into her mouth, caressing her tongue, she had no thoughts at all as she gave into the tingling that zipped from her lips to her core. No longer aware of her surroundings, she pressed her hips against his jean-clad leg, giving in to the desire to ease the need for friction.

He slipped his knee between her legs, the feel of her hot core on him causing his dick to ache, wanting to enter her warmth. Breaking away reluctantly, he nibbled for a moment as he willed his aching cock to behave. Finally pulling back, he said, "I hate to leave you, but Mitch and I are going to interview Walter's brother to see what we can find out."

Cocking her head to the side, she said, "You want me to take a look at his finances also?"

"That'd be great," he admitted. Pausing, he added, "You've made a big difference, you know?"

Smiling, she said, "I love working here with you."

"I don't just mean the business, but with me. In my life."

Her heart squeezed at his words, her smile beaming as she stood on her toes to capture his lips once more.

The door opened and a giggle brought Katelyn jerking back, but finding Gareth's arms not willing to let her go far.

"Well, you two...is this a business or a bordello?" Jillian laughed.

"Bordello? Who talks like that?" Katelyn quipped, shooting Gareth a sharp glance.

"What are you giving me the stink-eye for?" he asked.

Stepping back, smoothing her hand over her hair, she said, "Because you made me forget we are in the middle of the office!"

Grinning, he puffed out his chest, saying, "I like that...it's good for my ego!"

Play-slapping him on the arm, Katelyn turned to Jillian, asking, "So did you need Harrison Investigations or did you just come to catch me not working?"

Giggling again, she said, "I was wondering if you had any more items for the Cavalcade?"

"Yes, I've got them at home and was going to work on it this weekend." Waving goodbye as Gareth walked out the door, she turned to Jillian just as her best friend bounded over to offer a hug.

"So, things seem to be going well," Jillian said, smiling.

Answering her smile with one of her own, Katelyn nodded. "He makes me feel...well, just feel again."

Tears sprang to Jillian's eyes as she hugged Katelyn tightly, whispering in her ear, "No one deserves to be happy more than you."

Katelyn grinned over Jillian's shoulder, watching

Gareth's SUV drive down the road, her heart lighter than it had been in years.

Ringing the doorbell at the condo, Gareth admired the neatly trimmed lawns of the neighborhood. As the door opened, he recognized Ken Berry and introduced Mitch. Ken eyed them warily before inviting them in.

"We'll sit here," he indicated the living room. "Mom's sleeping in her chair in the back den and I'd rather her not hear us talking."

Taking a seat, Gareth allowed Mitch to take charge of the interview as he noted the many knick-knacks around the room. It appeared to be Sonya Berry's home, at least in decorating.

"Are you the main caregiver for your mother?" Mitch asked.

Nodding, Ken replied, "Yes. I never married and after our father passed away about three years ago, I decided...well, Walter and I decided that I would move in with mom."

"It looks like a nice area," Gareth said, but before he was able to say more, Ken interrupted with a snort.

"I'm not the big-shot that my younger brother was, so this'll have to do for me."

Mitch and Gareth shared a glance before Mitch asked, "What can you tell us about Walter? His habits? Anyone in particular you saw him hanging out with?"

"My brother and I weren't estranged, but we weren't close either. I worked in our dad's shop and kind of figured he would do the same. But he went to college instead and, well, after that, his life was different."

"Different?"

"You know...dinner parties with clients, golfing at the clubs. Hell, he must have belonged to at least three golf clubs and those places aren't cheap!"

"Are you much older than he was?"

Nodding, Ken sighed. "Yeah...I was ten years old when he was born. I was excited to get a baby brother, but my parents fell into the habit of giving him everything while I was raised with the work-hard ethic pounded into my head."

"Did you ever have any reason to think that he wasn't faithful to Eleanor?" Gareth asked.

Ken's face flushed as he looked down at his hands clasped in his lap. Pinching his lips, he lifted his head, saying, "Got no idea. But, then, I wasn't around him a lot. We didn't move in the same circles, if you know what I mean. But he and Eleanor would come over for Sunday lunches about twice a month and they seemed fine. He never gave any indication that they weren't happy."

"And Eleanor?" Mitch prodded.

Barking out a laugh, Ken replied, "She was over-the-moon for him. They both married late but she always had stars in her eyes when she looked at him. I know he made good money and she didn't work. By all appearances to me, they were happy."

Gareth eyed a picture on the wall of a younger Ken and Walter with their mother and another one of Walter and Eleanor next to it. With a quick glance around the room, he noticed there did not appear to be any recent pictures displayed. His attention was immediately brought back to the interview as Ken's voice rose slightly.

"No, I wasn't jealous of my brother, but I admit I wish he'd helped with our mom a little more." Sighing, he leaned back in his chair and said, "He'd give money, which was appreciated, but I know she wished he would visit more often considering how close we live. And, well hell, I could've used the time off. Sometimes it seems like I'm always stuck here."

A few minutes later, Gareth and Mitch said goodbye and drove back over the bridge.

"I can't see Ken wanting to kill his brother...there might be some money with the estate but most goes to Eleanor and he indicated he wanted more time off. With Walter dead, the care of their mother falls to him entirely," Gareth surmised.

"I was thinking the same thing," Mitch agreed. "And he says he has no idea who might want Walter dead. It seems no one really profits from his death...not really. Not his co-workers, and his wife certainly got his insurance, but would have had more had he stayed alive and continued to make money and have social standing."

"So, crime of passion?"

"If we knew who he was having an affair with, then we might be closer to finding his murderer."

22

The fire blazed high as more wood was added, warming the cool evening. The sun hung low in the sky, painting the evening in an array of ever-changing colors. The constant breeze off the bay skimmed over the gathering. Mitch's grandfather's old fishing cabin had been the sight of many beach parties for the Baytown Boys and their friends over the years.

Gareth sat in the sand with his knees bent, Katelyn between them, her back pressed to his front. Wrapping his arms around her, he placed his chin on her shoulder as they watched the sun dip. Her large-neck sweatshirt had slipped to the side and he bent to nibble on the soft skin exposed on her neck and shoulder.

Giggling, she playfully complained, "That tickles." As his movements halted, she quickly added, "But don't stop."

The bonfire was roaring, already casting shadows and light over the faces of those sitting around its warmth. Katelyn, with Gareth's arms around her, smiled at the large gathering. "You warm enough, babe?" he asked. With the fire ablaze, she nodded against his shoulder, unsure which was warmer—the fire or her back pressed against his body.

Jillian leaned against a large log, Grant tucking her in close to his side. Callan, Jason, and some guys from the Coast Guard played volleyball on the beach. Jade and Belle shared a blanket on the sand. Ginny sat in a beach chair, her legs stretched out in front of her.

Mitch walked from the deck with Tori, trays of snacks in their hands that they set on another blanket near the group.

"Got more beer!" Aiden called out, carrying a beer-filled cooler with Brogan toward the bonfire. Setting the cooler on the sand, they opened the top and grabbed a few to pass around.

Brogan walked by and offered a beer to Ginny who glanced up in surprise. Taking it, she nodded her thanks and her eyes followed him as he moved around the group offering more beer.

Katelyn observed Ginny's gaze on Brogan but as soon as he turned around, Ginny jerked her head toward the sunset. Brogan made his way back over, sitting on the sand next to the pretty police officer. Neither spoke to each other but Katelyn smiled at the way they both spared glances at each other and wondered if they would ever get together.

Zac came walking over, a young blonde on his arm. He looked over the gathering and said, "Hell, this looks just like old times."

A pang shot through Katelyn as she realized she thought the same thing...only now she was with Gareth and not Philip. Gareth's arms tightened around her and his warm breath tickled her ear as he asked if she was all right.

Twisting her head so that she was a whisper away from him, she smiled. "Yeah...I'm great," she replied, and realized she truly meant it.

Gareth's heart felt lighter as her words settled into him. He wondered if he would feel like Philip's replacement when with their friends, but was slowly beginning to accept that his place was solidified with the group...and in her heart.

"So, I hear Silas is all pissy about the golf tournament being cancelled," Jillian stated, bringing everyone's attention to her.

"Hell, Silas gets pissy about anything that doesn't go his way," Aiden quipped.

"We probably lost some money that would have come in from the golfers eating in town, but I don't think they really shop in town much when they come in for a tournament," Katelyn added.

Grant said, "Well, you can add in the resort manager as well, as far as being pissy. He bent the ear of the mayor, who in turn, jumped all over Mitch the other day about closing Walter's case."

The group turned toward Mitch, who said nothing, but snuggled closer to Tori on their blanket by the fire.

"Do you think it was someone he knew?" Belle asked softly, her eyes wide. "Or could it have been someone out there just killing people and he was in the wrong place at the wrong time?"

Mitch quickly replied, "You know we can't speculate

on an active investigation but, Belle, there's no evidence of some kind of a serial killer."

"So, we should be okay?"

Gareth picked up on her unease and reassured, "Everyone should be vigilant but, then, you should be anyway. But as Mitch said, there's no reason to think that anyone other than Mr. Berry was the intended victim."

"Well, he didn't just float up on the golf course," Callan said, plopping down by the fire. "Kind of makes me wonder if someone didn't have it in for The Dunes as well. Let's face it...dropping him off at the golf course really brought things to a halt."

"Was Walter going to play in the tournament?" Katelyn asked, twisting back around to Gareth.

Gareth sat up straighter, sharing a look with Mitch, Grant, and Ginny. *They hadn't even considered that angle!* "Don't know, Katie girl, but you can bet we need to find out," he whispered.

Turning off the downstairs light, Katelyn glanced over her shoulder as Gareth double-checked the front locks. Smiling, she caught his eye as he turned to face her, his smile matching hers. Her heart skipped a beat as electricity filled the air. The desire to have his body rock hers in the moonlight filled her senses. "I'm glad you're staying," she said, her voice soft.

"Nowhere else I'd rather be," he replied, walking slowly toward her, stopping only as his hands lifted to caress her shoulders. His thumbs moved in circles on her neck, the silky skin still slightly cool from the outdoors. "We need to get you warmed up."

Her gaze held his as she moved into his arms, feeling them slide from her shoulders to her back, pulling their bodies closer together. "Mmmmm," she murmured, her cheek pressed against his chest, his heartbeat pounding in her ear.

Bending quickly, he scooped her up, carrying her easily up the stairs and straight into the master bathroom. Setting her feet on the cushy bathmat, he bent over to turn on the faucets to fill the tub, throwing in some bath salts.

"A bath?" Katelyn grinned.

"I remember you said that a bath gets you warmer than a shower."

"I figured you had another way to get me warm," she teased.

"Oh, don't you worry, sweetheart...I've got my ways," he promised, grabbing the bottom of her sweatshirt and pulling it gently over her head as she raised her arms. Next came the camisole and her bra, landing in the laundry basket in the corner. She slipped off her shoes as his hands reached for her pants, the sound of the zipper slowly sliding down barely heard over the running water. His thumbs hooked into the waistband and her jeans and panties began their torturously slow journey over her curvy hips and down her legs.

Not wanting to rush a moment of her unveiling, he knelt, kissing her thighs, nibbling his way to her knees and down her calves. She lifted each foot as he pulled them off, leaving her standing naked for his perusal.

As he stood, he ran his hands over her curves,

appreciating each inch of soft skin until he stood over her once more. Holding her hand, he assisted her as she stepped into the tub, sinking down until the hot water engulfed her, resting her head against the rim.

She moaned in appreciation and he felt the sound in his groin. Toeing off his shoes, he slipped off his jeans as she rolled her head in his direction, her lazy grin now appreciating the view as much as the warm bath.

"You got room in there for one more?" he asked, pulling his sweatshirt over his head.

She eyed the play of muscles in his arms as they maneuvered the material and then gazed in awe at the muscles in his chest and abdomen. "Jeez, you're so ripped," she observed, her voice almost reverent.

Grinning, he leaned his naked body over the tub and repeated his question. "Any room for me?"

Jarring out of her admiration, she sat up, the water teasing her nipples. "Oh, yeah. For you...anytime."

Stepping into the tub, he slid down behind her and gently pulled her back against his front. With her head on his chest, he had a clear view of her glorious body as the water undulated around them. Not normally a fan of a bath, he had to admit this felt amazing and as her ass cheeks pressed against his ready-to-go cock, it was even more phenomenal.

Reaching over, she took a cloth and fragrant soap and began to lather. He reached around, taking the cloth from her, sliding it over her arms and chest. Dropping it, he used his hands to continue stroking her breasts.

Throwing her head back against his shoulder, she

pushed her aching breasts out, silently begging for more attention—he was eager to comply. Cupping their fullness, he circled his thumbs over her nipples alternating the soothing motion with a light pinch. Unable to keep her hips still, she pressed her thighs together in a feeble attempt to meet the need for pressure between her legs.

Sliding one of his hands down over her tummy, he cupped her sex underneath the water, teasing the flesh before inserting one finger. The flutter from deep within blossomed outwards as he nuzzled her ear, his warm breath mingling with the steam still coming from the hot water. Clutching his wrists, she held on as he continued his ministrations. Playing her body masterfully, he discovered her sweet spots—the ones that made her moan, the ones that made her wiggle with need.

Gently sucking on her earlobe as his thumb pressed on her swollen nub, she came undone, her body shivering in his arms as her orgasm consumed her, leaving her limp against his body.

Feeling the water cooling, he murmured, "Let me get you out of here and into bed before you get chilled again."

"I don't think I can move," she mumbled, her eyes still closed.

Chuckling, he placed his hands on her shoulders and pushed her forward, slipping out and wrapping a towel around his waist before bending to scoop her up. Placing her feet on the soft bathmat again, he picked up another thick towel, the small heater in the bathroom keeping them toasty. Kneeling, he started at her feet, drying each one off as she clung to his shoulders to keep her steady. Moving excruciatingly slow, he dried off each leg, kissing as he went. He inhaled deeply as he dried her trimmed curls, the scent of her sex mingling with the fragrant soap smell as intoxicating as any drug. Standing, he dried off her abdomen before giving each breast careful consideration. By the time he made it to her neck, her legs were a quivering mess barely able to hold her up.

Grinning, he scooped her up once more, stalking into the bedroom where he bent to throw back the covers before laying her on the cool sheets. Before she had a chance to chill, he followed her, covering her with his body.

His heat pressed into her as she begged, "Please...I need you...I need you now."

With his upper weight supported by his forearms on the mattress, he cupped her face, staring into her eyes. "You never have to beg me, Katie girl. I'm here for you." Lowering his lips to hers, he owned her with a kiss that was everything all at once. Soft and strong. Determined and delicate. Patient and primal. And she was lost to the feelings coursing through her body.

She spread her legs for him as he settled between her thighs, his arousal nudging her ready sex. Plunging his cock deep inside at the same time he plunged his tongue into her mouth, he almost exploded at the overwhelming sense of tightness combined with the unique taste that was all Katelyn.

Restraint cast away, he plunged as her feet on his ass and fingers clutching his shoulders urged him on. Sweat beads broke out on his forehead as he felt his lower back tighten and his balls draw up. His pelvis stroked her clit with each thrust and he felt her core squeeze as her head pressed forward, her lips landing on his neck, her teeth nipping at the tender flesh.

As her orgasm milked him, he rocked once more, groaning as the muscles in his neck corded. Continuing to thrust until the last of his cum filled her, he dropped onto her chest, barely registering the 'oomph' coming from her lips. Rolling to the side, he pulled her with him, so she was lying half on him, their legs tangled together.

As their bodies cooled and their heartbeats slowed, he brushed back her sweat-slicked hair from her face, peering deeply into her eyes. "I love you, Katelyn."

She smoothed her fingers over his lips as her own mouth curved into a smile and a tear slid down her cheek. "I love you too, Gareth."

His heart pounded at her words, his thumb gently sweeping away her lone tear. "I can't change your past, but I want to be your future."

"You're never in comparison with my past..." Licking her kiss-swollen lips, she added, "I once told Jillian and Tori that I had no idea if Philip and I would have even made our relationship last into the adult world. So, don't you see? I did love him...but as a very young woman. But now, I'm older...wiser...and definitely know what I want." Smiling again, she slid her hand from his shoulder to cup his strong jaw. "And what I want is you."

This time their kiss sealed not only their lips, but their hearts as well.

23

"I'm being sued!"

Katelyn looked up as the distressed woman burst through the door, looking so different from when she had first met her. Leaping up from her desk, she rushed over. "Eleanor, what do you mean? Who's suing you?"

"That, that, that...oh, my God!" Bursting into tears, she plopped down in one of the chairs.

Katelyn hurried, "Let me get you some water," and rushed to the back, slamming into Gareth as he came out of his office.

His hands grabbed her shoulders to keep her from landing on her ass. Bending to look at her face, he said, "What's wrong? Who's out there?"

"Shhh," she whispered. "It's Eleanor and she's crying. She says she's being sued."

Rearing back, he repeated, "Sued? By who?"

Shrugging, she replied, "I don't know. We didn't get that far. I'm going to get her a water from the fridge and then let's bring her back to the conference room."

Nodding, he headed back into his office to grab his laptop as Katelyn went to get Eleanor. Once settled, Gareth asked, "Eleanor, what's happening? Katelyn said you are being sued?"

Eleanor took a sip of the water and dug a tissue from her purse. Wiping her tears, she said, "I know you can't do anything, but I just needed to tell someone. It's all so awful...it's not like I haven't been through enough, and now this." Sniffing, she lifted her head and said, "I got a summons this morning. I'm being sued by Carrie Reynolds for a percentage of Walter's estate."

Gareth and Katelyn looked at each other, shock registering on both their faces. "But...but why would his receptionist sue?"

Anger laced through her voice as Eleanor said, "Because she claims to be not just his receptionist...but his daughter!"

As soon as Eleanor left, Gareth called Mitch. "Are you available? Eleanor Berry was just here and her new information may impact your murder investigation."

Nodding to Katelyn, he said, "Lock up. We're going to the police station."

"You want me to go too?" she asked in surprise.

"Yeah...I want your input as well."

Inwardly pleased, she grabbed her notes and within five minutes they entered the police station. Mildred Score, the station's indomitable receptionist and dispatcher, waved them back and they entered the work room, seeing Mitch, Grant, and Ginny already inside.

"Burt and Sam are out on patrol, but we wanted to hear your news as soon as possible," Mitch said, as he indicated for Gareth and Katelyn to sit.

"Carrie Reynolds, the young receptionist at Walter Berry's accounting firm, is suing Eleanor for a percentage of his estate, claiming that he is her father."

At that statement, the three officers looked as shocked as Gareth and Katelyn had when Eleanor told them.

"Daughter?" Grant repeated as though he heard wrong.

Nodding, Gareth replied, "Yes. She claims she is Walter Berry's daughter from a previous relationship between her mother and him almost twenty-one years ago."

Rubbing his hand over his face, Mitch leaned forward, his eyebrows lowered. "Eleanor had no idea?"

"No, this came as a complete shock to her. She's upset...it obviously happened a long time ago, but they were married at the time, so it means he had an affair. She doesn't understand why he would have kept this from her."

"But he must have kept it a secret from the others at work as well, because they would have certainly mentioned it," Katelyn supposed aloud.

"How might this information fit into the murder investigation?"

Gareth rubbed his chin, "I don't know, but I'd like to interview her—"

"And her mother," Katelyn interrupted, gaining the

attention of the others. Looking at Gareth, she said, "She was crying at the funeral and now we know it was for a man she was once intimate with...had a child with. Who knows what other underlying emotions are there? Anger, rejection...even greed."

The group simultaneously leaned back in their chairs, the implication hitting all of them. Mitch appeared thoughtful as he said, "I need to talk to both of them but," he looked across the table and added, "Katelyn, I want your input as well."

Unable to hold back her grin, Katelyn glanced over to Gareth, pleased at his smile as well. "Can we talk to them separate from you? After all, Gareth and I have no authority over them so we don't present a threat."

"That could be a good idea," Ginny piped up. "They might get more out of them initially. As soon as we start questioning, they could lawyer-up."

Mitch agreed and, with a nod, said, "Okay. Do it today and get back with me. If they have cause, I want to know about it."

"This is getting real, isn't it?"

Gareth looked over at Katelyn, seeing the tension lines on her forehead. Uncertain what she meant, he waited to see what would follow. He had already learned that she needed time on her own to process what was on her mind. Then, and only then, was she ready to talk about it.

After a moment of comfortable silence, she added, "What we're doing matters...it can affect lives."

Another moment of comfortable silence followed. "At first, I was just excited to be looking for clues as to where Walter might be, thinking he might be with another woman. I like Eleanor and didn't want to hurt her, but I got caught up in the thrill of the search. Then, when he turned up dead, I realized how serious it all is."

Turning in her seat to face him, she said, "This isn't just trying to fit some clues together...this deals with people's lives...their hearts."

Reaching across the console, he laid his hand, palm up, on her thigh. She immediately placed hers in his, linking their fingers and clutching tightly.

Responding, he said, "Remember that we are not going in accusing anyone of anything. We're simply on a fact-finding mission, still working for Eleanor right now. We don't determine the outcome, or what has happened in the past."

Sighing heavily, she nodded, her mind still in turmoil as she watched the gulls flying over the bay bridge.

"Come in. I would say *welcome*, but I'm not sure that's appropriate."

With that curious greeting by Cindy Reynolds, Gareth and Katelyn walked into the Reynolds' home and immediately viewed Carrie and her father standing in the comfortable living room. Once introductions were out of the way, they all sat, each observing the others.

Katelyn noted Carrie's pale face and her hands continually clasping and unclasping in her lap. Her face was pinched, her eyes darting frequently over to her mother. Jerry Reynolds sat comfortably by his wife's side, his arm draped around her shoulders as Cindy sat ramrod straight, her tight-lipped expression matching her daughter's. Cindy's blonde hair was perfectly coiffed, in contrast to Carrie's, which was in a ponytail. A quick glance around the room showed family pictures of the three of them over many years.

Gareth began, "For disclosure purposes, my client has given me permission to give her name. We are working for Eleanor Berry and she has now been served with papers claiming Carrie is Walter Berry's daughter. We're here just to find out more facts, if you will talk to us."

"Mr. Harrison, I have nothing to hide—"

"Hmph," Carrie snorted. The others looked over at her, but she remained silent.

Cindy proceeded again, "I *now* have no reason to hide, and will answer your questions."

Nodding slowly, Gareth offered a slight smile before beginning. "If you don't mind, can you tell us, in your own words, how the paternity claim has come about?"

"It's quite simple, actually. I met Walter at a business dinner when I was a senior in college. We had a relationship that lasted for a few months. He never told me he was married and I was naïve enough to not consider it. When I graduated, I was offered an internship and since we were not a formal couple, it was easy to leave and move to California at that time. I was already there when I realized I was pregnant."

"And you never told him?"

Plucking an imaginary piece of fluff off her pants, Cindy blushed slightly before looking back up. "Quite frankly, I was not in love with Walter. He was not a man I saw myself marrying. Oh, he was quite charming and was truly a good man...just not what I wanted." Shrugging, she said, "I was young and decided to have my baby on my own. I was offered a job back here in Virginia after the internship, but never ran into him again."

Katelyn saw Jerry smile slightly as he rubbed Cindy's shoulder, before she continued. "Carrie was only two when I met Jerry and fell in love. He loved Carrie as his own and together we became a family. He's been the only father she's ever known."

Gareth took in Carrie's knitted brow and decided not to ask her any questions until he had more information. *Looks like she's struggling to deal with all the new information.*

Turning back to Cindy, he asked, "So what made you decide to let Walter know...I'm assuming you let him know?"

Nodding slowly, Cindy replied, "About a year ago, I was out with Carrie having lunch and a man walked over. I looked up and, to my surprise, it was Walter. He had recognized me and when I introduced Carrie as my daughter, I could tell that he immediately made the connection." Lifting her shoulders slightly, she offered, "She looks like his side of the family."

Silence settled on the group for a moment before Cindy continued. "He called me the next day...I wasn't surprised. He of course wanted to know everything, but

I didn't want to have the conversation over the phone. I told Jerry and he agreed that I needed to be truthful. So, I arranged to meet Walter."

Carrie heaved a sigh and Katelyn's gaze jumped back to the young woman, her heart full of sympathy for how Carrie's world had changed in the last few days.

Cindy's eyes fell on her daughter and a look of sadness crossed her face. "Looking back, I should have told Carrie all along about her real father...but, to be honest, Jerry has been her real father. When I met with Walter, I did tell him about Carrie and, contrary to what you might believe, he was not angry about not knowing. Well, at first he was, but then he accepted it. Walter was a very pragmatic person. He even told me that he and his wife were unable to have children, so he said that he would like to help Carrie. She was still in college and he said his office needed a receptionist and he would help with college costs."

"Your news came as quite a shock to his wife," Gareth commented. "He did not tell her about his daughter."

"Sounds like I was just everyone's big ol' secret," Carrie bit out, her anger palpable.

Looking at her, Cindy explained, "Walter said his wife was unable to have children and he did not want to upset her."

"So, he gives Carrie a job and this gives him the opportunity to have a relationship with his daughter in a professional setting. What about now? What about the lawsuit?"

Pinching her lips, Cindy said, "Walter and I met several times over the past year—"

"Did you meet at a hotel?" Katelyn interrupted.

"Uh...no," Cindy stammered, blushing as her eyes cut over to her husband.

Gareth prompted, "Please continue about the lawsuit."

"Walter told me that he wanted to make sure that Cindy would be taken care of. I assumed he meant in his will. I never asked him directly, but that was my assumption...and my mistake. When he died, I kept waiting to hear from their attorney. When I didn't, I had my lawyer check and found out that Carrie wasn't mentioned at all."

Silence again lay over the group making Katelyn wiggle slightly, as though underneath an itchy blanket. Finally, leaning forward, she asked, "But why now? You've gone all these years without Carrie knowing about her real father...without his financial support. Why rock the boat now?"

"Because the fact of the matter is that he came into her life and he was her biological father. We did a DNA test, just in case we needed it, but he was so good to her that I never needed it. But now? He died and there is no mention of his daughter at all. I talked to Jerry and we decided that for Carrie's sake and for her future to be financially secure, we needed to proceed."

Turning to Carrie, Katelyn said softly, "Carrie, up till now, your mom's been answering the questions, but let's face it—you're an adult. What's your stance in all of this?"

Sighing, sounding more sad than angry, Carrie

replied, "I'm having a hard time with all of this. In the last week, I've lost my...boss, who I adored, only to find out he was, in truth, my father. And now, I'm suing his wife, who's completely innocent in all this mess, for money. It makes me feel...somehow dirty." She looked up at Katelyn and added, "But then, I'm his daughter. I'd like to be treated as such and since he knew I was, then why didn't he provide for me?"

Not answering her rhetorical question, Gareth glanced at Katelyn before saying, "We thank you for your candor. I'm sure the Baytown Police will be interviewing you as well, but I'll be reporting back to Eleanor Berry."

As Gareth and Katelyn walked out, Carrie grabbed her purse and said, "I'm leaving now also, Mom. I'm meeting Ed for dinner," and hustled out the door. Once outside, she jogged over to Gareth's vehicle. "I know this all makes me look like a selfish bitch. I really do feel sorry for Mrs. Berry...she's just as innocent in this mess as I am." With that, she walked briskly to her car.

Climbing into his SUV, Katelyn looked over and said, "Wow. Just wow. I don't even know what to think right now."

Gareth's gaze drifted to the side of the driveway near the back yard where he noted a boat sitting on a trailer parked next to the garage.

Cindy and Jerry stood together at the living room window and watched the vehicles pull out of their driveway.

"Do you think that went well?" Cindy asked her husband. A shoulder squeeze was his only reply.

24

The sun streamed in through the tall windows of Jillian's galleria, upstairs from her coffee shop. As Katelyn rounded the corner at the stop of the stairs, she saw the others gathered and grinned. Jillian had coffee and pastries laid out and Tori's mouth was already covered in powdered sugar.

"Sowwee," Tori tried to apologize, blushing at her lack of restraint when it came to sweets.

Laughing, Katelyn plopped down between Jade and Belle, reaching to the platter, helping herself as well.

"Rose is coming today," Jillian said, and right on cue, a pretty blonde bounded up the stairs.

"Thanks for inviting me!" Rose said. "I was in town today and grabbed coffee downstairs. Jillian invited me to come back for your get together. I hope I'm not crashing!"

"How's the ice cream shop going?" Tori asked, having successfully swallowed her large bite of pastry.

Rolling her eyes, Rose huffed, "I swear, the town

manager has me so twisted in knots, I want to throw in the towel and just try to open a shop in the northern part of the Eastern Shore!"

"No!" came several shouts all at once, startling Rose.

"Sorry," Katelyn said, "but this town needs new blood and an ice cream shop is perfect. Silas Mills drives everyone crazy, so you can't take it personally."

"Well, I know I told you that the first property I looked at had just been rented to the guy who owns the garage—"

"Jason," Jillian interrupted.

Shrugging, Rose said, "All I know is he wanted to open a tattoo parlor as well as the garage. But he's only got the garage going now and the storefront is just sitting there! I mean, it looks like he's got stuff in it, but I could be open now, growing my business now. Who knows how long it will be before he opens."

"He's a really nice guy," Tori said. "He helped me out when I was having some difficulties a couple of months ago."

"Well, nice or not...he's got the place I could afford. So, I'm still looking."

Turning to Katelyn, Jade asked, "So what's up with the murder investigation?"

"You know I can't talk about what we're finding out," Katelyn said, her voice uncharacteristically whiny. "Unless, of course, we discuss things you already know."

"Okay, fine. Let's talk about how the body got to the golf course," Jillian said, leaning back in her chair as she tapped her forefinger against her chin.

"Obviously by boat," Belle pronounced eagerly, sitting forward in her seat.

"Yes, but when, and what kind of boat?"

Tori said, "Could it have been in a small row boat or canoe?"

"I don't think so," Katelyn said as Jillian was shaking her head.

"Nope, not a small canoe. A boat...perhaps, but it would need a motor. It would take too long to travel by rowing."

"But they don't know where he was killed," Tori added.

"Why would someone want him killed?" Belle asked. "The newspaper article said that he was a beloved member of his organizations and his workplace."

Patting her hand, Jillian replied, "Oh, sweetie. Obituaries can make the devil look like a saint. No one's that perfect." Leaning back, she added, "But for someone to want him dead...well, there has to be motive, opportunity, and means."

"Ooh, look at you, sounding just like you stepped out of a TV crime show," Tori laughed.

"Hey, we're both with policemen—surely we've picked up some of the jargon!" Jillian laughed.

Rose, her expression uncertain, looked over at Jade, who had been quiet. Leaning over, Jade said, "This is how they roll."

"Motive is usually money or anger," Katelyn said, thinking about Walter's will, which had seemed so simple but, now, with the new information about Carrie, both reasons seemed to fit.

"Opportunity could be anywhere, since no one seems to know where he was when he told his wife and his coworkers that he was going on a weekend trip," Jillian surmised.

"Means is a hard clue to figure out because if he was hit on the back of the head, it could have been with anything," Katelyn stated.

"I vote for Colonel Mustard, in the library, with a candlestick," Tori quipped, her jest causing the others to laugh.

It did not take long for the mirth to end and somberness to settle over the group. "It's really sad," Belle said. "To think of anyone killed for whatever reason."

"Don't you think it has to be a man?" Jade asked. "The picture in the newspaper made Walter look like an average size man, but it would still take a lot to kill someone."

"Most murderers are men," Rose added as she scrunched her forehead in thought. "I'm sure I read that somewhere."

"Women are just as capable of anger and even hate," Belle said, her gentle voice belying her words. "Sometimes I think a woman would be more capable." As the others turned to her, curiosity at her statement, she added, "Men get angry quickly, but will often fight it out and then it's over. The flash of anger burns out." Lifting her shoulders in a slight shrug, she continued, "But women? Their flame of anger can burn for a long time. Even years."

As the subject changed and the others began talking about Tori and Mitch's upcoming wedding,

Katelyn's mind stayed on motive, opportunity, and means.

"Would you believe that I'm actually sick of going back over this bridge?" Katelyn asked.

Gareth chuckled and nodded his agreement. "When I first moved to the Eastern Shore I wondered if I would get tired of living in a small town and would want to head back over to the Virginia Beach area."

"Oooh, to go clubbing?" she joked, cutting her eyes to the side, suddenly wondering about his life before she met him.

"Hardly," he replied. "I was never much of a partier. My sister always accused me of being too serious, but," shrugging, "I never had much choice. The military certainly didn't change that. And, finishing up at Dover was not a barrel of laughs either."

Placing her hand on his leg, she said, "I'm sorry for you, but glad for all the soldiers, that you were the one making sure everything was taken care of."

"Don't feel sorry for me, sweetheart. I'm just glad I ended up where I did and found you. And just like you, I don't need to leave the Shore to find excitement."

Smiling, she turned to gaze out her window. "The wind is picking up. I heard we were supposed to get a storm soon." Shifting her attention back to Gareth, she said, "The girls and I were discussing the case—no, I didn't tell them anything," she rushed as he opened his mouth to speak.

Grinning, he nodded for her to continue. "Belle said

something that stuck with me. It was about how men can get angry and quickly get it out of their system, the anger dissipating. But that for women, anger can burn for a really long time."

"You got ideas about the case?"

"Well, I was just thinking about Cindy Reynolds."

"Yeah?"

Turning to face him, she said, "We only have her word that Walter didn't know about the pregnancy. Maybe Walter did know and rejected her twenty-years ago. Maybe she's been burning about this for that long. Maybe—"

"That's a lot of maybes," Gareth laughed. "But that's the way to investigate. Look for clues and then look for ways that things could happen."

"Do you mind if I talk to Carrie alone today? Maybe when you go back to talk to William?"

Gareth peered into Katelyn's blue eyes, noting the sparkle of life. "You got it," he said, enjoying the way her face lit with excitement. "So, how're you liking the investigating business so far?"

Shrugging, she said, "It beats waitressing." Seeing his look of concern out of the corner of her eye, she struggled to hold back a grin. Unable to accomplish that feat, she burst into laughter at his affronted pout. "I love it...you know that. And it keeps me from having to sit in trees!"

Shaking his head, he grinned. "Gotta admit, standing underneath your perfect ass that night was a sight to behold."

"I was shocked, to say the least."

Gareth watched as William shook his head slowly, his hound dog jowls making him look even more beleaguered.

"Walter never even hinted that Carrie was his daughter. I mean, I noticed he seemed to be particular to her." Blushing, he added, "I actually wondered if they were...uh...well, you know. But for her to not know either...it's all so strange."

"Do you know if you will keep her on?" Gareth asked.

"I can't see why not. None of this is her fault and she's a very competent receptionist." Shrugging, he added, "But, then, she's taking college classes so I would assume this is a temporary position for her." Sighing again, he said, "Seems likes lots of things are temporary now."

"And the firm?"

"I was Walter's partner and the firm will now be in my name." He leaned forward and whispered, "In fact, Sandra and I had some words yesterday about it."

Cocking his head to the side, Gareth prompted, "Words?"

"She assumed she would become a full partner but, in my opinion, she's too young and inexperienced. She'll remain a partner, but I'll look for another senior partner."

Gareth stayed quiet for a moment sensing William had more to say and he did not have to wait long.

"I know this sounds sexist, but I'm going to be looking for a male accountant to fill Walter's shoes."

His jowls shook once more as he explained, "There's just too many women here!"

"Thanks for the coffee...and the chance to run away for a few minutes."

Katelyn smiled at the young woman sitting across from her in the small coffee shop down the street from the accounting firm. Carrie, pale but still immaculately made up, sipped her coffee.

"Carrie, what can you tell me about Walter, your mom, anything?"

Toying with the napkin in front of her, Carrie sighed heavily. "I was looking for a part time job, figuring I'd be waitressing, but Mom called and said that she knew of a receptionist position. I didn't think I'd have a chance, but just to placate Mom, I went to interview. Walter..." swallowing audibly, she looked up, holding Katelyn's gaze. "It's still hard to say his name right now."

"I understand. Just take your time."

Clearing her throat, she said, "I'm fine...really. Anyway, Walter interviewed me. He was attentive, asked lots of questions and then told me I was hired. I thought I was just really lucky. A week after I started, he told me that the company would help pay for my college classes. Then I thought I'd hit the jackpot. He and Mr. Maskey were nice to work for even though Beth and Sandra were never as friendly."

"Why do you think that was?"

Rolling her eyes, Carrie replied, "You know how

women can be smiling to your face and then back-stabbing bitches to your back."

Katelyn blinked hard as she leaned back in her chair. *Really?* Having never experienced that kind of relationship, she once more realized what good friends she had. *God, I'm lucky!* Nodding dumbly, she indicated for Carrie to continue.

"Sandra lorded over me that *she* was a partner and I was nothing. Beth flirted with Walter but he was never interested."

"Are you sure? They both seem to think that he had a special relationship—"

"Oh, I'm positive! They would both bat their eyes and act like he had spent time with them, but I never believed it." She chuckled as she added, "Beth would get pissed when he spent time in a closed-door meeting with Sandra and Sandra would fume when he spent time with Beth going over the office finances."

Katelyn thought about what Belle said—*women can hold on to their anger.* Sipping more of her coffee, she gave Carrie a minute to drink as well before starting in on her mother.

"So, how did your mom tell you about Walter?"

Closing her eyes, Carrie leaned back in her seat, shaking her head. "She just called and said I needed to come home so that she and Dad could talk to me about something." Opening her eyes, she said, "Hell, I thought one of them had cancer or something. We sat in the den and Mom just started talking about a man she met when she was young and how she ended up pregnant. Honestly, the way she explained it to you the other day was exactly how she told me. Dad just sat there looking sad...I think he would have been fine with me thinking he was my biological father for the rest of my life."

"Did you get the feeling that Jerry was upset with your mom?"

"No...he's always let her call the shots. They have a good relationship, but Mom is the more dominant one. You know, the kind of relationship where if she needed him to, he'd bury a body for her."

25

Katelyn met Gareth as he left the accounting office, both climbing into his SUV at the same time. The dark clouds of earlier had continued to roll in as lightening began to zing across the sky. Just as they pulled out of the parking lot, rain pelted the windshield, creating a pounding rhythm.

Katelyn filled him in on her conversation with Carrie, ending with her relationship with her parents. "She shocked the hell out of me when she described Jerry as a husband who would bury a body for his wife if needed! But, then she explained it was just a saying and that she didn't mean it literally."

"Did she elaborate more?"

"She loves her parents and no matter what her mom has revealed, she says she'll always consider Jerry to be her father and Walter as her former boss."

"So, the lawsuit...is it more her mom than her?"

"Essentially, her mom has her convinced that

Walter wanted Carrie to have more. Supposedly Cindy and Walter had been in contact and Cindy thought the will was already changed." They sat silent for a moment as she bit her lip in concentration before she turned back to him and rushed, "Do you think that Cindy could have been the woman at the motel with Walter, even though she denied it?"

"Since there is no positive identification and the woman wore sunglasses and a scarf, then it's possible. By why go to such elaborate measures?"

"Maybe they didn't just talk. Maybe they rekindled their relationship."

A crack of thunder over the bay had Katelyn jumping as Gareth focused on the drive. The whitecaps on the waves crashed against the pylons and all thoughts of the case flew from her mind as she watched nature in effect on the water.

"Are you glad you stayed on the Eastern Shore?" His question came out of the blue, shocking Katelyn and she whipped her head around to look at him.

"Where did that question come from?"

Shrugging, he replied, "I want to know everything about you, I guess."

Smiling slightly, she said, "I think every teenager on the Eastern Shore dreams of leaving and ending up in a big city somewhere. And a lot have. When most of the Baytown Boys joined the military and left town, it felt lonely. And when Jillian went off to college, I felt left behind. Truly left behind. I dreamed of leaving too, but every time I looked at my mom's face when she thought about Aiden and Brogan, I knew I needed to stay. But I also discovered something..." she turned to face him fully. "For some of us, we grow up and realize that small-town isn't just a description of where we live. It's a description of *who* we are. I like knowing my neighbors. I like that when someone has a need, there's a whole town ready to step in and help." Laughing, she said, "I guess that's a long answer to your question, but yeah, I'm glad I stayed on the Eastern Shore. What about you? Do you miss West Virginia?"

Gareth almost answered with a rousing, *Hell, no,* but hesitated. "I do miss the mountains. I'd like to see my sister, brother-in-law, and their kids sometime...it's been too long." Glancing to the side, he cleared his throat and said, "Uh...I was wondering...well, after this case is over with, I was going to ask you to take a trip to West Virginia with me. We could spend a long weekend in the mountains and I could check in with my sister."

Pleasure slipped over her just as another crack of thunder rumbled through the sky. The raging storm outside was incongruous to the happiness in her heart. "I'd love to meet her," she said, reaching over to clasp his hand.

As they neared town, she said, "I was going to go into the pub and work this evening. You want to come with me and get dinner there? If it's slow, we can leave together."

"Sounds good. I'll drop you off and then go talk to Mitch. He'll want to hear from you about Cindy, but I can fill him in for now."

As he parked in front of the pub, she leaned over,

eager for a kiss. No longer caring who saw them, she pulled him close with her hand behind his neck, her lips moving over his.

Gareth recognized the shift in her willingness to claim him and wrapped his arms around her, allowing her to take the lead. Smiling against her lips, he pulled back regretfully as she sighed, her warm breath washing over his face. "Tonight?"

"Yeah," she mumbled, then blinked. "Oh, wait! I forgot—I've got a wedding meeting tonight with the girls. Can you pick me up at Tori's inn?"

"Are you going to be drunk?"

"No," she snapped, then sucked in her lips, giving a slight shrug. "Okay...maybe just a little. But then I'll let you have your wicked way with me."

"Can you imagine what it must have been like to find a dead body on the golf course?"

The chips and dip were gone, the wedding reception plans were finalized, and the third glass of wine had now brought out the random question.

Belle's eyes were wide as she looked over at Tori, who continued, "I mean, it was horrible when I had a guest who died in my inn, but his wife was screaming and he was lying in bed, so it didn't seem so shocking. But on the golf course!"

"If it was a crime of passion, I wonder who it was? A jealous husband or boyfriend?" Jade posed, pouring her next glass of wine.

"But why the trip? Why did he tell people he was going on a trip?" Jillian asked.

Belle surmised, "He tells his wife and his co-workers two different things to keep from having to answer questions and plans on meeting a secret lover?"

"Maybe there was more than one woman," Tori said, picking up the empty wine bottle. "Hmm, let me go grab more." Walking into the kitchen of the Sea Glass Bed Inn that had been left to her by her grandmother, she grabbed another bottle. She did not want her guests to hear their conversations, so the women had parked themselves on the patio off the kitchen. This was one of her grandmother's—and now her—private places that were only for family or friends...not guests.

Katelyn came up behind her and snagged another box of crackers. "Thought we might need more food to soak up all the alcohol we're drinking," she joked, taking another wedge of cheese from Tori's refrigerator.

Tori smiled at her friend and together they returned to the group, barely getting their fingers out of the way before Jillian dove into the snacks.

"I still think it could be a woman," Belle said. "A woman scorned...jealousy...maybe he made promises to a mistress that he no longer kept."

"Or he had more than one mistress!" Jillian said between bites. The group became silent as each woman's imagination began to run wild.

"Women kill for passion," Jade said. "A scorned woman could easily be the culprit, but it doesn't seem to fit. A woman might poison—"

"You don't think a woman would hit a man over the head?" Belle asked. "Spend a night at the trailer park where I live and you'd be convinced otherwise!"

"I heard Mitch and Grant say that Walter was supposed to play in the golf tournament that is now cancelled. Maybe it was a disgruntled golfer?" Tori surmised.

"A disgruntled golfer?" Jade snorted, barely keeping from spitting out her sip of wine.

The others laughed before Tori continued, "Hey, some of those TV detectives have murders to solve that are just as weird!"

"I'd say, it was more likely someone wanting to piss off Roger or Silas!" Jillian threw out.

"How do you do this?" Belle asked Katelyn. "I mean, you're investigating things that are hard to find out."

Shrugging, Katelyn said, "Gareth tells me that it's necessary to have ideas and let my imagination run wild, but then I can't fall into the trap of believing something until it's proven. So, I take all the things I think of and start trying to research one at a time until something is either proven or disproven."

"When does your PI class start?" Tori asked.

"In about three weeks. I really hope this case is wrapped up by then, because the class will take two full weeks and I don't want to be gone for that long while I'm still needed here."

Grinning, Jillian said, "Well, I don't know about the case, but I know Gareth will miss you no matter what!"

Katelyn's face softened at the thought of Gareth. Realizing she had the attention of the group, she cocked her head to the side. "What?"

"Nothing, sweetie," Jillian said, her eyes shining at her friend. "I'm just so glad to see you with a dreamy expression."

Katelyn almost denied the look on her face, but knew they were right. Sighing as she leaned back in her chair, she brought her wine glass up to her smiling lips.

"Hell, yeah!"

Grant shouted as the volleyball slammed into the sand at Jason's feet. The Baytown Boys, both old and new, had descended on Mitch's cabin on the bay after the latest American Legion youth ball game. The ratty volleyball net had seen better days, but still managed to stay, sagging, between the two poles buried in the sand.

Gareth grabbed the ball and volleyed it back over the net as the game continued. He, Jason, and Aiden were on one side with Mitch, Grant, and Brogan on the other. Callan, Zac, and a few others were standing around the grill and makeshift bar. After a few more minutes, the hamburgers were done and the volleyball game ended as the whole group gathered around the table, loading up their plates before sitting in the lawn chairs scattered about.

"So...did you find out if Berry was supposed to play in the tournament?" Zac asked right before taking a huge bite of hamburger.

Nodding, Gareth answered, "Yeah. I talked to Roger. Between him cursing about the *inconsiderate* body found on the golf course, he admitted that Walter was scheduled to play."

"You figure that has anything to do with why the body was dumped there?" Jason asked.

"We haven't ruled anything out," Mitch replied, noncommittally.

"But it's got to be significant that it was dumped there," Aiden argued.

Gareth took a swig from his beer and shook his head. "Not necessarily," he said. "The killer could just be looking for a place where the body might go unnoticed for a while."

"Then you gotta be looking at a man," Callan said.

Zac grinned, "Hell, I served in the Navy with some women that could carry a man." Looking over at the others, he continued, "They could bench almost as much as I could."

"Just 'cause you're puny—" Aiden began.

Jumping up, Zac balled up his trash and scored a shot with his toss into the garbage can before flexing his muscles. "I'll show you who's puny," he laughed, flexing his biceps.

The others laughed along with him as several began tossing their trash with shouts of, "Score!"

Brogan, thoughtful, asked, "You know any women around here that could lift a man into a boat...deadweight? I sure as hell don't."

Aiden grinned at his brother, saying, "Hell, you never get out. For all you know that pretty, little Ginny could out-bench-press you!"

Brogan blushed as he shoved up from his chair. "Shut the hell up, asshole," he said, elbowing Aiden in the back of the head as he walked by.

"Then it's like I said and you gotta be looking at a man," Callan restated as he joined Brogan walking back toward the beach.

Finishing their meal, Zac, Aiden, and Jason joined the others, another volleyball game beginning, leaving Gareth, Mitch, and Grant still sitting in the chairs.

"So...what motivation does a man have to kill Walter? Jealousy? Money?" Gareth mused aloud.

Rubbing his hand over his face, Mitch replied, "Maybe all of the above."

"Can't be money," Gareth said, setting his empty plate on the ground by his feet. "His brother only got a little bit and most of that will go to caring for their mother."

"What about his partner, William?" Grant asked. "He's now senior partner...gets to run the place the way he wants."

"Can't see him killing or getting rid of a body on a golf course," Gareth replied.

"He's got money. You can always hire someone to do your dirty work for you," Grant added, capturing Mitch's attention.

As the three continued to sit, their eyes on the volleyball game now being played against the backdrop of the setting sun, Gareth ran the possibilities through his mind.

Beth stood with shaking hands clasped together, building up her courage. "I know things. I've found things. Things that I think the police would like to know."

Before she gave the other person a chance to respond, she continued, "I'm not asking for much. But I feel a little compensation for what I know is warranted. Wouldn't you agree?"

26

"What exactly are we looking for?"

Gareth stared at the front of the small boat where Katelyn sat facing him, binoculars hanging around her neck. Her long hair hung in a braid down her back and his eyes dropped to her yellow tank top, underneath her hoodie, and cut-off jean shorts showcasing her long legs. Grinning, he said, "Well, I thought we would go around to the golf course, but I realize I have no chance of looking for any clues while you're sitting there like that."

"Like what?" she asked, her head cocked to the side.

"Like all my dreams rolled up into one gorgeous woman."

Katelyn's jaw dropped as her eyes lit. "Wow, that line alone was worth getting up at the ass-crack of dawn!"

"Well, it's true," he claimed, leaning forward to capture her lips. The boat rocked gently in the water as she threw her arms around his neck, his lips moving across hers. Pulling back regretfully, he kept his hand on the tiller. Throttling back, they drifted for a few minutes, the early morning sounds of the bay coming to life surrounding them. Gulls called from above before diving into the sparkling water. A blue heron stood statue-still with its legs in the surf, hunting for its next meal of fish.

Katelyn turned her face up toward the rising sun, letting the cool breeze toss her braid over her shoulder. With her eyes closed, she allowed the rocking movement of the boat to lull her thoughts along. Growing up on the bay afforded her the opportunity to spend as much time on or near the water as possible. Summers and weekends were filled with fishing off the pier, playing on the beach, learning to kayak and boat as soon as she could hold an oar.

A memory darted through her mind of Philip rowing her along the shore, landing in a small cove where she looked for sea glass. For a moment, with her eyes closed, she could almost imagine him sitting in the boat with her. But, instead of blond hair, his hair was brown. Instead of a teenage boy's body, a hard, muscular body sat across from her. When he called her name, the voice was deeper...more mature.

"Katelyn...you awake?" the voice called out louder.

Her eyes opened with a jerk, blinking rapidly as her body jolted when the words penetrated. Seeing Gareth staring at her, his eyes full of mirth, she sat up quickly.

"I thought you'd gone to sleep for a moment," he joked.

"No! Uh...no...just...um," she babbled. Guilt

flooded her, but she was uncertain what was worse—having trouble remembering Philip's face or dreaming of him when out with Gareth. Licking her dry lips, she turned toward the shore, saying, "Maybe it's time we headed in. I'm kind of hungry."

Gareth watched her carefully, noting her sudden unease. "Sure," he said, hesitantly, wondering what came over her.

Thirty minutes later, ensconced in one of the red, plastic booths of the diner, they ate in silence, each lost in their own thoughts.

The long stretch of beach was unoccupied as Katelyn bent over to pick up a piece of sea glass. *Dark blue—rare!* Her thoughts may have been as tangled as her wind-blown hair, but she clutched the glass in her palm, its bright color giving her a reason to smile.

Hearing a shout behind her, she saw Jillian and Tori walking over the dune toward her. Slowing her pace, she allowed them to catch up as she gathered a few more pieces of glass.

"I thought you and Gareth were going out boating today," Jillian said, her gaze already at their feet, her eyes searching for more sea glass.

"We did. We went this morning before breakfast."

"So what are you doing out here alone?" Tori asked.

Shrugging, she turned toward the wind, allowing the breeze to sweep her hair back so she could pull it into a ponytail easier. "We ate at the diner and then I decided I wanted some time to myself."

She noticed Jillian and Tori sharing a look, but pretended to not care. Facing downward, she continued to walk along the shore.

"Hey, sweetie," Jillian said, placing her hand on Katelyn's arm. "I'm not going to lie to you. Gareth called and asked if we would check on you. He said he thought you were upset about something."

Pinching her lips together, Katelyn stopped walking, facing the bay, sighing heavily. After a long moment where the only sounds were the gulls calling, hoping they had crackers for them, she finally turned back to her friends, admitting, "I'm forgetting."

Cocking their heads together simultaneously, Jillian and Tori remained quiet, letting Katelyn speak when she was ready.

Swallowing deeply, she repeated, "I'm forgetting...Philip."

The three women slowly began walking again, this time their search for sea glass more instinctive than purposeful. After some silence, Katelyn said, "I used to look at his picture on my bedside table every night when I went to sleep and every morning when I woke up. I did this for years and years and years. Before Gareth spent the night the first time, I placed Philip's picture in the drawer, not wanting to make Gareth uncomfortable. At first, the nightstand seemed naked, and now? I wake up and don't even think about it. I jump out of bed and am ready to greet the day, knowing I'll see Gareth."

Coming to the end of the beach where the cement factory had a fence, halting their progress, the trio turned wordlessly and began walking back down the beach in the opposite direction.

"And this morning, Gareth and I were out on a boat and at one point, it was so peaceful...so quiet. I closed my eyes and my mind drifted off with the sun beaming on my face. I was taken back to when Philip and I would go out on his old boat, but then I couldn't bring his face to mind. His blond hair was darker. And when he called my name, it wasn't his voice. It was deeper. It was Gareth's."

Stopping suddenly, she turned to the others and her voice cracked as she asked, "What does that mean?"

Jillian stood toe to toe with Katelyn and placed both hands on her arms. "Sweetie, I think it means you are finally moving forward. You're not being unfaithful to Philip, but you are letting him go. You've wrapped yourself in a blanket of grief for so long that it's all you know. Now, life is giving you more and as you embrace it, you shed the grief blanket a little more each day."

Sucking in her lips, trying to stave off the tears that threatened, Katelyn nodded. "I feel more alive than I have in so long."

Tori wrapped her arms around Katelyn from the back, resting her head on her shoulder, placing her in the middle of a hug-sandwich. "There's nothing wrong with feeling alive," she said.

"But what if I forget Philip completely?"

"You won't," Jillian promised. "This town is full of places and people he knew. You'll see him occasionally, on the ball field, in the diner, on a boat, and yes...sometimes when you're with Gareth. But honey, you're no longer living *for* his memory. You're living *with* his memory. And you can do that and love Gareth at the same time."

The three women held on to each other for a moment, silent emotions swirling around them as the breeze steadily blew inland.

Gareth leaned his arms on the wooden fishing rails of the city pier. The waves slapped against the pylons below and the gulls swooped down as a few fishermen cast their lines into the bay. The sun warmed him, although the breeze was cool, and as he dropped his gaze to the surf, he watched as schools of small fish moved as one around the rocks and crabs hovering nearby.

He felt a presence behind him, but before he could turn around, he heard a soft voice, instant recognition shooting through him.

"Hey." The sound was barely more than a whisper but pierced his heart nonetheless.

Turning around, he observed the beautiful woman standing in front of him, her usual self-confidence replaced with a pinched expression.

"Hey, back-attcha," he said. Leaning against the pier railing, he bent to catch her eyes. "You okay?"

Nodding jerkily, Katelyn replied, "Yeah. I was...well, you didn't have to send...I was fine."

"Hmmm," he said, giving away little emotion. He lifted his hand to tuck a wayward strand behind her ear. "You want to sit?"

Taking her hand, he led her a few yards down the

pier where a wooden bench overlooked the harbor. "Can I ask you a question?"

"Of course," she said, linking her fingers with his while her heart beat an erratic rhythm.

"Did you and Philip ever sit on this pier together?"

Uncertain of his reason for asking, she nodded hesitantly. "Yeah...we did. All of us did."

"And the ball field?"

Nodding again, she searched his face for a clue as to what he was feeling.

"Jillian's coffee shop...the diner...the town beach... Mitch's beach cabin...your pub..."

"Yes," she breathed. "Yes, to all of those." Suddenly afraid, she blurted, "Gareth, I don't know what you mean. Philip and I were kids together. Part of this town. So just about everywhere you look, I spent time with him." Hanging her head, her stomach sinking, she said, "Does this bother you?"

Turning his head to stare at her, he said nothing, causing her heart to pound more. "I can't change it, Gareth. I can't make this little town with all my growing-up memories go away. I can't make it any less a place I spent with Philip than I can change the history I have with Jillian."

Reaching up to cup her cool cheek, he rubbed his thumb over the smooth skin as he said, "I don't want you to forget, Katelyn. I know there will be things that you do with me that you also did with him. Places we'll be that you and he were together first."

Cocking her head, she peered at his face, trying to understand the meaning behind his words. His eyes held hers captive and she remembered the first time she saw them.

A crowded night at Finn's. Aiden cracking jokes and Brogan barking orders. Same old, same old. But then, Zac shouted a greeting. "Gareth!"

As the crowd parted, Katelyn came to a halt in the middle of wiping down the bar as a pair of crystal blue eyes held hers. Men had come and men had gone from the old pub over the years, never catching her attention, but in that instant, her cold heart jolted with long-forgotten electricity.

"I don't want you to forget," Gareth repeated. "I just want to make new memories with you, but I need to know you're okay with that as well."

"I forgot." Swallowing deeply, she tried again. "This morning...out on the boat...I forgot. I forgot Philip. When I closed my eyes, I didn't see him...I saw you. I didn't hear him...it was your voice that came to me."

"Are you afraid of forgetting him?" Gareth asked softly, his thumb still caressing her cheek.

"I was at first. It felt strange...not disloyal, but just strange."

"I'll do anything to make it easier on you, Katelyn," he promised.

Smiling, she felt a tear slide down her cheek, captured by his hand. "I don't need anything to be easier," she replied. "Jillian helped remind me that I no longer have to live for Philip's memory. Instead I can live with his memory and still love you as well."

"I love you, too."

Nodding as her lips curved, she vowed, "With all my heart."

Gareth's breath caught in his throat as he captured her lips, the kiss taking everything she had to give while offering everything in return.

27

"And I'm telling you once and for all, we need to wind this case up!"

Katelyn's grin toward Mildred as she entered the reception area of the Baytown Police Department dropped off her face at the sound of the very loud and very angry Corwin Banks, the town's mayor.

"And I'm telling you that we're working on it."

Katelyn recognized Mitch's voice, low but firm.

"This unfortunate incident has cost our town money with the cancelled golf tournament," Silas Mills complained.

"The Tall Ship and Pirate Festival starts this week-end," Corwin stated, "and I don't want the idea of a murder hanging over Baytown's head."

Katelyn rolled her eyes in unison with Mildred's at the mayor's whining voice. "How long have they been in there?" she whispered.

"Long enough for me to want to run for mayor in the next election!"

Giggling, Katelyn said, "Well, you've got my vote!"

Just then the conference room door opened, Corwin and Silas striding out. Seeing Katelyn standing in the lobby, Silas sneered. "I heard the barmaid was now working as an investigator. No wonder nothing gets solved!"

Katelyn swung around, fire sparking from her eyes. Planting her hands on her hips, she said, "I've spent my life in this town and I can guarantee I know the residents a helluva lot more than you do, you pompous a—"

Gareth cut her off as he walked out of the conference room with a, "Hey, Katelyn. Come on back."

She whirled around, her eyes narrowed as she stomped over to him. "Why did you stop me? I've had it with those two. Corwin's just a hot-air nincompoop, too stuffed with his own self-importance. But Silas? That man's a menace to this town!"

"No doubt, but let's not give him a reason to make life more difficult," he reasoned, kissing her forehead.

Blowing her cheeks out as she exhaled loudly, she nodded, her ire still firmly in place. Walking into the room, she observed Grant, Mitch, and Colt already inside, now knowing they were the ones Silas had been yelling at.

Mitch grinned and shook his head. "Don't make me have to arrest you for killing our town manager, Katelyn."

With a sugary-sweet voice, she replied, "Me? Oh, Mitch. I was just going to whack him in the head...not kill him. Surely you could ignore a little assault when it's warranted!"

The others laughed before sitting back around the table, looking at the whiteboard on the stand near the wall. Ginny, Burt, and Sam, the other officers came in and quickly took their seats as well. The mirth left the group as they stared at the names written before them, all leading down from the one at the top center: Walter Berry – victim.

Gareth's gaze followed the lines drawn to the ones in Walter's life with motivation and opportunity and his eyes kept landing on Carrie and her parents. "Why now?" he mused aloud before realizing he had garnered everyone's attention. "I keep wondering why Cindy tells Carrie now about her dad. She said it's because they ran into each other, but why didn't she say anything before? She finally tells Walter twenty years later that he's a father...goes to the trouble of getting Carrie the job...even has Jerry on board. But it's the timing I don't get."

"Cindy never felt strongly enough about it to contact Walter and have him contribute, never once over all the years. But after he dies, she sues the estate for Carrie to share in the inheritance," Mitch stated. "I agree—it's odd."

The group continued to sift through the clues, interrupted only when Colt's radio called out. 10-54; 10-55. He listened and then turned to Mitch. "Possible dead body. The coroner is being called." His gaze shot around the room as he stood. "Address is Eleanor Berry's house."

Gareth reached over, grasping Katelyn's hand, stilling the constant fluttering. "We don't know anything yet, so just hang in there," he warned.

"What if it's Eleanor? Someone killed Walter and now his wife and we didn't solve it in time?" Her voice shook with fear as she watched the scenery fly by.

The Berry's home was only fifteen miles north of Baytown, but the drive seemed interminable. Finally, turning onto the driveway, Gareth parked far enough away for the law enforcement vehicles and ambulance to have plenty of room. As Katelyn started to open the door, he pulled on her hand, catching her attention.

"Babe, remember—we're not officially on the case like Colt is. Even Mitch is out of his jurisdiction here. We are just contracted to assist Eleanor and now the police. But we have to stay out of their way. Understand?"

She wanted to scream, but held on to her frustration. Nodding, she agreed. "I understand," she said, squeezing his fingers before jumping out of his SUV.

Rolling his eyes, he quickly followed, hustling to where Colt and Mitch were standing. The coroner was kneeling on the ground by a woman's body and Katelyn's pace began to slow.

"My house! Why would someone do this and leave them at my house?" a woman's voice cried from the front door.

Gareth and Katelyn's eyes shot up as they watched a North Hampton female deputy put her hands on Eleanor's shoulders and gently move her back into her house.

"Eleanor?" Katelyn gasped, turning toward Gareth,

whose attention was on the ground before them as the coroner stepped back, waving toward Zac to bring the stretcher.

Beth. The dead woman lying in Eleanor Berry's yard was Beth.

Katelyn felt dizzy with everything going on, but she shook it off, determined to maintain professionalism.

"You okay?" Gareth whispered into her ear. Nodding jerkily, she tried to speak then cleared her throat before trying again. "Fine...I'm fine." Twisting her head, she said, "Can I go see Eleanor?"

"Sorry, but we need to wait until we get the all-clear from Colt."

"But she needs me—"

"Katelyn," Gareth said softly, taking her arm and pulling her gently out of the way as more cars came into the driveway. "She is our client, not our friend. I know it's hard, but you can't get personally invested in the situation. This is a murder scene. She's going to have to be questioned—"

"Questioned?" Katelyn's voice rose.

With his hand on her upper arm, he turned her so that she faced him with her back to the house. Bending slightly, he captured her eyes. "Think like an investigator. She will need to be questioned. What was she doing...where she was last night...when she found the body...all of that."

Sucking in a deep breath before letting it out slowly, she nodded. "You're right. You're right." Dropping her chin to her chest, she studied her shoes for a moment, her thoughts a tangled mess. Lifting her gaze back to his, she asked, "Maybe I'm not suited for this."

Moving his hand to the back of her head, he pulled her into his chest, his heartbeat solid against her cheek. "You're smart, intuitive, and fearless. You're doing great. You've only been doing this for three weeks. Don't let this mess with your head."

Swallowing deeply, she looked back into his face, willing his strength to seep into her. "You think I've gotten too close?"

"I think you identify with her. With her grief." Seeing the flash in her eyes, he rushed on, "That's not a bad thing, Katelyn. But when investigating, you'll find a lot of heartache. A lot of grief. And you can't let it all drag you in."

Before they had a chance to talk more, Grant walked over, his gaze jumping between the two of them. "Body's been identified as Beth Solaski. Bookkeeper and office manager at Berry and Associates Accounting, but, then, I reckon you know that."

Nodding, Gareth confirmed. "Yeah, we've interviewed her a couple of times. But I've got no idea what the hell she's doing here. Does it look like she was murdered here or brought in?"

Grant's gaze cut over to Katelyn, noting her pale complexion. She noticed that he had stopped talking and shifted her eyes to his. "Grant, I'm okay. I'm not going to pass out or anything. I admit I'm shocked and really want to comfort Eleanor, but please, continue."

Shooting her a quick nod, he said, "All I can say right now is that it looks like she was murdered somewhere else and brought here. There's no blood around the wound on her head."

"Tire tracks?" Gareth asked.

"Not in the gravel, but the ground near her body appears to have been disturbed to avoid any shoe prints."

"So she was brought here for the specific reason to scare Eleanor?" Katelyn asked, her eyes now flashing with anger.

Shrugging, Grant said, "Way too early to hazard a guess right now."

"When can I see her?"

Just then, the North Heron deputy who had been with Eleanor walked over. "Are you Katelyn MacFarlane?" Seeing her nod, the deputy said, "Mrs. Berry would like you to be with her while she's being questioned."

With a hasty glance toward Gareth and obtaining his nod, she followed the deputy into the house, sliding down on the sofa with Eleanor.

The tearful woman offered a wane smile directed at Katelyn, grasping her hand before turning to Colt. Katelyn noted Mitch stood in the background, out of his jurisdiction but here since Walter had been found in Baytown and the two murders were most likely connected.

"Mrs. Berry, it would be best if you would begin by telling us exactly what led to you discovering the body," Colt commanded, his voice steady and soothing.

Nodding, she reached out with a shaking hand to take the coffee cup offered by another deputy and took a fortifying sip. "I didn't hear anything last night at all. I've..." she blushed before continuing. "I've been taking sleeping pills at night since Walter's death. My doctor prescribed them because I just couldn't sleep. I was never a good sleeper when he was out of town on business and with him gone now...well, I just can't sleep."

"What time did you go to bed?"

"Right after eleven," she replied definitively. "I know because I watched the headlines of the eleven o'clock news, but turned if off after only a few minutes. The main story was about some crime and I just can't deal with anything like that anymore."

Taking another sip of coffee, she winced and Katelyn noted it appeared to be black. She remembered how Eleanor liked her coffee from the visits to the office and she quickly hastened to the kitchen, grabbing the creamer from the refrigerator and the sweetener packets from the counter. Placing them in front of Eleanor, she received a smile in appreciation. They waited as she doctored her coffee, taking another sip with a sigh of contentment.

"I usually rise about seven in the morning and sit on the back porch as I have my breakfast and coffee. Our...well, my newspaper gets delivered about nine o'clock and if I have no plans for the day, then I go out and get it then. Today I was a little late. I'm still writing thank you notes for the condolence flowers and memorial donations that came in. It was probably closer to ten o'clock before I walked out the front door to go to the mailbox to get the newspaper." Shuddering, she continued, "That's when I saw her."

Wiping her brow, she continued after another sip of coffee. "At first, I thought someone had fallen—my brain simply couldn't comprehend what I was seeing. I ran over and that's when I could tell she wasn't breathing."

"Did you recognize her?" Colt asked.

Shaking her head, Eleanor said, "No...at least, not at first. I ran back into the house to call 9-1-1. To be honest, I didn't go back out until the ambulance showed up." She turned her glazed eyes toward Katelyn, and asked, "Who would do such a thing? And why here?"

28

The silence in the cab of the SUV was ominous.

Gareth looked over at Katelyn, uncharacteristically quiet as they drove back to Baytown. Parking in front of the office, he turned off the engine, noting she made no movement to get out.

"Katelyn?" he said softly as he reached over to take her pale hand in his much larger one, causing her to jump.

"Wow," she said, turning to face him, an embarrassed half-smile on her face. "I was a million miles away."

"I know your mind is turning everything over... same as mine. But we also need to take a look at some of the other cases we've got going right now and let the police do their job."

Nodding, she started to open her door when he squeezed her hand, pulling her attention to him again. He leaned over and kissed her forehead. "Don't worry...

with all of us working this case, we'll find out what happened to Walter, and now to Beth."

"And to Eleanor," Katelyn insisted, her stormy blue eyes holding his. "Because whoever is doing this, is doing it to her as well."

With a final squeeze, they alighted from the SUV and entered the office. Leaving her at her desk, he made his way into the back room, making two cups of strong coffee. Taking one to her, he took in her tired smile as she took the proffered steaming cup.

"Shouldn't I be doing this for you?" she joked, smiling her appreciation.

"You looked like you needed this more than I did," he joked in return. Looking over her shoulder, he asked, "What are you going to work on this afternoon?"

Sighing, she replied, "I need to check emails, update the website, send out invoices on the two cases you just finished. And, to be honest, I need to get ready for the PI course that starts in two weeks. I'll do the course and, since I've been shooting since I was a kid, I should pass the firearms registration with no problem." She sucked in a deep cleansing breath and let it out slowly before continuing. "I'm ready, Gareth. I'm ready to move forward."

Smiling, his heart swelled with pride watching the light return to her eyes. Leaning down, he captured her lips, tasting the intoxicating mixture of coffee and the cinnamon gum she had been chewing.

She leaned into his kiss, her hands clasping his forearms before sliding up, landing on his shoulders. With his easy acceptance, she realized just what the gift was that he had offered weeks earlier. The gift of a new life...the gift of a new beginning.

Gareth sat in his office as guilt slid over him, but he pushed it away. He had told Katelyn to work on something other than Walter's case, but he could not tear himself away from thinking about the connection between Walter and Beth.

While Katelyn had been inside the house with Eleanor, he had been outside with the deputies processing the scene.

Beth had been killed elsewhere and then brought to Eleanor's yard. The gravel driveway offered no prints or forensic evidence. With no close neighbors or security lights, no one had seen anything. *Why was Beth killed?* The most obvious reason was she knew something about Walter's death. *So why didn't she go to the police with her information?* Because she wanted to get something out of it—probably money. *So, if Beth was blackmailing the killer, what did she have on them?*

William certainly had the business, now that Walter was gone, but at his age he was planning on retiring soon and from what Katelyn had discerned, he had plenty of money for him and his wife to travel and live well. Sandra had hopes of moving up in the business. With Walter gone and William close to retirement, perhaps she planned on having it all to herself. There was certainly no love lost between her and Beth.

Scribbling his notes down on a pad of paper, he wrote Carrie and Cindy's names. Cindy thought Carrie would receive an inheritance from Walter and perhaps decided to hasten his demise to push up the timeframe. Beth did not know about Walter paying for Carrie's education...*I wonder what else she discovered when she started looking. Maybe Walter had more going on than just Carrie's college payments.*

Leaning back in his chair, the hard wood dug into his back. New office furniture had been on his list of things to purchase, but hiring Katelyn had put that on hold. Thinking of her sent a smile across his face.

"Katelyn!" he shouted, then regretted his tone when she skidded around the corner of his door her eyes wide.

Seeing him sitting at his desk, her feet almost slipped out from under her as she came to a stop. "What the hell? I thought you were having a heart attack!"

"Sorry, baby," he laughed. "I was just thinking about the case and wanted to get you to help me out."

Cocking her hip, she tapped a fingernail on the doorframe. "I thought we weren't going to work on this case today?"

Grinning, he replied, "I only said I thought you should work on other things." Sobering, he added, "I felt like you needed a break from thinking about Eleanor. But, I've been pondering some things and I thought you might like to help with some computer searches, if you've got time."

"Absolutely," she enthused, ready to get back on the case. "I sent out the invoices, checked our email and other than another business wanting some info on a former employee, we don't have anything new."

He shook his head, wondering how he ever got along without her, but then she smiled and he wondered how he ever got so lucky as to have her in his life.

Gareth looked at the screen, but his attention was on Katelyn's presence as she leaned over with her chin on his shoulder and her breasts pressed against his back. Her soft scent filled his nostrils and he blinked twice to bring the words on the screen into focus. Now, he wondered how he would ever get any work done with her in such close proximity.

"Look," she called out, her breath washing against his ear. Pointing to bank-recorded transactions, it appeared Walter's brother, Ken, had moved money around recently. "Do you think that's significant?"

"Hard to tell from this. He handles their mother's affairs and it looks like he combined her accounts with his after Walter died, probably to make things easier. It doesn't look like he is trying to defraud her."

"Ugh!" she exclaimed. "I'm sick of staring at the computer screen. It's almost dinner, let's close and head on to Mom and Dad's place."

Lifting his eyebrow, he quipped, "And did I know about dinner at your parents?"

Katelyn had already turned to head toward the door to lock it. Shrugging, she called back, "It's just my family—you already know them." Whirling around, she exclaimed, "Oh, but I did forget to tell you that my grandfather will be there also."

Sighing, Gareth closed his eyes for a moment, expecting the familiar sensation of nerves combined with irritation at the idea of a family gathering. But thinking about the MacFarlane clan, all he felt was... ease. Surprised, he called out, "Coming!" and closed his laptop for the night.

"Pirates? Seriously?"

"Of course! I always dress up as a serving wench on Pirates Day in Baytown," Katelyn declared.

Gareth first eyed her emphatic stare before sliding his gaze over to a smiling Aiden and brooding Brogan. *Nothing unusual there.*

"It's good for business," Aiden quipped. "Throw out a few 'aarrghs' and wear a pirate costume and the business booms. The families bring in the kids for lunch and then we have an Irish band come in at night and really crank up the level!"

"Arrrgh, my ass," Brogan growled. "It's the rum that'll bring in the crowd this weekend. Might be a tradition, but wearing a costume, forget it."

"Oh, come on, bro," Aiden grinned. "Last year you put in a gold hoop in your ear and drove the ladies wild."

At that, the family burst into laughter as Gareth watched the easy camaraderie amongst the family members. While it was nothing like what he remembered families doing, he appreciated the way they accepted him as one of their own. Watching Katelyn walk back over to the fire pit, carrying a tray of dessert with her mom, his heart leaped at the sight of her dark hair glistening in the firelight. As she turned her deep blue eyes toward him her smile lit her face, shooting straight to his heart.

"You've got it bad, my man," Aiden said, drawing Gareth's attention away from Katelyn for a moment.

Meeting Aiden's grin, he said, "So where do I get a pirate's costume at this late date?"

Laughing, Katelyn said, "Oh, don't worry...I'll take care of you!"

The conversation lulled for a few minutes as the gathering settled in for dessert.

Finn MacFarlane, Katelyn's grandfather, looked over at Gareth and, waving his fork toward him, said, "Tell me about your family, son. Did they all come from West Virginia?"

Katelyn's gaze shot toward Gareth as her hand reached out to find his, knowing he hated talking about his family.

Corrine rolled her eyes and said, "Papa Finn, not everyone has to be Irish, you know?" She turned toward Gareth, saying, "My background is English. I thought Finn was going to have a fit when Eric proposed. But then, he found out that I knew how to make a Guinness stew that would put his mama to shame!"

"Oh, blasphemy, girl!" Finn cackled. "To be truthful, I was born here, but my grandfather came over from Ireland and worked on the railroads that made Baytown great. Then, when the bay bridge was being built, he worked in the cement factory. My father bought out the old building in town and started the pub."

Smiling, Gareth squeezed Katelyn's hand, and replied, "I envy your family...all of your family." Knowing he had all eyes on him, he continued, "I've shared my background with Katelyn, but it's not very happy, so I tend not to talk about it much. My dad had a factory job and died in a work-related accident when I was ten. Mom started drinking and then kept trying to find someone to take care of her. Her new husband turned out to be only good for supplying her with more alcohol and using us for...well, let's just say he took his frustrations out on us."

"Oh, Gareth!" Corrine exclaimed. "I'm so sorry!"

He caught Aiden and Brogan's contemplative stares and wondered what they thought. *Do they think I'll be the same? Well, they might as well get the whole story now.* Plowing ahead, he continued, "My sister was fifteen when Dad died and she married her high school boyfriend as soon as she turned eighteen. I think it was probably because she wanted out of the house, but it turns out she chose well. He's a good man with a good job and they have two children."

"Gareth, honey, you don't—" Katelyn began.

Cutting her off, he gave a little tug on her hand and as she leaned into him, he placed a sweet kiss on her lips. "Baby, I've got no reason to not be honest with your family. This is about where I came from."

Turning back, he said, "Mom drank a lot and made excuses when my stepfather took out his frustrations on both of us. At twelve, I wasn't big enough to do anything, but by the time I was sixteen, I was a pretty good size. I'd been boxing, weight lifting, and running for several years. An older man lived in our trailer park and he'd served in the Vietnam War. He took me under his wing and taught me how to defend myself. So, I did." His blue eyes turned dark at the memory, but he saw no recrimination in the eyes of anyone around the fire pit. "It was the last time he ever tried to punch me and I didn't see him abuse my mom anymore either. But he kept her in alcohol, so I guess his revenge worked."

Leaning back, pulling Katelyn's hand over to his thigh, where he linked his fingers with hers, he smiled. "Got out, moved around a bit, then joined the service, did my tours, and found this place. I keep in contact with my sister, but my mother died of alcohol poisoning about three years ago. As to my stepfather? Got no idea where he is, nor do I care." Letting out a huge sigh, he shifted his gaze between Katelyn's parents and grandfather. "I guess we'd better get it out in the open, if my background bothers you."

"Son, I admired you before, but I admire you even more now," Eric stated. "You did what you had to do to survive and prosper and looks to me like you did a damned good job!"

Finn shifted in his seat, a grimace set on his face. Looking around the patio at his family, his eyes settled on Gareth. "I told you my grandfather came from Ireland to work on the railroads, but what I never told you is that I remember him as being a man with a mighty temper...who tippled too much to boot."

"Tippled?" Katelyn asked, head cocked to the side.

"Drank too much," Brogan grunted.

Finn eyed his oldest grandson, nodding slowly. "Yeah...he drank. Got into fights. I remember my dad telling me that he had to go down to the bar to drag his father back from too many long nights of drinking. And when he drank, he started out as a happy drunk, but then became an angry drunk as time went on. I never saw this side of him growing up, and back then, people kept hold of their family secrets." Sighing heavily, he said, "I remember going over one day after mass 'cause my grandmother hadn't come and when she opened the door, she had a huge bruise on her cheek. Told me she fell on the stairs. Grandpa came down the stairs from the bedroom and looked at her face. He walked over and lifted his hand, gingerly touching her bruise. 'Oh, Molly, darlin', what happened?' he asked." Finn shook his head once more and said, "He never even remembered what he had done. When I was much older and my grandfather had passed, I overheard my parents talking about my grandparents. I walked into the room and told them I wanted to know the truth."

Katelyn, tears in her eyes, stared at her grandfather as he shared his story, knowing he could have easily kept quiet. But, in Finn's tale, he opened the door wide for Gareth. She twisted her head around to his, seeing his smile directed at her.

"Sir," Gareth said, now facing Finn. "I appreciate you telling me your story."

"Hell, son," Finn said, his hand slapping down on his knee. "None of us are perfect and we don't have perfect families. But my dad learned from his dad's mistakes and I vowed to be the kind of man my father was. Proud to say that Eric has also taken up that mantle. And same goes for my two grandsons, although God only knows when they'll settle down with wives!"

The heaviness of the conversion lifted at Finn's jab at Aiden and Brogan. Aiden leaned back in his seat and quipped, "I've got too much awesomeness for just one woman to handle!"

Brogan cuffed his brother on the back of the head as he rolled his eyes. "You are one cocky bastard," he complained, but Katelyn saw the twinkle in his eyes.

Leaning her head onto Gareth's shoulder, his breath washed across her ear as he said, "You got good people in your life, darlin'."

Squeezing his hand once more, she turned to hold his gaze and placed a soft kiss on his lips. "Yeah, I do. You are good people."

29

Everywhere he turned, he ran into a pirate.

Gareth walked down Main Street, glad it had been closed to through traffic, considering the number of children running all around. If he did not know better, he would have thought it was Halloween with all the costumes everyone was wearing, most of which were pirate outfits. Screams of "Arghhh" and "Ahoy, maties" were heard from every shopkeeper standing outside their store.

"Gareth!"

He turned and saw Jillian coming out of her coffee shop with a tall, iced drink in a plastic cup held out to him. She was dressed in a wench's costume and he raised an eyebrow. "Has Grant seen you like that?"

Grinning, she laughed as she quipped, "Oh, don't worry about me. This is tame compared to some, as you'll find out. Here—have an iced coffee on the house."

Accepting the proffered drink, he silently preferred

a cold beer, but found the coffee to be refreshing. Nodding his thanks, he continued down the street. He noted all five officers of the BPD as well as some of the North Hampton County deputies on hand to patrol the town. Tourists flooded the streets, but the crowd appeared easy to manage. Waving to those he knew, warmth passed through him as he realized how many people he recognized, and who greeted him in return. Several of his fellow American Legion members stopped to chat and introduce their families.

Anxious to meet up with Katelyn, he hastened down the street. She had left early in the morning to help set up the Finn's tent to sell beer at the Pirates Festival. Gareth had offered to come, but she insisted he wait until she was free for them to walk around and enjoy the festivities.

Crossing the street, he walked over the unused railroad tracks toward the town's harbor, glancing at the many vendors' tents along the way, where food, drinks, souvenirs, local artwork, and beach items were being sold. Spying a large crowd around the biggest tent, he recognized Brogan's bark and Aiden's laugh. Rounding the corner, he was easing toward the counter when he stopped in his tracks, his jaw dropping at the sight in front of him.

Katelyn, in full pirate wench regalia, her long, dark curls hanging down her back, was grinning at the crowd of men as they waited in line for their beer. Dressed in a scoop neck blouse and tight, lace-up corset showcasing an impressive cleavage, paired with a long skirt, she continued to check IDs as Gareth stood rooted to the spot. *Fucking hell!*

Two young men began pushing each other, jostling in the line, but before Gareth or her brothers could react, she reached down and grabbed a long, wooden sword from under the counter, swinging it above her head. "Maties, stand in line like good, little pirates, or I'll carve you up and serve you to the fishes." The crowd laughed and the pushing ceased.

Brogan groused, "If you weren't wearin' that fuckin' costume, we wouldn't have this problem!"

"Yes, and if I wasn't wearing this fuckin' costume, we wouldn't be selling as much beer!" she retorted, hands on her hips as she glared at her brother.

"Yeah, well, maybe he'll talk some sense into you!" Brogan growled back, nodding toward the edge of the crowd where Gareth was standing, his eyes narrowed on her.

"Hey, sailor!" she called out as soon as her eyes locked onto his. "You want to take a poor wench out on the town, now that her shift is over?" She rounded the counter and ran straight into his arms.

Capturing her plump, red lips, he fought to keep from pressing her too closely, knowing he was already in a losing battle with his cock reacting to the sight of her. Pulling back slightly, his gaze dropped to her cleavage and he scolded, "You've been in that costume all morning and didn't tell me?"

Pushing back, she placed her hand on her hip and threw attitude, "And just what would you have done if I had told you?"

Grabbing her by her waist again, he crushed her to his chest. "I'd have ravished you before you left the house and then come out with you, so that I could have challenged any man who looked at you to a duel." He paused, his brow crinkled, before amending, "Nope— that's too civilized. I would have simply taken my sword to any man who dared to stare at your impressive... uh...assets."

Hooting with laughter, she stood on her tiptoes and kissed him once more. "Spoken like a true pirate!" She reached behind the counter and grabbed her purse and a shawl, which she wrapped around her shoulders, tying it in front.

As they made their way through the crowd, they stopped at the Methodist Church's tent to buy fish and chip baskets, then over to the Elementary School's tent to buy sodas. On their way over to the picnic area, Gareth stopped at the American Legion Auxiliary's bake sale tent and added a bag of cookies to their bounty.

Katelyn glanced dubiously at their lunch as they sat down and said, "If I eat all of this, then I'll pop my corset!"

Eyeing her costume once more, Gareth shook his head. "If you think you're about to pop, let me know so I can get you home first—then you can pop whatever you want!"

Throwing her head back in peals of laughter, she missed the stares of friends and family sitting around, all with smiles on their faces and shared pleased glances.

"So, tell me about the pirates in this area," Gareth

asked. "We didn't learn too much about them growing up in West Virginia."

Sitting on lawn chairs and blankets on the town's beach, the large crowd waited for the fireworks show over the water to begin. Katelyn now draped a heavy cape over her shoulders to keep the chill night air at bay. She snuggled closer to him and he obliged by pulling her in tight. Most of their friends and families had staked a claim to a large section, smiling and waving at the others from town.

Katelyn, grinning at Gareth's interest, said, "The pirates in the 17th century found that this area was a natural hiding place for the growing colonies. Ships would enter the bay and be surprised by the pirates that would sail out, easily capturing them. The Barrier Islands on the other side of the Eastern Shore were perfect for keeping an eye on ships going up and down the Atlantic coast, and this area was perfect for their attacks on the bay."

Twisting around to face him, she continued, "In fact, Blackbeard would hang out in the Baytown Harbor—though of course there wasn't a Baytown back then—and scuttle many ships trying to get up the James River to Williamsburg, which was the capital at that time."

Gareth chuckled, saying, "I had no idea you were such a trove of pirate knowledge."

The others around began pitching in with their own pirate tales, the group filling the night with stories and laughter. He looked around, recognizing the towns-people, whether from friends, his business, or from the American Legion. *Home...this is what it means to be home.*

The warmth of his thoughts slid over him and he leaned over, kissing Katelyn's cheek as the cool breeze blew in.

"Supposedly, Blackbeard's crew had developed such a taste for Madeira, a Spanish wine, that they attacked a ship right out here," Jillian pointed to the harbor next to them, "and they only took all the wine before scuttling the ship."

"Can you blame them?" Tori laughed. "I love Madeira!"

Aiden, plopping down on a blanket, added, "The first piracy happened in the mid-1600's. Some Maryland plantation owner in the area sent one of his minions to capture a small boat owned by a Virginian. That sparked the next two hundred years of pirates on the bay."

"Damn, brother," Katelyn called out. "When did you get so smart?"

"Hey, I'm not just another pretty face!" Aiden quipped, as Brogan threw a wadded-up paper napkin at him, and the others laughed.

"I had no idea there was this much about real pirates," Gareth admitted.

"Lots of them dealt with the colonists," Zac threw out, tossing his beer can into the trash bag. "They'd steal from ships and sell the good to the colonists, who were just as glad to get non-taxed items. Kinda like another way to stick-it-to England."

"I remember learning in school that real pirate life was not nearly as glamorous as the movies made it out to be. The vessels were dank and moldy, disease and injuries were prevalent and then, when they landed, they faced death," Mitch added. "Plus, a lot of their time was boring…just lying in wait for a ship to come by. Not really planning too much, but waiting for the right opportunity."

Mitch's words rolled around in Gareth's head, tickling an idea, but then the fireworks began and he was enraptured with Katelyn's laughter as she clapped in glee. Realizing he had never seen this side of her, he smiled, tucking her in closer. The two shared a smile as they were wrapped up in the bright flashes over the bay, creating their own celebration, and missing the knowing smiles from the others in their group.

The soft light coming from the bathroom illuminated the bedroom, casting a glow on Katelyn standing in the middle of the floor, her shawl abandoned, leaving her in her enticing wench costume.

Gareth placed his hands on the elastic neckline and gently pulled the material off her shoulders, baring the pale skin below. Kissing her neck, he moved his lips down over her collarbone, sucking gently on her pulse-point, before moving lower.

Dropping her head back, she offered herself to him, relishing in the feel of his warm lips trailing over her body, tingles shooting through her. Holding onto his shoulders, she leaned back further, allowing him more access.

He slipped the soft, cotton blouse lower, her nipples dark against her pale breasts in the moonlight. His lips continued to follow his hands as he kissed a path until latching his lips over one nipple, sucking it deeply into his mouth.

He felt, as well as heard, her moan as it vibrated deep in her chest. Bringing her head forward, she clutched him tighter as his lips alternated their magic between her breasts.

"I've never been ravaged before," she said.

His hand moved to her belted corset and he mumbled, "How the hell can I ravage you if I can't figure out how to get the outfit off?"

She giggled as her fingers deftly untied the laces, allowing the wide material cinching her waist to fall to the floor. "I think a real pirate would have just ripped it off," she said, "but I'm glad you didn't. It's my only wench costume and I'll need it next year."

Hooking his thumbs in the elastic waist of the skirt, he easily slid it over her hips, discovering the blouse went to the floor as well. "The skirt was over a dress?" he mumbled against her breasts, as his kisses continued and he pushed the material to the floor as well.

"It's a chemise," she explained, gasping as his lips dropped lower. "Kinda like a blouse and a slip all in one —mmmmm."

With a swift movement, Gareth scooped her up into his arms, depositing her gently onto the bed. He jerked his long-sleeve t-shirt over his head, dropping in into the pile on the floor. Making fast work of removing his pants, he soon loomed over her as he crawled onto the bed, straddling her thighs.

His hands skimmed her legs as he bent to continue the kisses from earlier, this time beginning with her tummy and moving upward over her breasts until latching onto her lips once more. He moved his knees to nudge her legs apart and she willingly allowed him access as she raised her feet against his ass.

His fingers dipped to her slick folds finding her ready for him. Unable to keep the grin from his face, she looked up at him questioningly.

"You're ready for me," he stated simply.

"For you? I've been ready since you first told me you wished we'd stayed home today so you could have your way with me!"

Lifting his eyebrows, he said, "You've been wet for me all day?"

Nodding, she replied, "Didn't you notice me squirming earlier?"

"I thought you just couldn't get comfortable on the beach blanket."

Giggling, she said, "Well, that's true, but it wasn't due to the sand. It was because just seeing the way your eyes traveled over me made me hot...and wet...and ready!"

"Remind me to always ravish you with my eyes," he muttered against her lips, as he plunged his tongue into her mouth. His fingers sunk into her waiting sex, mimicking the action of his tongue, both used to drive Katelyn wild.

She welcomed the heaviness of his body over hers, the weight warm and comforting. Shifting her legs apart further as he settled between her thighs, her body tingled in anticipation and she lifted her hips slightly as she pressed her core against him.

Plunging his swollen erection deep inside, her

groans filled the night. Leaning her head up, she nipped his shoulder with her teeth, hearing his groans added to hers. Her core felt the friction as he reached places she was sure had never been breached before. His pelvis rubbed against her clit, the pressure building as she clung to his back, her fingernails digging into the thick muscles.

Gareth pushed up on his elbows as he watched her face at the exact moment her orgasm rocked her body and she bit her bottom lip, her eyes pinned on him. Heat crept from her stomach upward, a blush turning her cheeks rosy.

As she cried out his name, he roared through his orgasm, continuing to thrust until every drop was spent. Falling to the side, he engulfed her in his embrace, his body pressed close as their heartbeats slowed together.

Once rational thought returned, he stared down at her naked beauty, displayed in the moonlight, shaking his head ever so slightly. She leaned up on her elbows, her brow knitted.

"What's wrong?" she asked.

"Never thought I'd get so lucky," he confessed. Seeing her still confused expression, he said, "If I think back hard enough I can remember the love between my parents, but after Dad died, things went all to hell. I never really thought much about love after that."

She reached her hand up, cupping his jaw, running her fingers delicately over the rough stubble of his beard, keeping silent as he continued to speak.

"I spent so much time when I first came to Baytown just hoping to get the business up and running, that I never thought about dating. And I sure as hell never thought I had a chance with you."

"Me? Why not?"

"Because you're beautiful...smart...funny. You're one of the Baytown Girls, someone everyone knows. And I'm just an outsider—"

"I noticed you right away," she blurted, halting his words. "I saw you in the bar on one of the first days you were in town." Blushing, she continued, "I never thought I could feel this way."

"And here we are," he muttered against her lips.

"And here we are," she repeated, relishing his kiss.

30

Lying in wait. Waiting for the right opportunity.

Gareth woke up the next morning, the words about the pirates filling his mind. He felt Katelyn move in his arms as she snuggled closer to him. He gazed at her dark, sexy, sleep-tousled hair flowing across the pillow, its silky tresses tickling his shoulder where her head rested. He fought the urge to run his fingers over her cheek, not wanting to wake her.

Shifting slightly, he continued to allow his mind to roam. *Someone wanted Walter dead. A crime of passion probably would not have afforded someone the time to arrange for a boat, so we've gone on the assumption that it was planned, start to finish. But, what if someone was waiting for the right opportunity. The boat could be ready. The plan to dump the body at the golf course could have already been decided upon. If someone were patient, the timing would have presented itself. But who?*

"Hey, you."

Katelyn's sleepy voice sounded, startling him out of

MARYANN JORDAN

his thoughts. Turning his head, he gazed into her eyes, his heart slipping further into love. "Hey, yourself."

"You had such a pensive look on your face when I woke up."

"I was just thinking about something said last night about pirates and was, for some crazy reason, thinking of how it might pertain to Walter's death."

Blinking several times, trying to focus on Gareth's words as she came more fully awake, she puzzled, "Pirates and Walter's death? What on earth does one have to do with the other?"

"Well, nothing really," he chuckled, realizing how ridiculous it sounded. "But I thought about how the killer may have been ready to kill Walter for a while but was just lying in wait for the perfect opportunity."

"So not a crime of passion and not completely planned either?"

"Yeah," he sighed, realizing the idea did not get him closer to identifying the murderer.

Katelyn rolled over on her back, staring at the ceiling for a moment, her mind now turning over possibilities. "Who would be the one who might have a reason to kill Walter but not necessarily be in a hurry?"

She rolled her head to the side suddenly at the same time he turned toward her.

"Carrie!" she declared at the same time he said, "Cindy!"

Looking at each other, they laughed. Sitting up and pushing back against the headboard, Gareth said, "What if Cindy was tired of waiting to see if Walter was going to give more money to Carrie?"

"Yes, but killing him would leave them exposed if

he hadn't changed his will, which he hadn't," Katelyn argued. "But what if Carrie wanted him dead...not just for money...but for revenge?" She sat up as well, sitting cross-legged on the comforter, facing him.

"What's her motive?"

Licking her lips as she stared out the window momentarily, she said, "Anger, instead of money. Maybe she's pissed that he left her mother to begin with. Maybe Walter did know about her and didn't want her back then."

The two sat in pensive silence for a moment, before Katelyn flopped backward onto the comforter and growled, "There just aren't enough clues! This is all speculative!"

Gareth grinned as he moved over her body. "Clues aren't always so easy to find...you just have to keep looking." Kissing her, he mumbled against her lips, "We've got to put the exploring to rest right now. We've got to get ready for the game."

Moaning, she complained, "I'd rather stay in bed with you and keep searching."

"Babe, if we stay in bed, looking for clues is not what we'd be doing!"

Laughing, she agreed as she rolled out from under him. "Okay, slave driver. I'll fix some breakfast before we head to the ball field."

An hour later, Katelyn yelled for one of the American Legion youth to run to the next base as the hit ball sailed to the backfield. Jumping up and down, she cheered the teenage girl on as several of the outfielders scrambled to get their gloves on the ball.

As the girl rounded the bases and crossed home plate, Katelyn grabbed her in a huge hug, hearing the cheers from the stands. As the game ended, she walked over to her friends sitting on the bleachers waiting for the next game.

"Congratulations," Tori said. "Your kids are doing really well out there."

"Thanks," she replied, "I think it's been really good for some of the older teen girls to help the younger ones. And Ginny's a great coach." Her eyes moved across the field, lingering on Gareth, as he worked with some of the boys on the sideline. Her brothers and most of the Baytown Boys were out in force today, all of them working with the youth leagues.

"So," Jade nudged Katelyn from the side. "How are things with Gareth? You two looked really cozy last night on the beach."

Smiling, Katelyn replied, "Good. Really good."

"And no more guilt?" Jillian asked, arriving with a large cardboard box lid filled with coffees from her shop.

"Mmmmm," Katelyn moaned in appreciation, sipping her coffee as she eyed her friend. "No guilt. Life has to move on and I'm now embracing that philosophy."

Jillian leaned over and kissed Katelyn's forehead. "You have no idea how happy that makes me," she replied, sitting down on the bleachers. Lifting her face toward the field as she sipped her own coffee, she declared, "Now, where're our men?"

After a few minutes, Belle piped up, "You know, every time I'm here, even though the Baytown Boys are now the coaches and not the players, I'm always taken back to high school days here on this field."

Several others agreed, but Katelyn stayed silent, turning Belle's words over in her mind as her eyes sought out Gareth, smiling and laughing with the others on the sidelines. *Philip was my past...Gareth is my present...and I hope my future.* With that thought in mind, she knew what she needed to do that afternoon. As the next game came to an end, Katelyn sought out Gareth and with a smile, said, "Are you going out with the guys?"

"I was...unless you needed me?"

Shaking her head, she slipped her arms around his waist and stood on her toes to touch her lips to his. "Well, I always need you, but you go on. I've got some things I need to clean out of my closets and I think I'll spend the afternoon at that task."

"You need any help?"

"Nah, I've got it. Come over whenever you're done."

With another quick kiss, they separated. Waving toward her friends, she hurried off to begin her task.

The unmoving air was stifling and a coat of dust covered everything. *How long has it been since I've been up here?*

From the looks of things, the answer was "too long". Katelyn's house included an attic but living alone she had rare use for the space. Several large, plastic storage totes stood in the center of the room, like sentinels guarding the space. Not wanting to get coated in dust herself, she brought a towel for sitting on and another one for wiping off the box lids.

Opening the first one, she peered inside, a slight smile curving her lips at the contents. She reached in, pulling out her—well, Philip's—high school jacket, his football and baseball pins clipped to the front. Holding the material up to her nose, she wondered if it would still smell like him. Mostly, she was hit with just a scent of age, but as she buried her nose deeper into the inside lining, she caught a whiff of Philip's aftershave. Grinning, she remembered when her brothers started wearing aftershave, hoping to catch the attention of girls.

She carefully folded the jacket, knowing it would go into the pile for Philip's parents to keep. Another peek inside and she lifted out the high school football t-shirt that he had worn and when he left to join the Army had given to her. *Lordy, I wore that to bed almost every night!* The material was soft, almost threadbare in a few spots. Holding it close for a moment, she sighed heavily and placed it in a garbage bag she had brought up with her. It was the first item to go into the bag and her fingers itched to snatch it back out. She closed her hand around it again, pulling it a few inches out—hesitating —and then pushed it forward again.

Steadying her breathing, she fought the urge to close everything back up and run downstairs. *No...I can do this. I can go through the memories and put them in their place. It's time.*

Next came the high school yearbooks that she used

to have proudly displayed on a bookshelf and, once Philip died, had buried in the attic, no longer wanting to be reminded of their happy, bygone teenage years. Flipping them open, she realized they contained so many memories, not just of Philip, and moved them to a pile to take downstairs to place with her childhood photo albums.

Underneath the yearbooks, she pulled out an old scrapbook, smiling at the forgotten hobby. She had cataloged their relationship in the pages with carefully preserved movie ticket stubs, the play program from a musical he took her to in Virginia Beach, concert tickets from when a group of them sat in a Norfolk stadium, prom pictures, and a multitude of other memorabilia. She ran her finger along the trim edges and remembered the hours she and Jillian spent making their scrapbooks. The realization hit her that Jillian's scrapbook about she and Grant was still relevant now that they were together.

With a sigh, she carefully pulled the photographs out of the book before placing it into the garbage bag. It was easier to let go since old movie tickets and programs no longer held the same appeal as they did in her teenage years.

The final box was the most difficult to go through— letters. This tote contained the notes passed in class, the letters she had written to him and he gave back to her for safekeeping when he joined the Army, as well as the letters, cards, and copies of emails he sent to her when he was in service. It was difficult at first, trying to decide what to keep and what to get rid of but, as she plowed through the pile, it became easier. She ended up only keeping a few that he had handwritten, where she felt as though his personality shown through, had another pile for his mother, containing some where he chronicled his military days, and the rest went into the bag to throw away.

A sound from below hit her ears, followed by a shout. "Hey, babe? You here?"

"Gareth! I'm up in the attic. Come on up!"

A moment later, his head poked up through the folding, stair door, saying, "I didn't realize there was anything here but a crawl space. This is great—you could build this out into another room up here!"

She looked around, nodding in agreement. "I never thought of that since I haven't needed the extra space."

He climbed the last few steps and walked over, his gaze landing on the boxes next to her. "Whatcha doing?" Before she could answer, his eyes landed on the high-school jacket and he instantly understood she was going through Philip's things. "Oh, I'm sorry, babe. I'll leave you alone."

"No, no," she rushed, patting the towel she was sitting on. "Please, sit with me."

He lowered his body next to her, reaching out to rub her shoulder. "Katelyn, you don't have to show me or tell me anything."

"I know...and that's one of the many reasons I love you," she said, her face soft with a slight smile. "I was sitting at the ball game and it occurred to me that I no longer look at the field and expect to see—or miss—Philip. Instead, all I think of is you. And that was when I knew it was time to deal with what was up here. I would never want you to stumble across it and wonder what I had kept and why."

Moving in closer, he whispered, "I never want you to lose your past. It's what made you who you are."

"I agree, but Gareth, the memories I need to keep are in here," she touched her heart. "And they'll share the space with all the new memories that I have to make. But these?" She looked at the boxes, "are just things that I no longer want to hide from. I either need to throw them away, give to Philip's parents, or find a new place in my life for whatever I want to keep."

He leaned over and kissed her forehead, saying, "Well, then I'll leave you to it. But when you're finished, call me and I'll come help you take the boxes down." He stood and, with a last glance and wink backward, he climbed back down the steps.

Turning back to the boxes, she sighed. "He's a good man, Philip. I know you would have liked him...and approve of what I'm doing now." With those words whispered into the air, she turned back to her sorting.

An hour later, everything sorted and with Gareth's help, she was ready to celebrate. "Let's go sit out on the pier," she suggested.

Readily acquiescing, they walked the few blocks to watch the sunset over the bay. Carrying a blanket to wrap over their legs, she quickly snuggled into his arms.

"You doin' okay?" he asked.

"Perfect," she replied, knowing it was the truth. She felt a hitch in his breath and turned to peer deeply into his eyes, reaching up to cup his jaw. "Really," she assured. Inhaling the salty air deeply, she added, "I feel freer than I have in years and I have you to thank for that. Falling in love with you has given me the push to let go of the past and face the future."

Gareth inched forward, his lips claiming hers. The kiss started slow, building heat as he nibbled on her bottom lip before sucking it into his mouth. Pulling back, just enough to whisper, "I want to be your future, Katelyn MacFarlane," he moved back in.

31

"Eleanor!"

Katelyn, sitting at her desk, had answered the phone, surprised and pleased at the caller. "How are you doing?"

"As well as can be expected, I suppose. I have started the process of going through some of Walter's things."

Katelyn startled at this news, thinking about her weekend's activity, years after Philip died. "Do you need any help?"

"No, no. It's good for me to go through everything a bit at a time. The reason I called was Walter had been in the Air Force after high school and I forgot that he had been in the American Legion Chapter when we lived in Norfolk. Anyway, he didn't go to the local meetings when it was started up here, but I thought it would be nice to make a donation in memory of him to the Baytown Chapter."

"Oh, Eleanor, that would be wonderful," Katelyn

acknowledged. "Zac Hamilton is the Finance Officer. If you like, I can ask him who you would need to make the check to."

"That would be perfect, thank you. I also wanted to invite you over for coffee sometime soon. I can only spend so much time in this house, trying to decide what to do."

"I'd love to, Eleanor. Next week I start classes for becoming a private investigator and will be unavailable. Would sometime this week work out for you?"

"Let's plan for tomorrow? About ten o'clock?"

"Perfect. I'll talk to Zac today and let you know tomorrow what he says."

Telling Gareth where she was going, she walked the two blocks to the fire station. Waving to the few volunteers working on the fire truck, she made her way over to the ambulance, where she found Zac restocking his supplies. Telling him about the forthcoming donation, she laughed at his exuberant response.

"Hell yeah, we'll take a donation! The youth teams alone could use it, for sure. Once we get it, I'll present it at the next meeting and the chapter will decide what to use it on. Then we'll let Mrs. Berry know."

With a quick hug goodbye, she walked back to the office after a detour to Jillian's coffee shop. Stepping inside, the dark interior was warm against the chill of the autumn air. The sound of the coffee grinder mingled with the late breakfast crowd. The scent of freshly brewed coffee filled the air and Katelyn's gaze searched for Jillian.

The old building had originally been a store in the late 1800's and fell into disrepair over the years. The store passed through multiple owners and eventually ended up bought by Jillian's parents. Determined to return the store to its former glory, they kept the solid wood paneling, carved wooden support poles, and the glass display cases on the sides of the long room downstairs. They turned the rest into a coffee shop and Jillian's mother began baking pastries to sell along with the coffee.

Antique tables and amber sconces on the walls to soften the sunlight that came from the front gave the quaint shop its ambiance. Jillian had worked in the shop as a teenager and when she came back after college her parents turned most of the business over to her.

One of the servers noticed her and waved toward the upstairs. Jillian had restored the second floor to the same glory as the coffee shop downstairs and showcased local artists' paintings on the dark paneled walls. Glass cases exhibited pottery and other artists' work. She found Jillian, in her galleria, working on a display. "Hey, girl," Katelyn greeted.

"Hey, yourself. What brings you here this time of day?" Jillian wiped her hands on her pants and motioned for Katelyn to join her at a little table overlooking Main Street.

"I had an errand to run and decided to bring something back to the office. I know it's a bit early, but I ordered a couple of sandwiches when I came in."

Cocking her head to the side, Jillian asked, "Are you okay?"

Nodding, Katelyn brushed her hair off her shoulder and said, "Actually, I'm great. I spent time yesterday sorting through Philip's things that I had stuffed into the attic."

Jillian reached out and took Katelyn's hands in hers. "Oh, sweetie."

"It was time. Honestly, it was past time. But it was good. I went through all the letters, the mementos, everything. I saved a couple of things like the yearbooks and pictures. But there were a few things that I'm taking over to his parents and then I threw away the rest."

The two women sat quietly for a moment, the sun streaming through the window warming them. "You know, Brogan once told me that he warned Philip that he'd kick his ass if he ever hurt me, but then he didn't get the chance." Seeing Jillian's confused look, she chuckled ruefully, and added, "I didn't understand either, but Brogan said that Philip did hurt me when he died. And Brogan wasn't able to do anything about it."

After another moment of speculative silence, Katelyn said, "I realized when I read Philip's letters yesterday, that he lied to me. He said he'd love me and be with me forever. Oh, I know, he didn't really lie, but the fact is that life can intervene and it feels like someone has broken a promise." As the words came out of her mouth, she jolted as a thought flew through her mind.

"I know who did it!"

Gareth looked up from his desk as Katelyn came flying into the room, her cheeks flushed and her eyes bright. Panting, she looked as though she had been running. "Huh?"

"Walter...I know who killed him."

Jumping up from his seat, he rushed over, placing his arm around her waist and drawing her near. Feeling her heart pounding against his chest, he asked, "Were you running?"

Nodding, she wrapped her arms around his waist as well, feeling the warmth and strength from his body as she willed her breathing to slow. "Yes. I was over at Jillian's and as we talked, I suddenly had a thought and realized I know who killed Walter."

Gareth led her out of his office to the workroom across the hall. "Let's sit here. I'll get you some water." Once she was seated, he grabbed a water bottle out of the refrigerator and handed it to her. Several long gulps later, she set the bottle on the table and looked up.

"Okay...now bear with me, so I can explain what my thought process was."

He settled into a chair and said, "Okay. Go for it."

Licking her lips, capturing the last water drop, she began. "It started yesterday as I was going through Philip's things. I read the letters and cards he sent when he left to join the service. And they all promised that he would come home to me...love me forever. And I was struck with the realization that he did not keep his promise." She waved her hand in the air, saying, "Of course it wasn't his fault, but nonetheless, something had been promised and not fulfilled. And that really hurt me. And in my grief, I admit that at one time I was angry with him."

She sighed heavily adding, "Anger toward someone

who is dead might sound bad, but it really is one of the stages of grief. I moved past that, but in studying grief, I do know that some people do not move through the stages...they get stuck. So, some people might get stuck in anger."

Taking another sip of water, she said, "And then you were talking yesterday morning about how maybe, like the pirates, someone had been waiting for the right opportunity to kill Walter. Not a quick crime of passion, but a slow burn where they just waited."

Seeing the confusion still on his face, she plunged ahead. "Okay, so then I was talking to Jillian, telling her all this and it suddenly hit me. Someone was angry with Walter. We know he had been seeing a woman, so what if this woman thought something was going to happen. Promises unfulfilled. And so their anger built, simmered. A plan was formed and then at the right time, they killed him."

Reaching out, he took her hand, giving her fingers a squeeze. "Okay, I get where you're going with this, but who are you thinking of?"

"Carrie. Carrie Reynolds."

Gareth was silent for a moment, his cautious nature at odds with Katelyn's enthusiasm. Her leg bounced in excitement as she held his hand tighter. "Keep going," he prodded.

Leaning back in her chair, she said, "What if Carrie found out Walter was her father. Not after he died, but before."

"But would killing him do anything? After all, he was helping to pay her college tuition."

Jumping up from her seat, she paced. "Oh, big deal,

a thousand dollars a month, when he could be paying so much more!" Whirling around, she leaned her hip against the counter and continued, "Okay, think of this. She finds out he is her dad and suddenly is mad that he knew and has done nothing more than just give her some college tuition money. She starts to stew about it. Gets really angry. I mean...shouldn't he want to do more? Shouldn't he want to have a special relationship?"

"So, how's the murder happen?"

Sucking in her lips for a moment as her mind spun, she said, "If her mom actually told her before his death, like they led us to believe, then she's angry because he doesn't treat her any differently than any other employee. And, if her mother had also told her that he'd agreed to leave Carrie something, then to her, maybe he's better off dead than alive. So she begins to plot. She tells him she wants to meet to talk. Maybe they were going off to meet that weekend...that's why he didn't say anything to Eleanor."

"And you think that at that meeting, she killed him? What about disposing of the body?"

"I think Cindy and Jerry helped her. She killed him and then panicked. She once described Jerry as a man who would hide a body...maybe she wasn't lying. He's considered himself her father and is besotted with her mother. Wouldn't they do anything to cover up for Carrie?"

Gareth leaned back in his chair, and sighed. "I get where you're going with this, Katelyn...I honestly do. But there are a lot of *ifs* in your theory."

Walking over, she knelt next to his chair, laying her

hands on his knees as she stared up into his face. "I feel it, Gareth. I feel like this murder was out of anger. A slow burning anger. Anger for a promise not kept... whether real or imagined."

Smiling down into her face, he nodded slowly. "Okay...here's what I'll do. I'll go to Mitch right now and go over your theory with him. Let's see what he thinks, because I don't want to act right now without the police involved. Okay?"

"Okay," she agreed as she squeezed his knees. "But here's one more thing I thought of. With the lawsuit for her to have a share in the will based on paternity, then there's only one person standing in her way for a larger claim."

"Eleanor," he breathed.

Nodding, she said, "I'm afraid for her."

With a soft kiss, he assisted her up from her kneel and they walked together to the reception area. Leaving her at her desk, Gareth headed to speak to Mitch.

"Katelyn's got a theory."

Mitch, Ginny, and Grant listened carefully to Gareth as he explained the conversation he just had with Katelyn. 'I know it's not much to go on, but lacking any conclusive evidence...unless you all have something..."

"We haven't found any specific sums of money transferred from Walter to anyone, including those he works with," Ginny reported. "And we looked at his private, shared, and business accounts. There was no evidence of blackmail or that he was involved in anything financially illegal. The Berry's accounting business checked out as well. So, his payments to Carrie have been the only oddity in his finances and, while Cindy explained how that came about, we only have her word for it. Maybe Carrie was upset that more wasn't coming, if she knew ahead of time that he was her biological father."

"If so, she's a damn good actress," Gareth admitted. "When I talked to her, she gushed about Walter. That's what I kept going back to when Katelyn was telling me her suspicions."

"People can pretend all sorts of things when they're afraid of being caught," Grant stated. "Protesting innocence or a love for the victim is common."

"If the case is not so much about money, but about revenge...anger...maybe even betrayal, then the Reynolds' family are high on the suspect list," Mitch agreed. Looking over at Gareth, he asked, "You want to go with me to Berry and Associates to talk to Carrie and then over to the Reynolds' again?"

Grinning, Gareth said, "Just let me tell Katelyn where we're going. Who knows? Maybe her intuitions will solve this case after all."

Jerry opened the door, his smile dropping as soon as his eyes landed on the visitors. "Chief Evans...Mr. Harrison." He stepped back and allowed them entrance into the house.

Cindy walked from the back, wiping her hands on a

dish towel, her grimace in contrast to her words of welcome. "I was just fixing us some tea. Would you like some?"

"No, thank you," Mitch replied. "We have a few more questions for you."

Inclining her head toward the living room, she led the group to the chairs. Perching on the edge of her seat, she said, "How can we help you?"

"We wanted to talk to you again about the timing of when Carrie discovered Walter was her father."

Eyes narrowed, she answered, "I told you...we talked to Carrie after Walter died and found out he had not changed his will."

"We were hoping to find Carrie here so that we could talk to her also," Mitch prodded.

"Why on earth would she be here on a work day?" Cindy quipped, her lips pinched.

"We went to the accounting firm and were told that she was out sick today," Gareth explained. "When we went to her apartment, she was not home and her car was not in her parking space."

"Oh...uh...well..." Cindy met Jerry's eyes, her brow scrunched.

Gareth observed the couple carefully and was convinced they were truly confused. "So, you don't know where she is today?"

"No, but she's an adult," Cindy snapped. "She doesn't tell us every step she takes."

"We understand," Mitch said, his voice steady. "Is it possible that she could have discovered the truth about her father before you told her?"

Jerry's eyes widened as Cindy reared back. "What? That's ridiculous!"

"But it is possible," Gareth pressed.

"She was completely stunned when we told her," Cindy explained. "She didn't act like she knew. In fact, she was angry with him, even though he was dead, and with me. Even at Jerry."

"But that could have been an act. It's possible that she discovered the truth and kept quiet, pretending anger...or perhaps became truly angry, when it all came out from you? That is a possibility, right?"

Cindy opened and closed her mouth several times but nothing came out. She looked over to Jerry, his face tight as he spoke, "Anything's possible, Chief Evans."

32

Oh, she's got company.

Katelyn's car crunched over the gravel in the driveway to Eleanor's house and she observed another car parked out front. She hesitated, trying to decide what to do. She had planned on seeing Eleanor for coffee tomorrow but, once Gareth called to tell her where he and Mitch were going, she became antsy.

Unable to concentrate, she tried to organize some of Gareth's files, but found herself staring off into space instead. Finally, giving in to the restlessness clouding her mind, she decided to pay an impromptu visit to Eleanor. But now, looking at the darkening sky with the clouds covering the sun, she wondered when the predicted storm would hit. The forecast called for tropical storm winds and heavy rain lasting into the next day. She hoped to visit today since tomorrow would be an indoor only day.

Now, parked behind another car in the narrow driveway, bordered by trees, she wondered if she should interrupt. *I'll just pop in and say hello. She probably has lots of friends just drop by.*

Walking to the front door, she raised her hand to ring the doorbell when she noticed the front door was not quite closed all the way. Ringing the bell, she waited but Eleanor did not answer. Pushing on the door slightly, she stuck her head inside.

"Hello? Eleanor? It's Katelyn." No reply. "Eleanor?" she raised her voice, but still no reply came. Debating between her nosiness and what was socially acceptable, she opened the front door slightly wider and stepped inside. Calling out once more, silence was all that greeted her. Unsure if she should continue or back out, she cocked her head to the side, listening for a clue of someone present.

A faint sound of voices could be heard and she took another step into the house. Shaking her head in derision, knowing she had been taught to never enter someone's home uninvited, she nonetheless continued toward the kitchen. Rounding the corner, she ascertained the voices were coming from the back porch. A few boxes were stacked in the hall, permanent marker labels on the outside. **Men's clothes. Men's shoes. CDs. Books.** Katelyn remembered Eleanor had said she was going through some of Walter's things.

A golf bag was propped next to the boxes with a pair of golf shoes on top. A few extra golf clubs were also piled next to the bag. Still hearing the sounds from the patio, she wondered, *Should I go back out the front and walk around?*

Her breeding overcame her curiosity as she turned to back out of the kitchen quietly and head toward the front door. A tote bag, partially opened, on the kitchen counter, pushed almost out of sight, caught her attention. Blonde hair protruded from the opening. Thick, sandy, blonde hair. As if drawn by an invisible magnet, she stepped over to the tote and lifted the material. Inside was a wig, haphazardly stuffed into the large bag. Licking her lips, Katelyn glanced behind her, still hearing the voices from the backyard.

Peering deeper into the bag, she pulled out a lipstick...cheap, drugstore brand. Popping off the cap, the bubblegum pink color was exposed. Sucking in a quick breath, she realized whoever was here talking to Eleanor may have been the woman with Walter at the hotels. The edge of a wallet was peeking out from underneath the wig. With another glance behind her to check the sliding glass doors leading to the patio, she reached inside to pull it out. Red leather. Expensive. Opening it, she glanced at the driver's license, and gasped.

The bay bridge stretched out in front of them, white-caped waves crashing against the pylons.

"It's a good thing we're getting back before the storm hits," Mitch said, expertly handling the police SUV in the high winds sweeping over the road. "If it gets stronger, they'll shut down the bridge."

"That happen much?" Gareth asked. "I've never been out here in a hurricane before."

"Not too much, but it does happen. We don't always get a direct hit from a hurricane, but often get the remnants of ones that come up the coast. When that happens, they'll close off the bridge and we hunker down. Right now, this is just predicted to be a tropical storm."

"What about flooding?"

Mitch nodded. "Had a flood back in 2014."

The two fell into silence as they went down into one of the tunnels, the SUV getting slapped with the strong winds when they emerged. As Mitch continued the drive toward the Eastern Shore, Gareth stared out the window, his mind not on the impending storm outside, but on the uneasy feeling in his gut that the case was about to erupt.

Stepping closer to the sliding glass door, staying in the shadow of the kitchen, Katelyn leaned as far as she dared to peek outside. Eleanor was sitting in a patio chair, the floral pattern of the cushion in stark contrast to her black pants and blouse. Shifting slightly, Katelyn spied Carrie sitting in a similar chair facing Eleanor. Two half-filled glasses of iced tea sat on a table between them. Panic caused her heart to pound as she tried to think what to do.

Slipping her hand into the pocket of her raincoat, she felt for her phone while stepping backward so her words would not be heard. Pressing the shortcut for 9-1-1, she halted as she backed into a wall, dropping the phone back into her pocket.

Whirling around, she startled as hands reached out to grab her arms. The wall turned out to be a man.

Glaring at her he growled, "What the hell are you doing here?"

Katelyn stared, dumbstruck, at Ken as his grip tightened. The pain in her arms provided the opening for anger to overtake her surprise. Kicking out, her boot hit its target and he immediately let her go, dropping to grab his shin as he cursed.

Whirling, she ran toward the door but the sound of gunfire behind her and the splintering of wood next to her halted her flight. Turning around, she stared at the gun in his hand. Directly behind him, the sliding glass door opened as a wide-eyed Eleanor looked on.

"What..." Eleanor began, her surprised expression morphing into anger.

"Caught her in here snooping."

Katelyn glanced behind the couple, observing Carrie still sitting in the patio chair, not moving. Narrowing her eyes, she bit out, "What have you done to her?"

Shooting a look over her shoulder, Eleanor turned back and said, "She's just having a little rest...for now."

Ken, his eyes still on Katelyn, said to Eleanor, "We don't have time for this. We've got to keep on schedule."

Reaching over, Eleanor took the gun from his hand, and ordered, "Get the duct tape from the top kitchen drawer. Tape her wrists together and then you can get going. We're still on schedule."

"What are you doing, Eleanor?" Katelyn pleaded. "This makes no sense. You...why you...why did you kill your husband?"

As Eleanor stepped closer, Katelyn watched as her

face contorted with anger. "He betrayed me. What we were. What he promised."

Not understanding, Katelyn's gaze dropped from Eleanor's eyes to the gun in her hand, fighting to stay brave when her knees began to quake. A slight shake of her head indicated she still had no idea what Eleanor was talking about.

Ken came back into the room, a roll of grey duct tape in his hand. "Hold out your arms," he ordered. Katelyn complied, secretly glad he was taping her hands in front of her and not behind her back. She placed one wrist slightly over the other, a small separation between them, which she hoped he would not notice.

"Was it for the money? The inheritance?" she asked, lifting her eyes back to Eleanor.

"He promised me that I was his only love...that there'd be no one else that he loved more than me." Snorting, she continued, "He had no idea that I've taken birth control during our entire marriage. I never wanted kids and had no plans to share him with anyone else." Her eyes seemed to be pleading with Katelyn for understanding as she repeated, "And he promised me that I was his only love."

Biting her bottom lip as Ken wrapped and then ripped the tape, she continued to maintain the space between her wrists, giving them a bit of wiggle room. He walked away, tossing the roll of tape on the counter. Turning to Eleanor, he jerked his head toward Katelyn and said, "What about her? What the hell are we going to do about her?"

"I still don't understand, Eleanor," Katelyn said,

hoping to keep them talking. She looked over Eleanor's shoulder at Carrie still sitting in the patio chair. The winds had increased and, by the look of the clouds, it would soon be raining. She could not tell if Carrie was dead or just knocked out.

Eleanor noted where Katelyn's attention was and, as though she knew the unasked question, she replied, "She's not dead...yet. She's only drugged."

Her gaze shooting back to Eleanor's face, she asked again, "But why?"

Eleanor's chin quivered as she answered, "Walter and I were happy. Just the two of us. He said he would always take care of me. We had our wills made out and everything would come to me. Then I found out he had a daughter. A daughter! He kept that from me. He didn't tell me he set her up with a job. And then he started paying for her college. When would it stop? I knew he was falling for her...glad to be a father after always telling me he was fine with it just being the two of us. He didn't want me to work, so I've always counted on him to take care of me. And now with her?" she jerked her head toward Carrie, "I'd be stuck with her sucking away the money for the rest of my life."

"So, you killed Walter? That's your reason for killing your husband?"

A flash of uncertainty flew through Eleanor's narrowed gaze as she bit her lip, looking toward Ken. "I...I..."

"Shut up!" Ken said, drawing Katelyn's attention.

Wondering if he were the instigator, rather than Eleanor, she said to him, "Then again, with Walter out of the way, you knew you were taken care of...especially with your mother still living."

Ken glared at her before shifting his gaze to Eleanor. "You told me this would be easy money. You told me that if Walter's daughter got an inheritance, I'd get nothing."

"Of course, that's true!" Eleanor bit back. "And I took care of you, didn't I?"

Understanding began to dawn on Katelyn as she listened to their conversation. Still unable to tell exactly who had planned Walter's murder, it was evident they had played on each other's insecurities. Working her wrists, she inched backward, but had no clue how to extract herself from their clutches.

Suddenly, Eleanor shouted, "Enough!" Looking at Katelyn, she said, "You're a problem, my dear, that I didn't want to have to deal with. But now we have no choice." Turning to Ken, she ordered, "Put her in the trunk."

Eyes wide, Katelyn felt a sigh of relief escape her lips as he walked to open the sliding glass door and headed toward Carrie. Eleanor stepped over to a kitchen chair, where she picked up a raincoat and slid her arms inside. Picking up the blonde wig, cut in a similar fashion to Carrie's, it dawned on Katelyn that Eleanor was dressing as Carrie.

"What's your plan?"

Eleanor's lips curved into a smile as she said, "Why, Carrie will be driving home, where she will park her car in her garage for any neighbor to see and then, when the garage door is down, she'll leave the car running."

"And you'll be the Carrie that they see. Then you'll slip out and no one will be the wiser. It'll look like a suicide."

"Now you're getting the idea."

"But a toxicology report will show the drugs you gave her in the tea. That's how you drugged her, isn't it?"

Another flash of uncertainty filled Eleanor's eyes before she straightened and replied, "It won't matter. Nothing will point her back to here. I asked her over under the pretense of getting to know my husband's daughter but told her, due to the lawsuit, she shouldn't tell anyone she was here."

Her mind racing over the past month, Katelyn's gaze dropped to the tote bag still on the counter. "The wig... you were the one at the hotel? You..."

Nodding, Eleanor's smile slid back into place. "This took planning, my dear. Ken and I made trips to a flea-bag hotel with no security. It was easy to charge it to Walter's account and make it look like one of the women he works with was having an affair with him."

"And Beth?"

Lifting her shoulders delicately as though Katelyn had mentioned something unpleasant, she added, "She called to say she wanted to meet. Said she'd found a discrepancy in the office accounts. I was suspicious and had Ken meet me at the location I chose." Lips pinched, she spat, "Stupid woman! She thought to blackmail me. Me!"

"So, you killed her and brought her back here?" Katelyn asked, incredulity filling her voice. "Why on earth would you do that?"

Throwing her head back in a cackle, Eleanor said, "It's perfect! Who would suspect me? It was obvious the body was brought here from somewhere else, so why would the police suspect me? After all, it was me who called them and then cried about someone trying to frighten me." She stepped closer to Katelyn, her face now sad, and added, "Don't you see? I had to. He lied to me...he told me it would always just be me...just the two of us."

"But Eleanor, he didn't lie to you. He didn't know he had a daughter."

"He gave her a job...he met with her mother. The next thing you know, he would have wanted to have her over for dinner...birthdays, Christmas. And then, then...I know he would have wanted to do something more permanent. He would have changed his will... leave what he could to her. She," jerking her head toward the patio where Ken was in the process of lifting the unconscious Carrie over his shoulder before walking around the side of the house, "would have always come between us." Shaking her head sadly, she whispered, "Always..."

Katelyn, her body quaking, stared as she realized the woman standing in front of her had slipped into an alternate reality...*hell, she's fucking crazy!*

33

Just as Mitch and Gareth turned off the highway toward Baytown, Mildred came across the police radio.

"North Hampton called. A 9-1-1 call came in, but the caller did not speak. The operator could hear a partial conversation in the background. The phone was traced to Katelyn MacFarlane."

"Shit!" Gareth cursed, pulling his cell phone from his pocket. Having silenced it, he checked his messages. "She was going to Eleanor's." Looking toward Mitch, he said, "Whoever killed Walter may have come back for Eleanor!"

"Ten-seventeen. Eleanor Berry's home. 142 East Beach Cove Road. Ten-thirty-three. Alert NHSD." Making a u-turn on the uncrowded street, Mitch immediately pressed the accelerator, hurrying to the scene.

"I thought she was going to see Eleanor tomorrow," Gareth said, fear gripping his heart.

"Maybe she went early because of the storm," Mitch

offered, his lips tight as he barked more orders into his radio. "Colt and his sheriffs will meet us there. Mildred'll send Grant and Ginny as well."

"At least we know it can't be Cindy or Jerry since we just left them," Gareth growled, as his mind worked through the suspects. "But Carrie? Fuckin' hell! Katelyn was right!"

"Got her into the trunk of her car."

Katelyn grimaced as Ken came back into the house, his nervous gaze shifting all around. He looked over at her before turning to Eleanor.

"You've been talking to this nosy bitch for too long. We gotta get outta here. There's a storm brewing and I told you this was a fuckin' bad day to try to do this."

Eleanor rolled her eyes before facing him, speaking as though to a child. "Ken, it's fine. We're almost finished here anyway. Now, be a dear and keep an eye on Katelyn while I get ready."

Passing the gun to him, Eleanor walked to the kitchen counter and grabbed her tote. Smoothing her hands over the wig, she then applied the bubble-gum pink lipstick. Zipping, then belting, Carrie's dark coat, she turned and faced Katelyn. Laughing, she threw her hands out to the side as she twirled. "Voila! And now I am Ms. Reynolds...at least to anyone who sees me!"

Katelyn had to admit the transformation was good, even if Eleanor was almost twenty years older than Carrie. From a distance, no one would think twice about assuming it was Carrie. Certainly not any of

Carrie's neighbors who might see her drive into her garage. The reality crashed into her that unless she did something, both she and Carrie would die tonight. *And Gareth would have no idea where to find me.*

"We've got to go. What are we going to do with her?" Ken growled, spittle flying from his mouth as he faced Eleanor. "You've planned everything down to the last detail and now her showing up is gonna mess it all up. So, what are you gonna do about her?"

Eleanor stood, tapping her fingernail on the kitchen counter, her lips pulled in as she considered her options. "I thought about taking her with us, but that would be too much of a complication. If she were found dead in Ms. Reynolds' trunk, it could possibly point back here." The tap-tap of her nails continued, before she glanced out the window toward the pier at the impending storm, the rain beginning to hit the patio. "She'll have to be taken care of like Walter. Only, when you take her out in the boat, you can just dump her over the side. Weighted, of course."

"Now? You want me to take her out now?"

"Yes. I'll start to Ms. Reynolds' house and as soon as you deal with this one, come and pick me up."

"There's a fuckin' storm coming," he whined, his eyes narrowed. "I can't take a boat out in this!"

"Fine! Then kill her, but outside the house on the pier so the rain can wash away the evidence. When we get back, we'll get rid of her then."

Ken walked over, grabbing Katelyn by the arm as Eleanor left through the front door. "Let's go." He pulled her through the sliding glass door, both immediately drenched with the rain. The wind whipped from the side, causing Katelyn to stagger against him.

Looking ahead, she saw that he was dragging her toward the pier where a small, flat-bottomed boat was tied to a pylon. *If he gets me close, I'm dead!* Tripping, she landed on the hard, wooden planks, her fingers close to one of the oars haphazardly left on the pier. Even with her hands taped, her fingers were able to latch around the handle, the feel of wood as familiar as the baseball bat behind the bar at Finn's.

Struggling to stand, she whirled around, whacking the oar against the back of Ken's head, unheeding of the injury it might cause. "Aughhhh!" she screamed as the wooden oar made contact and he dropped like a stone to the pier.

Not checking to see if he was just injured or dead, she stumbled back down the pier and across the yard, slowing as she neared the corner.

Eleanor was not in sight, but Carrie's car was still parked in front of the house. Realizing she had parked behind Carrie's car, pinning her in, Katelyn's heart leaped. She tried to twist her hands from the tape, but the rain made the process more difficult.

Skirting around the side of the house again, she peeked through the kitchen window, observing Eleanor digging through Katelyn's purse. *She must be looking for my keys!* Katelyn grinned, feeling the sharp jab of her keys in her raincoat pocket along with her phone. Her smile dropped from her face as soon as Eleanor realized they were not in her purse and she barely jumped out of sight as Eleanor walked to the patio door, staring out toward the pier. *Shit, she'll see*

Ken! Hoping the rain would impair her vision, she pressed against the wall of the house as Eleanor opened the door.

"Ken! I need her keys! Ken!"

Hearing Eleanor shouting, Katelyn knew it was only a moment before Eleanor discovered Ken's crumbled body. The slanting deluge of rain was the only reason Eleanor had probably not realized it was him lying on the pier.

Peeking around the corner, she saw Ken moving slightly. *He's not dead!* Unsure if that was a good thing or not, Katelyn knew she had to hide. *If they kill me, Carrie'll never have a chance to be rescued!*

Turning in circles for a few uncertain seconds, she ran to a nearby magnolia tree and reached up to a limb, grasping it with her taped hands. Using her feet on a lower branch, she pushed up until the thick, waxy leaves hid her from view.

Gareth grimaced as he willed Mitch to drive faster. The SUVs wipers were flying back and forth, slinging water from the windshield as the raging storm pelted down. Finally, pulling into the Berry's driveway, Mitch maneuvered to the side allowing a NHSD sedan to pass him.

Mitch growled, "Jurisdiction," halting any complaint from Gareth.

Colt and several of his deputies were moving into position around the front of the house, as well as a few hurrying to the back, as Mitch pulled up. As the house came into sight, Gareth strained to focus on the movement at the front door, seeing Carrie hustling out into the storm and Katelyn's car parked in the driveway.

"Carrie Reynolds, stop and put your hands into the air!"

Eleanor halted, her face morphing into confusion and Colt took his opportunity. With her focus on the deputy standing with his gun trained on her, Colt quickly came from the side, hitting Eleanor's wrist. The gun flew across the ground as Eleanor screamed, dropping to her knees as she held her injured wrist.

"Where's Katelyn?" Gareth shouted, running through the storm toward her. He and Mitch skidded to a halt as Eleanor's wig slid to the side. "What the hell?"

Mitch stepped to Colt's side as he cuffed Eleanor and pulled the wig off. Gareth stared, stunned, as the woman they assumed was Carrie morphed into Eleanor.

"Eleanor? It was you?" he gasped. Startled, he shook his head, refocusing as he growled, "Where's Katelyn? What did you do with her?"

"I don't know…"

Gareth grabbed Eleanor by the upper arms before Colt could stop him. "Where is she?"

Her eyes narrowed to slits as she glared at the law enforcement around her. "Ken was taking care of her. Ask him!"

Colt's radio alerted them to a body found in the backyard, ambulance needed immediately. Dropping Eleanor's arms, Gareth and Mitch raced around the house as the storm raged, seeing several deputies squatting around a body near the end of the pier.

Unheeding of the rain slamming into him, Gareth's feet skidded to a stop as the EMT talked to Ken, who was now sitting up, holding the back of his bleeding head.

"Where is Katelyn—"

"Bitch hit me in the back of the head with an oar," Ken grumbled, his wobbly voice low.

Gareth stood and stared out over the bay, swinging his head back and forth as he tried to think of where she could be. The water was grey, whitecap waves crashing against the pier with sideways rain pummeling all in the path of the storm. Chest heaving, he tried to steady his thoughts but—

"Gareth!"

Jerking his head around, he tried to ascertain where the sound originated. All he could see was the rain soaked yard. Looking at Mitch, he shouted, "Did you hear that?"

Mitch opened his mouth to answer when he was interrupted.

"Gareth!"

This time the scream definitely came from the yard. Both men ran down the pier, their feet slipping on the wet grass. Whipping his head back and forth, slinging water from his face, Gareth looked for Katelyn, but to no avail. Shouting, "Katelyn?" into the wind, he listened for a response, his heart pounding against his chest. *Where the hell is she?*

"Gareth! Up here!"

"Where?" he shouted, his hands on his hips,

turning in circles on the patio. Wiping the water from his eyes, he blinked trying to focus.

"The magnolia—up here!"

Looking at Mitch, he swore, "Goddamnit, what the hell is a magnolia? Where the fuck is she?"

Mitch looked to the side of the yard, seeing a tall, untrimmed magnolia, its limbs bending against the storm. Pointing, he shouted, "It's a tree—there!"

Racing to where Mitch pointed, Gareth steadied himself with his hands against the tree trunk, the thick leaves providing respite against the driving rain. Looking up, he viewed Katelyn's marvelous ass as she perched on a limb a few feet above his head.

His chest heaving, he grasped the trunk to hold up his weight as his legs gave out from under him. Lifting his head, he wiped the water from his eyes again, this time not sure if it was all rain or perhaps a few tears mingled in.

"Baby, what the hell are you doing up a tree?"

"I'm stuck. I was trying to hide when I saw Eleanor searching for Ken, but my wrists are still taped together—"

Immediately on alert, Gareth swore. "Fuck, Katelyn." He climbed up the limbs, standing on the branch below her and searching her face. Wet, dark strands of hair hung in her eyes as she blinked the water away. Her wobbly smile hit his heart and he grasped her cheeks as he pulled her in for a kiss. "Scared as shit, babe."

"I thought I killed him...but he was going to kill me and dump me overboard—"

"Shh, not now. Let's get you down." Looking at her

wrists, he noticed the bloody skin where she had tried to shuck the tape. Pulling out his keychain, he opened a penknife and deftly sliced the tape between her wrists before slicing through the small branch that was stuck onto her pants. Moving behind her, he assisted her down, one limb at a time until their feet were firmly on the ground.

"Just like old times," she tried to joke, but the words caught in her throat as she looked into his eyes, seeing fear mixed with relief. She yelped as he swung her up into his arms, stalking toward the house, the storm howling all around.

"No, no, put me down. Gareth—Carrie's in the trunk of her car. We've got to get her out!"

Mitch, water pouring off his police cap, stood next to Gareth, hearing Katelyn's determined cry. "Which car is hers?" he barked.

"The one in front of mine!"

Nodding, as he looked behind her, he said, "They're getting her."

She turned, seeing Zac jump from the ambulance, running over to Mitch and Colt. She ran forward as they opened the trunk to find Carrie taped and still unconscious. The men turned to Katelyn as she said, "Eleanor gave her something. It was in her tea, to make her sleep. I don't know what it was."

Nodding, Zac and the other paramedics lifted her from the trunk and quickly placed her in the back of the ambulance.

Remembering Ken, Katelyn grabbed Gareth's arms. "Ken Berry," she gasped. "He was working with

Eleanor. He was going to kill me but I hit him with an oar!"

As the wind howled and the rain pummeled everyone in its path, Katelyn watched as Carrie and a still-grumbling—but not dead—Ken were taken away in ambulances, while Eleanor sat in the back of a NHSD vehicle. And then she turned toward Gareth and collapsed.

34

Katelyn, sitting in the pub, surrounded by her family and friends, finally smiled as the feeling of safety crept back over her. The tropical storm had been down-graded, but the rain and wind still howled outside. She knew most in attendance would have stayed in their homes to ride the storm out, but as soon as the news spread, all gathered at Finn's.

Corrine and Eric came barreling in to check on their daughter. Aiden picked her up, snatching her from Gareth's arms, and twirled her around until Gareth, grumbling, pulled her back into his embrace. Jillian and Tori rushed in, hugging Katelyn before settling in Mitch and Grant's arms. Belle and Jade also came, slamming the door behind them, shutting out the rain.

Gareth assisted Katelyn to a chair, making sure she was comfortable before shifting his gaze about the room. He knew the town got behind one of their own, but Katelyn had it in spades. A hometown girl with years at the diner and pub...everyone loved her smile.

Zac made his way in with Jason and Callan in tow, all tossing head jerks of approval toward Gareth. Ginny made her way in, her eyes landing on Brogan before sliding toward Katelyn.

Brogan, surly as ever, placed a plate of Katelyn's favorite fish and chips in front of her, with a side of the chef's special slaw next to it. Bending over, he kissed his sister's head, his shaking hands giving the only indication of his fear for her. His eyes landed on Gareth and he said, "Gratitude, man." With a slight head nod toward Ginny, he moved back behind the bar.

"How long had she been planning all that?" Tori asked.

Taking a sip of the warm cider Aiden had given her, feeling as though she might never get warm again, she replied, "From what she said, she was suspicious when she called his office a few times and he wasn't there. She then followed him and discovered he met several times with Cindy Reynolds. Always in public, but it was enough that she thought he was having an affair. Then, she found out it was worse. A daughter."

"How is that worse?" Corrine asked, her eyes glued on her own daughter.

Shrugging, Katelyn said, "That's where her issues came to play. A mistress could be gotten rid of...or at least wouldn't have had any claim to Walter's money. But Eleanor wanted it all. She wanted his love as well as his money. And a daughter could ruin that. A daughter was the one thing that Walter might end up loving more than her."

Aiden chimed in, "Sounds fuckin' bonkers, if you ask me." He ducked as Brogan walked near, but kept his smile in place.

Nodding sadly, Katelyn could not help but wonder what drove Eleanor to such extremes.

"But the hotel receipts, trying to build a case against someone else...that took a great deal of plotting and planning," Jillian said, stealing one of Katelyn's French fries.

Shaking her head, Katelyn agreed, "Yes, it did. What I struggle with is that she cared for her husband, but felt as though he betrayed her in the greatest sense. He not only had an affair many years ago, which was long over, but had a child from that union. To her, it was the ultimate betrayal, and he needed to be punished."

"She knew he had not changed his will, so she had to get rid of Walter before he decided to. But, she was smart enough to know to divert all suspicion away from her. Hence the elaborate setup," Gareth added, his arm wrapped around Katelyn, his fingers splayed on her shoulder, gently rubbing. "Playing on Ken's insecurities and money problems, she convinced him to go along with it. It was the two of them going to the hotels, her dressed in a blonde wig, to cast suspicion on someone else."

"I don't get that Ken guy at all," Brogan piped up. "To kill his own brother."

"She did the killing, but Ken was willing to get rid of the body. He got his hands on a small motorboat and took the body over to the golf course. That was just one more dig toward Walter. His brother was the country club socialite, while Ken was the stay-at-home, take care of their mother kind of man. Eleanor probably knew that Ken had resented his brother for years," Gareth explained.

"The lawsuit threw a monkey wrench into her plans," Katelyn said, abandoning her food to lay her head on Gareth's shoulder, offering him a small smile as her hand on his thigh squeezed.

"But you solved the case!" Jillian pronounced, gaining an eye-roll from Mitch and Grant. "Okay, fine, the Baytown Police helped," she giggled as Grant grabbed her waist, pulling her toward him.

"Oh, no, I didn't!" Katelyn refuted. "I just ended up at the right place at the right time. Or rather, perhaps, the wrong place at the wrong time!"

"Don't want my baby sister having to do anything like that again, but thank God for her bat-swinging skills!" Aiden quipped.

Leaning in to whisper in her ear, Gareth said, "And her tree climbing skills."

"I told you I'd bring all kinds of different skills to the job," she quipped, then moved to speak so others could not hear. "And later, I'll show you some of my special, just-for-you-skills."

Smiling as he leered, she leaned her head back on his shoulder, her gaze roaming around Finn's, her heart full of the friends and family gathered.

One Month Later

"Harrison and MacFarlane, Private Investigations. Katelyn MacFarlane speaking. How may I help you?"

Gareth walked by, winking at Katelyn as he watched the sign painter finish adding her name to the door. Taking the invoice, he turned and walked back over to Katelyn's desk as she finished the call. She reached her hand out, but he shook his head.

"Now that you're a partner, you shouldn't have to handle all the invoices as well."

Making a play for the piece of paper, she placed her hand on her hip as he held it away from her. "Well, as the office manager, I happen to know that we can't afford to hire someone else right now...so, I'll still handle the payments."

Stepping closer, he pressed his body right up to hers, towering over her as he said, "We'll need to figure it all out as we go, but with you now licensed private investigator, we'll share the office duties...at least until we can afford someone else."

Wrapping her arms around his neck, she pulled him closer. "We can economize by you moving in with me. Every penny counts, you know?" she teased.

One Year Later

Gareth watched the sign maker as he painted the finishing touches on the front door.

Harrison and Harrison Private Investigations.

"I like it," a soft voice came from behind. Gareth turned, seeing Katelyn walking across the street, a Finn's lunch bag in her hand. He moved to take it from her, planting a kiss on her forehead.

The painter finished, and wiping his hands on a worn rag called out, "All done, Mr. and Mrs. Harrison. It looks real good, if I do say so myself."

Katelyn smiled as she nodded. "Yeah, it does." Turning to Gareth, she said, "We've been married for three months and I swear, it still feels strange to be called Mrs. Harrison."

"A good kind of strange?" Gareth asked.

Lifting on her toes, she kissed his lips lightly. "Yes," she smiled, "a good kind of strange."

Gareth wrapped his arms around her as they entered the building, nodding at the older woman sitting at Katelyn's former desk. "Mable," they greeted together.

Mildred's sister had come to live with her but quickly discovered she was bored. Like Mildred, she had worked as a receptionist for a police force where she previously lived and missed the excitement. Becoming Gareth and Katelyn's receptionist worked for all.

Patting her purple-grey hair, she stood and greeted them. "You've got an afternoon appointment and after that, Mitch would like to see you concerning some work as well."

"When is the next appointment coming in?" Katelyn asked.

"Not for another hour, so you have time to eat," Mable replied, her smile landing on the young couple.

"If you don't need me, I'll run over to have a bite with Mildred."

Waving her away, Gareth started to walk toward the back when Katelyn's hand pulled on his arm. "Hey, now that we're alone, I wanted to talk to you."

Placing the Finn's bag on Mable's desk, he gave his undivided attention to Katelyn. Cocking his head to the side, he said, "What's up, babe?"

Suddenly nervous, she placed her hand over her stomach and blurted, "I'm pregnant."

The silence in the office was deafening for a moment before he grabbed her in a bear hug, twirling her around. "We're gonna have a baby?" he yelled, his eyes twinkling as his heart pounded in both joy and fear.

Nodding and laughing at the same time, she confirmed, "Yes. I went to the doctor this morning while you were out. I didn't want to say anything until I was sure."

Setting her down gently, he held her face in his hands. "Oh, Katelyn, you've made me the happiest man."

Tears stung her eyes as she said, "For so long, I never thought I'd have this. Career...husband...baby. But you found the clue to my heart."

"And what clue was that, sweetheart?" he whispered, his breath warm against her face as his lips moved closer.

"Love," she whispered back, leaning into his kiss.

Don't miss any news about new releases! Sign up for my Newsletter

Don't miss the next Baytown Boys
Baytown Boys
Finding Peace

For bar owner, Brogan MacFarlane, hard work and nightly beach runs help drown the war memories he would rather forget.

But there was one thing in town that provided a distraction... the pretty cop with the haunted eyes.

Ginny Spencer carried her own battle scars deep inside and kept people at arm's length. If only the surly bartender with the Irish blue eyes did not make her long for more.

When a peeping tom in town escalate to assault, Ginny is determined to find the culprit, but it opens wounds she'd rather forget.

Brogan, seeing her pain, steps in and allows her to soothe his nightmares as well.

When two scarred souls come together, their love gives them the peace they've been seeking.

Baytown Boys...
Military duty called them away to war zones, but after tours overseas, the group of friends found their way

back home as men, seeking the peaceful little seaside town. Now, the band of brothers, together once more, work to provide a place for less fortunate veterans to call home.

Please take the time to leave a review of this book. Feel free to contact me, especially if you enjoyed my book. I love to hear from readers!

Facebook

Email

Website

ALSO BY MARYANN JORDAN

Don't miss other Maryann Jordan books!

Lots more Baytown stories to enjoy and more to come!

Baytown Boys (small town, military romantic suspense)

Coming Home

Just One More Chance

Clues of the Heart

Finding Peace

Picking Up the Pieces

Sunset Flames

Waiting for Sunrise

Hear My Heart

Guarding Your Heart

Sweet Rose

Our Time

Count On Me

Shielding You

To Love Someone

For all of Miss Ethel's boys:

Heroes at Heart (Military Romance)

Zander

Rafe

Cael

Jaxon

Jayden

Asher

Zeke

Cas

Lighthouse Security Investigations

Mace

Rank

Walker

Drew

Blake

Tate

Hope City (romantic suspense series co-developed

with Kris Michaels

Brock book 1

Sean book 2

Carter book 3

Brody book 4

Kyle book 5

Ryker book 6

Rory book 7

Killian book 8

Saints Protection & Investigations

(an elite group, assigned to the cases no one else wants...or can solve)

Serial Love

Healing Love

Revealing Love

Seeing Love

Honor Love

Sacrifice Love

Protecting Love

Remember Love

Discover Love

Surviving Love

Celebrating Love

Follow the exciting spin-off series:

Alvarez Security (military romantic suspense)

Gabe

Tony

Vinny

Jobe

SEALs

Thin Ice (Sleeper SEAL)

SEAL Together (Silver SEAL)

Letters From Home (military romance)

Class of Love

Freedom of Love

Bond of Love

The Love's Series (detectives)

Love's Taming

Love's Tempting

Love's Trusting

The Fairfield Series (small town detectives)

Emma's Home

Laurie's Time

Carol's Image

Fireworks Over Fairfield

Please take the time to leave a review of this book. Feel free to contact me, especially if you enjoyed my book. I love to hear from readers!

Facebook

Email

Website

Made in the USA
Coppell, TX
28 January 2022

72551003R10218